THE TRUTH ABOUT LIES

ALY MARTINEZ

The Truth About Lies
Copyright © 2018 Aly Martinez

ISBN-13:978-1725789555
ISBN-10:1725789558

The Truth About Lies is a work of fiction. All names, characters, places, and occurrences are the product of the author's imagination. Any resemblance to any persons, living or dead, events, or locations is purely coincidental.

Cover Designer: Hang Le
Photography: Wander Aguiar
Editing: Mickey Reed
Proofreader: Julie Deaton
Formatting: Stacey Blake

THE TRUTH ABOUT LIES

PROLOGUE

Penn
One minute after I lost her...

"Lisa!" I roared into my empty bedroom. My phone shook wildly in my hands as I watched in horror on the tiny five-inch cell phone as she hit the floor, blood pouring from her neck. Unable to tear my eyes away from the screen, I paced like a caged animal. "You motherfucker!" I screamed, rage and agony extinguishing any humanity I had left. "I will fucking destroy you!"

They couldn't hear me—not with her headphones still connected to the phone. But they didn't have to hear me for the judgment to be cast.

My heart stopped as she suddenly coughed, gurgling blood.

"Oh God," I choked out, dropping to my knees as though it could bring me closer to her. I couldn't fathom how much pain she had to be in. I wasn't the one covered in stab wounds, yet the pain radiating inside me felt like I was being burned at the stake. "It's okay, baby. I'm right here. It's going to be fine." Lies. "You just hang on." My voice cracked. "Just…a few more minutes."

She was on her side the way she so often slept. It looked like I could slip into the space in front of her and sleep for all of eternity. Her limp arm would have rested on my chest, her leg angled up over my hip, her chest flush with my torso. And we could have slid into oblivion together.

I would have gone. Willingly. If for no other reason than just to go with her.

My desperate mind swirled, failing for what had to be the millionth time to figure out how to crawl through the phone and carry her to safety.

But rational thought? It tore me limb from limb.

I was vaguely aware of the two men digging through her belongings and flipping the room in search of God only knew what, but the adrenaline ravaging my system tunneled my vision and left me unable to focus on anything other than her.

I couldn't stop blinking.

As if each millisecond of darkness would erase the last twenty-nine minutes.

As if I could rewind time, start over, and magically change the present.

As if I could actually save her.

Suddenly, the door to her hotel room flung open and two police officers—with guns raised, triggers poised—charged inside.

My whole defeated body came alive, hope surging through my veins, launching me to my feet as the sound of gunfire rang through the speaker on my phone.

The darker blond of the two men dropped immediately.

The one in the grungy T-shirt stormed toward the

officers, triggering another round of bullets.

A victorious war cry tore from my throat as he collapsed to his knees and swayed from side to side for a moment before the knife fell from his hand. Then he keeled over on top of it.

"Yes!" I screamed, the sweetest relief slamming into me. "Oh thank you, God." I breathed as my head became dizzy.

That was it.

It was finally fucking over.

The cops rushed in and secured both of the dead men before dropping to their knees beside her. I watched, my lungs burning for oxygen, bile clawing its way up my throat, as they checked for a pulse.

Hope thundered in my ears, but the shake of their heads as they huddled around her told the saddest story of all.

For twenty-nine minutes, from over a thousand miles away, my heart had beat in that room with her.

And as he spoke into the radio on his shoulder, telling the dispatcher that she was gone, my heart died in that room with her as well.

"Nooooo!" I bellowed, my face vibrating as my soul tried to tear free of my body.

She couldn't be gone. They had to be wrong. They had to be wrong.

I gripped that phone so tight that the corner of the glass cut into my fingers, and chanted, "No. No. No."

I desperately needed the screen on my phone to go dark and finally disconnect the nightmare.

I needed her to call me back and laugh at me for being too protective and overreacting.

I needed to stop looking at her lying on that hotel floor, blood—God, so much blood—pooling all around her.

But I knew, down to the marrow in what felt like my rotting bones, if I severed that connection, I'd never see her again.

On weak legs, I stumbled back, found the edge of our bed, and sank down.

I continued to stare.

I continued to blink.

And I continued to pray for a miracle that I knew would never come.

As the seconds passed, my body became numb yet I was simultaneously in more pain than I thought a human could survive.

And as the adrenaline ebbed and reality sank in, I wasn't sure I wanted to survive at all.

CHAPTER ONE

Cora

Four years later...

"Shit!" I cried as I threw the covers back and sprang from the bed.

The most obnoxious drone was coming from the alarm clock across the room. I knew better than to keep it on either of the mismatched nightstands next to my bed. The snooze button was my only addiction. But it seemed I'd finally mastered the fine art of sleeping through the alarm.

"Shit," I repeated when I tripped over my accounting textbook. I vaguely remembered the thud of it falling over the side of the bed as I'd dozed off while studying.

Stupid. Stupid. Stupid. I couldn't afford to make that mistake again. What if—

No. No what-ifs. I lived in today. Not in the past. Not in the future. Today.

Lifting the mattress off the floor, I used my toe to shove the book underneath, careful to make sure it was deep enough that the lump it caused was unnoticeable.

After that, I snatched my new turquoise silk robe off the old rocking chair that served double duty as my "clean"

1

laundry hamper and shrugged it on. I shouldn't have bought that robe; it cost a small fortune even if it had come from the discount store. But I hated sleeping in anything more than a tank top and panties. With as many midnight "emergencies" as I dealt with, including those where I'd forgotten what I was wearing and run out of my apartment practically naked, I decided that it was time to invest in something that at least covered my ass.

Dragging my long blond hair up into a ponytail, I hurried to my bedroom door. It took two hands to force open the stubborn deadbolt and then slide the chain free. Making a mental note to get some WD-40 on that, I added it to the priority section of my to-do list, which was roughly long enough to wrap around the Earth—twice.

My bare feet padded against the short hallway's distressed hardwood. It wasn't the purposeful type of distressed meant to make that tiny apartment appear charming and rustic, but rather the kind that said it had been at least three decades since anyone had treated that flooring with anything other than contempt. But there was only so much a bottle of wood oil could do. And in the twelve years I'd lived there, I'd tried pretty much everything.

Holding my robe closed with one hand, I knocked on the door to the girls' room. They hated sharing such a small space, but after listening to the constant bickering and arguing over the last six weeks, I was sure I hated it more. In a two-bedroom, eight-hundred-square-foot apartment, our potential sleeping arrangements were limited.

"Girls, get up! I overslept. You're gonna be late for school."

Silence. Where the hell had that been at two in the

morning, when they were still up fighting over a curling iron?

"River. Savannah. Up. Now! If you miss the bus, I can't take you this morning." I rapped my knuckles louder on their door, but at thirteen and sixteen years old, they could have slept through me crashing into their room on a wrecking ball Miley Cyrus style. "Girls! Come on. I don't have time for this. Get up and get dressed." I gave the tarnished knob a loud rattle only for it to turn in my hand.

My skin crawled and panic slammed into me as the door creaked open.

No lock. No deadbolt. No chain.

Nothing to protect those two innocent children from the monsters who lurked around us.

My heart clawed its way into my throat as I flew into the room. The sight of River's dark hair splayed across her pillow, her pink cheek barely showing from beneath her polka dot comforter, momentarily quelled my fears.

However, the twin mattress on the floor beside hers was heartbreakingly empty.

"Where is she!" I shouted, snatching the blanket off River. She'd been wrapped up like a burrito and went tumbling to the floor.

"Jesus, Cora," she complained, rubbing the sleep from her big, brown eyes.

I squatted in front of her and squeezed her cheeks with one hand. Forcing her to look at me, I slowly repeated, "Where…is…she?"

Her eyes cut to Savannah's bed before flashing wide with a similar terror that was spiraling inside me. "I…I don't know."

"Did anyone come in?"

She shook her head.

"Are you sure?"

Sounding more like a child than she had in years, she squeaked, "Positive. Do you think maybe he…"

She didn't have to say it. I was way ahead of her with that nightmare.

I sucked in what I hoped would be a calming breath and attempted to focus on the most logical explanation.

But we didn't live a logical life. The horrifying and extraordinary were far more common than the ordinary.

Savannah had been living with me for six weeks, but this wasn't the first time she'd snuck out. And, God, I prayed she'd only snuck out.

"It's going to be okay," I assured River with a lie.

Her long, black lashes fluttered as she nodded. "She's probably just hanging out on the first floor."

Great. Now, she was reassuring me.

I patted her cheek and rose to my feet. "You get dressed. I'll go find her. Pack both of your lunches. 'Kay?"

"Yeah," she whispered instead of the usual argument.

After a brief stop to grab the building keys from the fireproof safe in my closet, I was out the front door. The cold concrete scraped my feet as I marched down the stairs. I'd only made it to the second floor when one of the new girls whose name I'd yet to memorize tried to stop me.

"Cora!"

"Not now," I clipped.

She leaned over the metal railing as I jogged down. "Water's pouring from the ceiling in my room."

I winced. That building was falling apart as it was; we

didn't need a flood to speed the process.

"Call Hugo!" I replied, never slowing.

"He's busy fixing Kerri's air conditioner."

"Forget her air conditioner. Unless Hugo is holding up this building with his bare hands, flooding takes precedence over everything else."

"Right," she scoffed and then disappeared.

In my haste when I reached the ground floor, I took the corner too tight and the railing bit into my side. Even with my new tan thanks to a spring heat wave, it'd leave one hell of a mark. But pain was nothing new for me. Unfortunately, neither were bruises.

"Cora!" Brittany called as I stormed past her open apartment door.

"Not now!" I replied.

She jogged to keep up with me. "Ava's not home yet."

My eyes were anchored to the apartment at the end of the hall as I said, "That rich Hispanic guy took her on an overnight."

"What!" she shrieked. "Why didn't she tell me?"

I rolled my eyes. "Uh, because aforementioned rich Hispanic guy took you on an overnight a few weeks ago and didn't ask for you again when he emailed Marcos last night."

"That fucking bitch!"

I glanced over my shoulder and found her stock-still in the middle of the breezeway, her lips pursed tight.

Outstanding.

"We'll talk about this later," I said, slamming my fists on the door to apartment 108. The smell of weed wafting from the crack at the bottom gave me a twinge of hope. "Chrissy, open up." I fumbled with my ring of keys, searching for the right one.

Angela strutted out of her apartment next door and leaned her shoulder against the doorjamb. She was still fully dressed in a barely there skirt and a crop top from a night of work.

"Everything okay, Cora?" she asked.

I pounded on Chrissy's door again but aimed my question at Angela. "You seen Savannah?"

"No, but I just got home a few minutes ago." Her plump, red lips split into a glowing smile. "I was *crazy busy* last night."

She was seeking approval. Something I usually gave her freely no matter how nauseated it made me. I just didn't have it in me to give it to her while I was in the middle of a nervous breakdown.

After finally locating the right key, I unlocked the door and charged inside. Well, almost charged inside. The door caught on the chain lock, causing me to face-plant into the wood.

"Son of a..." I exclaimed, lifting my hand to my face. Blood was dripping from my nose. Without thinking, I wiped it on the sleeve...of my brand-new robe.

Fan-fucking-tastic!

Bleeding and now pissed off more than ever, I yelled through the crack, "Chrissy! Open this goddamn door!"

Her splotchy face filled the narrow space. "For fuck's sake, can't a girl get some peace and... Oh, hey, Cora," she purred condescendingly, revealing two rows of yellowed teeth as she smiled.

My hands fisted at my sides, and the desire to plant one

of them in her mouth damn near overtook me. "Is Savannah with you?"

She lifted a joint to her lips, took a drag, and then replied on a puff of smoke, "What happened to your nose?"

"I'm not in the mood for your bullshit, Chris. Is she with you?"

Her husky smoker's voice became saccharine. "Well, you did tell me not to let her hang out here anymore."

This bitch.

"Not an answer," I seethed.

Calm was my specialty. When you're something of a housemother to over thirty working girls, the number varying by the day, you learn to pick your battles. Missing money? You wade in. Missing lipstick? You steer clear. Catfight over a john? You let them hash it out. Catfight over a john where one woman pulls a butcher knife and chases the other woman around the building? You learn to trip a bitch with a water hose.

I was accustomed to catty. Especially from Chrissy. But right then, a volcano of violence was dangerously close to erupting inside me. I did not have time for her little games. But if she wanted to play…I was damn sure going to win.

"You have two seconds to tell me if she's in there before I call Dante."

It wasn't a threat. It was a death sentence. And not one I would issue lightly. But there wasn't much I wouldn't do for Savannah.

She blinked, but her smile vanished. "She came to me in the middle of the night. What was I supposed to do?"

My breath tore from my throat in a combination of

relief and rage.

"Let me in," I demanded.

"Cora, seriously. I didn't—"

I silenced her with a glare. "Do *not* make me tell you again."

The door closed, and I heard the slide of the chain before it swung open.

Purposely, I clipped her with my shoulder as I shoved inside. God, that place was a hellhole. None of the apartments in that three-story, fifteen-unit building were anything that could be considered nice, but most of the girls took pride in the little they had and transformed their spaces into something habitable. Not Chrissy though. I couldn't be sure if she'd ever mopped the floors. Forget about the kitchen or, God forbid, the bathroom.

My stomach rolled as the stench of marijuana and filth invaded my nostrils.

And then it rolled for a different reason.

On a sofa that had once been brown but so much of the pleather had peeled off that it was now mostly white mesh, Savannah was sound asleep surrounded by beer cans and fast food wrappers, a pipe still clutched in her hand.

I wasn't her mother. However, that scene would have been any parent's worst nightmare. But, for me, without a sign of new track marks like those she'd come in with, her only being drunk and high was a massive victory. Hell, for a moment, I considered throwing a "welcome home" party when she woke up. That is until my stomach sank as I took in her black sequined dress so small that it barely covered her breasts and her ass at the same time and the red stilettos kicked off on the floor.

Blood thundering in my ears, I spun to face Chrissy. "You took her out to the street?"

She waved me off and stabbed out the joint in an ashtray. "She said she wanted firsthand experience from a professional."

Fury radiated through me at lightning speed. "Firsthand? Are you kidding me? Firsthand would have been letting her watch you sit on your ass while you wait on Marcos to text you with a job. You haven't worked a corner in over decade."

She glared. "No. But that's where we all started. She won't be any different."

Stepping up into her face, I roared, "She's sixteen! She's supposed to be in school, not working a corner!"

She cocked her head to the side and bulged her eyes, her lips twitching with humor. "Well, good news: She only *stood* on a corner, Princess Cora. She didn't fucking *work* it."

My body started to hum. The beating I had taken when Marcos found out I'd snuck Savannah out of Dante's house was unrivaled. However, in the six weeks she'd been giving me hell, I'd never regretted it. I had two years to do the impossible and save the unsavable. And I'd be damned if I was going to let Chrissy guide her into the flames of hell for no other reason than misery loved company.

"How many times do I have to tell you that she's off-limits?"

"And who decided she was off-limits? Sure as shit not her. She sneaks her ass down here every damn night, begging to go to work. She belongs on the first floor, Cora, not up in that ivory tower of yours on the third."

9

That was what all the girls thought. They assumed I didn't have the same struggles they did. No. I wasn't out fucking to pay my rent, but I was a slave to the Guerreros just as much as they were.

Though she wasn't completely wrong. In a lot of ways, I was a princess. But only because I had a direct line to the king. It would cost me. Dearly. But for Savannah…

Holding Chrissy's challenging stare, I called out the open door, "Hey, Angela!"

"Yeah, Cor," she answered immediately, proving that our altercation would be today's first stop for the gossip train.

"Do me a favor and help Savannah back up to my place?"

"Yeah, no problem," she chirped, eager for the opportunity to help.

Flashing Chrissy one last smile—and I do mean one *last* smile—I exited her apartment, lighter than I'd felt in weeks.

I hadn't made it more than two steps before someone was calling my name.

"Cora, there's water leaking through my ceiling."

And someone else. "Cora, Hugo isn't answering his cell."

Annnnd someone else. "Cora, I want that lying bitch Ava out of my apartment!"

"Cora…"

"Cora…"

"Cora…"

It was never ending.

Closing my eyes, I made my way up the stairs, mentally prioritizing the morning's list of dramas. It was always the same order of importance: Safety. Structural. Sanity. With no one's life in immediate danger, first up was the flooding.

On a sigh, I asked the group, "Where's Hugo?"

Three different voices replied in unison, "Kerri's."

Someone else added, "Though I don't think I'd go in there unless you want an up-close-and-personal of Hugo's hairy ass."

I froze midstep, a vise in my chest cranking down as I turned around. "Come again?"

It was New Girl—Christ, I really had to learn her name—who pushed to the front of the pack and answered, "Cora, seriously? I know I haven't been here long, but none of our air conditioners work. And you think Hugo got off his lazy ass at seven in the morning to fix Kerri's? I'm sorry. I know my apartment is flooding and all, but I will grow a set of fins and a pair of gills before I get on my knees for that fat, sweaty pig."

I was twenty-nine years old and I'd been in the sex industry for fourteen years. Nothing should have shocked me anymore. Especially not a man manipulating a woman to get his rocks off. That was a given. Yet I still asked, "Why the hell would you have to get on your knees?"

She glanced around at the other girls. "Uh...because it's the only way you can get him to fix anything."

I blinked at them, completely and utterly shocked.

They all blinked back, completely and utterly shocked that I was shocked.

Shit. They thought I knew. And worse: that I'd actually allowed it to happen.

The air in my lungs turned toxic, and my head began to pound.

Every day.

Every night.

That was my life.

The stress, the responsibility, the failure.

The weight of being everything for everyone was suffocating. The desperate desire to give up taunted me with every sunrise. But this wasn't a life I could just walk away from. Trust me. I'd tried.

Pinching the bridge of my nose, I stared up at the concrete breezeway, pleading for help that was never going to come.

At least not for me.

"Cora?"

My eyes snapped open and I found River standing on the stairs, a mug of coffee stretched out in my direction.

"Water's coming through the wall in our kitchen," she said nonchalantly. "I threw some towels down. But you might want to get Hugo up there soon."

I searched her eyes for any clue that she knew that Hugo's preferred currency was a blow job. Thankfully, I found none.

I'd done what I could to keep her in school and away from the rest of the bullshit, but she was far from innocent. Her brown hair was tied up in messy bun, and she was wearing a backpack over a pair of stylishly tattered jeans and a loose T-shirt that read *I really don't care.* That young, sweet girl was being raised by what most of America would call the dregs of society. Whores. Hookers. Prostitutes. Whatever the new term of the week was. But we were all just people stuck in a shitty situation with no one else to lean on.

Except they *all* leaned on me.

Suddenly, I remembered why I sacrificed my soul on a daily basis.

Because I hoped like hell they wouldn't have to.

After drawing in a deep breath that rejuvenated not only my burning lungs, but also my resolve, I took the coffee from her hand and announced, "Savannah's fine."

"I heard." Her gaze drifted over my shoulder to the women who were starting to disperse. Their problems were still mostly unresolved, but more often than not, that was their constant state of being.

I jerked my chin to the stairs. "Come on. I'll walk you down."

She quirked a dark eyebrow. "The kitchen?"

"Oh, please. It will take at least five minutes for Hugo to haul his ass up the stairs. I've got time."

She aimed pursed lips down at her black Chucks and started toward the stairs. "Why are you bleeding?"

I touched my nose with my free hand, thankfully finding it dry. "You want the truth or a lie?"

"Truth."

"I ran into the door. But if you'd asked me for a lie, I would have said I got elbowed in the nose while wrestling Chrissy to the ground, just before hog-tying her and then using her hair as a mop to clean that disgusting apartment."

She laughed quietly as we walked side by side to the front of the brick building. We stopped at the end of the concrete that divided our hell from the rest of the world. When she tipped her head back to catch my gaze, her smile faltered. I could almost see the anxiety crawling across the smooth curves of her olive complexion.

"Hey," I soothed, giving her shoulder a squeeze. "What's wrong?"

"You know Chrissy isn't going to stop," she whispered. "The others, they don't put up with Savannah. But Chrissy—"

The vise in my chest threatened to crack my ribs. She shouldn't have to worry about people like Chrissy. But that was her reality, regardless of how much I hated it.

"I'm going to take care of it."

Her face paled. "Please don't call Marcos."

I rolled my eyes. "Relax. I didn't say anything about Marcos."

Her big doe eyes searched my face for the lie. She wouldn't find it, but it was definitely there, skillfully hidden beneath the surface right beside a mountain of my fears and regrets.

Looping my arm around her shoulders, I gave her a side hug that wasn't nearly long enough—for either of us. It was all I could give her though. "Go. Get out of here before you miss the bus. I'll take care of Chrissy. You take care of geometry."

"Corrrra," she drawled in warning.

"Riiiiver," I mocked, giving her a gentle shove toward the dirt parking lot.

She walked backward, keeping her brown eyes locked on my blues. "You'll be here when I get home, right?"

I scoffed. "Aren't I always?"

"So far, anyway," she mumbled.

Guilt burned like an inferno in my chest, but I smiled through the pain. "I'll see ya at three."

She stared at me.

I stared back.

A million words were spoken during that moment of silence: promises, pleas, apologies, explanations, and everything in between.

All of it was the absolute truth.

Which was exactly why two tears rolled down her cheeks as she lifted her hand in the air, spun on a toe, and jogged toward the bus stop.

CHAPTER TWO

Cora

"I want Chrissy gone!" I demanded before the back of Marcos's hand landed across my cheek.

Savannah screamed from the couch as my head snapped to the side. Pain exploded in my neck when my chin hit my shoulder.

His lanky body folded at the hip, and his face contorted like the monster he was. "I don't give a fuck what you want!"

Once upon a time, I'd been in awe of how beautiful Marcos was. All of that straight, black hair and thick lashes lining eyes so dark that I couldn't see the pupil. But then again, all the Guerrero brothers were gorgeous.

Dante, Marcos, and Nicolás were the personification of every poor girl's dream. Tall and lean with chiseled jaws and strong shoulders that were not only sexy but oozing with power. Add to that the flashy cars, expensive clothes, and never-ending string of promises and it made them the golden ticket. But that gold had tarnished all too quickly when I'd discovered the intrinsic evil that was born and bred inside them.

All except Nic.

After catching my balance, I rolled my aching shoulders back and stood my ground. "I can't deal with her anymore. I've warned her, Marcos. Repeatedly. Either she's gone tonight or—"

I didn't get to finish. He snaked a hand out and fisted the top of my hair. My scalp turned to fire, feeling like it was going to tear free. I swallowed my cry as he forcefully tipped my head to the side.

"Or what? What the fuck are you going to do about it, Cora?"

Nothing. That was all I could ever do.

But just like his hand in my hair, I had the power to twist Marcos in knots. "What do you think Dante's going to say if he finds Savannah on the street with Chrissy and starts asking questions about how she got here?"

His jaw became stone, and his black eyes narrowed.

Dante Guerrero. He was everyone's trump card. The girls used his name to keep johns in check, Marcos used his name to keep me trapped in that prison, and I used his name to keep Marcos on his toes.

We all feared Dante in one way or another. Including Savannah, who was sitting on the couch, her legs hugged to her chest, makeup running down her cheeks. Her body locked up at the mere mention of his name.

Dante was especially her problem since she'd landed on his radar. He did love a beautiful redhead, apparently regardless of her age.

Luckily, he had enough women and drugs to keep him distracted for the rest of his natural life. And, as long as I could keep Savannah out of his sight, chances were he'd

17

forget about her.

Or he'd show up drunk or high in the middle of the night and find her when I was alone and helpless to do anything but watch him take her.

I had two years to keep her out of his reach. Two years until she was an adult in the eyes of the law. Two years in which I could mold and shape her into believing she could do better than this life. Two years until she could avoid being sent back to her even more disturbing parents. One year until she could finally free herself—the way I never could.

Marcos glared at me. And, with pain radiating through my body, I fearlessly glared back.

He knew I wasn't bold enough to call Dante. But he also knew just how desperate I'd had to be in order to make the threat.

"Fuck!" he boomed, giving me a hard shove that sent me stumbling across the room.

Savannah shot to her feet and caught me before I hit the wall. "Cora," she whispered through a sob.

Using her to regain my balance, I cracked a smile that caused my busted lip to scream with pain. "It's okay. I'm okay. Relax."

She nodded, her messy auburn hair brushing her shoulders. At five-six, she towered over me by at least four inches, but as we both turned to face Marcos, she intertwined her fingers with mine like a little girl, breaking my heart that much more.

Unwavering, I stayed the course. "I need her gone, Marcos. Not for me. Not for Savannah. But for the safety of every girl in this building."

Sighing, he pinched the bridge of his nose. "For fuck's sake, Cora. I don't have time to deal with your petty bullshit."

"Believe me, if this was something I could handle, I never would have dialed your number. But she's been walking this line for a long time and you know it. It's time we cut her loose."

His malevolent eyes slid to mine and the air took on an icy chill as he whispered, "We?"

I sucked in a deep breath. The words burned like a wildfire and they hadn't even met my lips yet. I didn't want them to be true anymore. I'd wanted to change them every day for over a decade.

But, without a shadow of a doubt, they were the only reason I was still alive.

I swallowed down the acid and then allowed my breath to carry the filthy truth into existence. "My name is Cora *Guerrero*, is it not?"

My tear ducts stung, but they knew better than to release any moisture. Crying was only allowed in my bedroom, with a pillow over my face, my ass to the floor, my back to the wall, a chair propped against the door, and three locks securely in place. No one—especially not a Guerrero—got to see that.

My throat was thick as I continued, "If Nic were still alive, you know what he would do."

Marcos's flinch was subtle, but it was there.

I didn't just see it—I felt it.

And I reveled in it.

He could beat me.

He could control me.

He could keep me trapped in his world for the rest of his life.

But, with one syllable, I could slash him to the bone without ever lifting a finger. It had been thirteen years since Nic died, and he was still my only protection.

Marcos let out a loud growl. "Don't fucking bring Nic into this."

"He's already here," I shot back.

His jaw ticked, and his nostrils flared. "You know it was my little brother who recruited Chrissy?"

"Yes. And I know it would be *my husband* who threw her to the curb for disobeying a direct order from a member of the family."

Cocking his head to the side, he prowled toward me.

I guided Savannah behind me. My heart raced, and adrenaline sprinted through my veins. But I showed him *nothing*.

Stopping in front of me, he dipped low and brought his face down to mine. "You were his whore, Cora. One of *many*. Just because he put a ring on your finger does not make you part of *my* family."

"You have no idea how much I wish that were true."

Suddenly, he reared back, his palm once again aimed at my face.

On the inside, I cowered.

On the inside, I screamed.

On the inside, I begged him to finally let me go.

But, on the outside, I shut down.

I didn't dare flinch. I didn't even blink. Any weakness I

possessed would only be used against me. He could hit me until I was shattered into a million pieces, and when it was all over, I'd rise again, find a way to put myself back together, and carry the fuck on because no one else was ever going to do it for me.

I was on my own and had been for the majority of my life. Too many times, I'd been emotionally twisted into an unrecognizable heap. But no man would ever break me.

So I stood there, Savannah trembling at my back, my head held high, staring into the pits of his demonic, black eyes, prepared to accept his wrath for no other reason than it was the only way to survive.

Just before impact, his hand froze, inches from my cheek. A sinister smile lifted one side of his mouth as he tipped his chin to Savannah. "You sure she's worth all this?"

Her front became flush with my back, and her hand gripped my hip impossibly hard. She'd probably never had anyone in her life say she was worth anything.

But then again, she'd lived sixteen years without me.

"I'm positive."

Her shoulders shook with an unshed sob, and I reached back, patting her thigh while keeping my gaze locked on Marcos.

For several beats, he held my stare. His every blink was a challenge—and a command.

But through it all, I didn't beg.

I didn't cry.

I didn't bargain.

I did, however, give him what he wanted.

Cutting my gaze to the floor, I allowed my shoulders to

21

sag as I used my hand to cup my bruised cheek.

It wasn't much, and it cost me nothing, but that single submissive gesture was enough to give him back the control he so desperately needed.

Though, make no mistake about it, I was the victor.

His black dress shoes, which cost more than my entire wardrobe, disappeared from my line of sight as he strolled toward the door.

"I'm turning Chrissy out," he announced as though it had been his idea.

Quiet relief flooded my body, and I did my damnedest to hide my smile. "Okay."

And then, all too quickly, I didn't have a smile to hide.

"Shift the girls around. I'll send over two more in a few days to take her place."

My stomach sank. New girls meant new problems. New troubles. New fights. But worst of all, new girls meant he'd found more women to drag into this hell.

As much as it killed me, there was nothing I could do to prevent that. All I could do was keep my head high and my judgments low and accept them with open arms into the very life I'd sell my soul to escape.

Besides, my feeling sorry for the new girls wasn't going to keep them safe.

Which reminded me...

"You need to replace Hugo."

He slowly turned to face me with a scowl. "Don't push your luck with me."

I shrugged. "Okay. But he's been fucking the girls in exchange for repairs."

His body jerked, and then the muscles at the base of his neck strained against the collar of his pressed white button-down.

If I had led with this problem, we'd never have gotten to Chrissy. Marcos didn't give the first damn about any of my girls being taken advantage of. He did, however, care about his cousin blatantly breaking one of his precious rules.

For the Guerrero men, pride and control were everything. And disrespect—family or not—was a mortal sin.

Chrissy he'd take care of. She'd be put out to pasture, as Nic had often called it. Basically, she'd be left on a corner and ordered to never come back. Though, if I knew that woman at all, she'd join another stable before the sun went down. But Hugo… Well, his life hung in the balance of how generous Marcos was feeling that particular afternoon.

With long strides, he stormed from my apartment. Outside, four men fell into step behind him. His entourage changed so fast that I didn't bother learning their names. Not that I needed to. They didn't talk to me.

"Don't forget about Chrissy!" I yelled after him.

He didn't acknowledge me directly, but he snapped and flicked a finger to the beefy guy on his left as they marched down the stairs single file.

"Oh my God," Savannah breathed when we were alone. "I'm so sorry, Cora. Are you okay?"

"Yeah, I'm good," I replied on pure instinct before I did the physical inventory. My head was pounding, my eye was aching, my vision was partially filled with black dots, and my nose was still messed up from earlier that morning. But overall, I was as fine as I was ever going to be.

"Go to your room and lock the door," I ordered.

"I...I...um," she stammered.

Smoothing my pale-pink tank top down, I snapped, "We'll talk later."

"But—"

"*Later*," I repeated. "Now, go."

Thankfully—or my head and my slipping patience—she didn't argue any further. With my back to her, I listened to her footsteps move down the hall. Then there was the click of her door shutting followed by the tick of the lock, the clack of the deadbolt, and then the slide of the chain. Only then did I leave the apartment.

The sound of yelling greeted me before I hit the breezeway. Usually, the chaos was a hacksaw to my nerves, but after the day I'd had, it was music to my ears.

Chrissy shouting.

Marcos cussing.

Hugo lying.

It was the raging winds of the sweetest storm.

And like the princess they claimed I was, I stood at the rusted railing that overlooked the parking lot of my castle, my long, blond curls whipping in the wind, my body aching, but not nearly as much as my heart. I sucked in a deep breath and got lost in the maelstrom of my kingdom.

I felt nothing as I watched Marcos land fist after fist against Hugo's face. The only thing that could have been better was if Hugo had landed a few punches of his own.

"Cora!" Chrissy screamed as Marcos's man guided her to a car with his hand in the back of her hair. "Cora, please!"

I wanted to feel guilty. Maybe I hadn't tried hard enough

to make her understand how serious I was about Savannah, but I refused to drown myself in the cesspool of what-ifs.

I couldn't save everyone, regardless of how hard I tried. Women like Chrissy were destined to destroy themselves, and I wasn't about to stand by and allow my girls to be slayed by her shrapnel.

Emotionless, I watched them sling her into the back seat of a black Mercedes, and seconds later, Hugo's unconscious body was unceremoniously tossed into the trunk.

In the commotion, most of the girls had emerged from their apartments.

None of them spoke.

Nor did any of them step up on Chrissy's behalf.

The few I could see on the bottom floor were huddled together like a team in pajamas, their hair up, their faces clean of makeup.

All fights were momentarily forgiven.

Problems forgotten.

Enemies becoming sisters.

And as the car kicked up a cloud of dust, we'd lost one of our own, but we were stronger than ever.

Or at least *they* were.

"Cora," someone called.

"Cora," came another voice.

And then another. "Cora."

With my head spinning in a million different directions, I ignored them and walked back to my apartment, making a beeline straight to my bedroom.

Calmly, I shut the door, locked all three locks, and then—careful not to let Savannah hear me—slid the rocking chair over and propped it under the doorknob.

No sooner than I nabbed a pillow off the bed and brought it to my face, the floodgates opened.

I sank down the wall, my shoulders shaking violently as sobs overtook me. They were skillfully silent. Wild, yet perfectly controlled from far too many years of practice. The sudden emotional release was agony when all I truly needed was a single second of relief.

Every tear was earth shattering, all-consuming, and torn from my soul.

And still, after all this time, they changed absolutely nothing.

But then again, nothing ever would.

CHAPTER THREE

Penn

"Penn," Drew called from the other side of the door. "You ready?"

I blinked at the cheap commercial carpet beneath my bare feet.

It was a different hotel in what felt like a different lifetime. God knew, I was a different man. But the carpet was always the same.

Ugly. Dingy. Coarse.

Beautiful, heartbreaking...

Her.

Wiping the sweat beading on my forehead, I yelled, "It's open!" I got busy pulling on my socks as the door cracked open, and Drew's lanky frame appeared in my peripheral vision, holding two cups of coffee.

He propped his shoulder against the jamb. "You get any sleep?"

I shoved off the bed and walked to the dimly lit bathroom to grab my boots. "Few hours in the truck."

"Mm," he replied. "She was gone by midnight. You could have come back—"

"Can't sleep in a hotel room. Not new information." After sinking down on the corner of the bed, I slipped my brown leather boots on without allowing my gaze to stray to the carpet again. "Besides, me sleeping in here might hinder your ability to fuck your way through the female population of Chicago."

He laughed and walked inside, using his foot to shut the door. "I spent the last two years behind bars where the only tits I saw were on a three-hundred-pound man named Bubba. I have some making up to do."

I took the offered coffee and set it on the nightstand. "Should I be concerned that you were checking out Bubba in the shower?"

His cup stopped halfway to his mouth. "Jesus Christ. Was that a joke?"

I finished with my laces and then sat up, resting my elbows on my thighs and allowing my hands to dangle between my legs. "I don't know. I guess that depends on how nice you thought his tits were."

He stared at me in awe for several seconds, and then a slow Drew Walker smile split his face, but his eyes turned dark. "Shit, it's good to see you again, brother," he choked out through the emotion.

I cut my gaze to the side to hide the way his happiness wrecked me. It sure as fuck didn't *feel* good to see myself when I looked in the mirror. "Listen, I'm going to grab some breakfast. What time do we have to be there?"

I felt his presence close in on me, but I gathered my wallet and keys to avoid eye contact.

"You don't have to do this, Penn."

My head snapped up. "You know I do."

He stepped into my path, forcing me to pull up short. "Go home. You still have the house, right?"

Drew was younger than I was by two years, but that little shit had me in height.

I had him everywhere else.

Pressing a palm to his chest, I gave him a hard shove. "Move, asshole."

He shook his head. "I appreciate you coming to pick me up, but you should go back. Start a new company."

"You mean like the one I lost? Yeah, spectacular idea."

"No. I mean like the one you *gave up* the day she died."

My hand on his chest became a fist around his T-shirt. "Shut your damn mouth."

"You know it's true."

"No. What I fucking know is I need a goddamn job, Drew. Same as you. And not twenty-four hours ago, you said your *buddy* on the inside found us one. Don't start this *go home* bullshit with me now."

His brown eyes held my blues, neither of us willing to back down. "You don't belong here."

"I don't fucking belong anywhere!" I roared, giving him a hard shake before releasing him.

Like I'd been shot, anger tore free of the numbness making me feel everything, fresh as the day I'd failed her. My chest heaved, and my heart went to war with my rib cage. Lacing my fingers on the back of my neck, I tucked my chin to my chest and stared down at that fucking carpet.

One in. One out.

"Please!" she'd screamed as the silver blade of his knife

29

disappeared inside her stomach.

One in. One out.

"You'll never be alone," she'd whispered in her vows the day we'd gotten married.

One in. One out.

"Just a little longer," she'd soothed the day I'd watched her drive away for the very last time.

One in. One out.

I squeezed my eyes shut and focused on the emptiness that filled my vision.

One in. One out.

Slowly, the familiar numbness began to creep back over me like a force field rejuvenating my defenses and allowing me to breathe again.

"I need this, Drew."

"Okay. Shit, man. Relax. It's just... It's a maintenance job at a whore house and you've got an engineering degree from MIT. I'm thinking you're a little overqualified."

Opening my eyes, I shook my head. "I'm not that man anymore. That guy died a long time ago. In a shitty hotel room just like this one."

"So bring him back to life." He shot me a crooked grin. "Jesus did it."

Fucking Drew.

Cracking my neck, I sucked in a shaky breath. "Don't do this. Not today."

His cheeks puffed as he blew out a ragged sigh. "All right. I gotchu." He gave my shoulder a squeeze. "But, for the record, she'd kick your ass if she saw you like this."

"I know," I half choked, half laughed. "I fucking know.

And it's time."

After nabbing my coffee off the nightstand, he once again passed it my way. Lifting his in the air, he smiled—a true, genuine smile I hadn't been able to form in years—and toasted, "To new beginnings."

I tapped my cup with his. "To the end."

CHAPTER FOUR

Cora

"So, yeah, Hugo's officially gone," I said into the phone wedged between my shoulder and my ear as I started up the steps to my apartment. Grocery sacks dangled off my arms, weighing me down. The third floor was the safest, but, God, it was a pain in the ass—literally and figuratively—to haul groceries up three flights of stairs each week.

"Good," Catalina replied and then paused awkwardly.

I knew what was coming. It happened every time an unknown number popped up on my phone. I had no way to contact her, just the address and a combination to a storage locker across town where I'd drop her envelopes of cash.

"Look, I hate to ask you this, but Isabel was sick last week and—"

"How much?" I whispered, glancing around as if someone could hear her.

Her voice was thick and shaky as she replied, "Maybe just two hundred bucks or so. Honestly, whatever you can spare."

I'd give her five hundred.

"Yeah. That's no problem. I'll drop it off tonight after the girls go to bed."

Her breathing shuddered, tears no doubt falling from her russet-brown eyes. "I don't know how to thank you."

"Just stay alive. That's all I need."

"I love you, Cora."

"I love you too." I didn't dare say her name.

She'd been on the run since the day she'd testified against her father, Manuel Guerrero. If she was ever found, it would be her death sentence. And not just because her brothers, Dante and Marcos, would never stop looking for her. Her husband, who had once been tight with Manuel—but later, as the district attorney, put him behind bars—was hell-bent on finding her as well.

She was my only lifeline outside of that building. My survival depended on her ability to remain in the shadows. And I would do whatever it took to keep her away from them, including risking my life to bring her money.

Because, one day, she was going to be my only way out of this nightmare.

Catalina severed the call just as I hit the landing to the third floor. Sucking in a breath, I packed down the emotion that accompanied those calls. If I thought about it too long, those moments would destroy me.

In my weightlifting exercise of the day, I lifted my hand—and all seven thousand pounds of bags—to remove my phone from my ear and then kicked on the bottom of my apartment door. "Little help!"

All the locks clicked and then Savannah swung the door open.

A blast of mildew assaulted me. "Christ, it stinks in here."

"You told me not to open the windows while you were gone." She started grabbing bags from my outstretched arms.

She'd been on her best behavior in the two days since Chrissy had been kicked out. And considering that the water had to be shut off to half the building due to rusted-out pipes, I wasn't about to complain. With thirty women sharing two bathrooms and the strong possibility of mold from the flooded floors and drywall giving my girls the black lung, I needed all the extra help I could get.

As I passed, River didn't lift her head from her bowl of cereal. Unlike Savannah, River had been avoiding me since Chrissy's departure. Or, more accurately, since she had first seen the giant bruise Marcos had left on my cheek.

I knew the silent treatment all too well—including how it would end.

She'd freeze me out for a few days, and then I'd make homemade lasagna and garlic bread. She'd cave and sit in the kitchen while it cooked, not speaking, but no longer avoiding. And then, when our plates were empty and we were both in a carb coma, she'd tell me a truth: how much she hated it when I allowed Marcos to put his hands on me in order to protect the other girls.

And then I'd tell her a lie: that I wouldn't do it again.

Truth and lies—it was how we worked.

"Hey, Riv," I called, setting the bags on the counter. "Can you do me a favor and grab the bleach out of my trunk? And leave the door open—this place reeks."

She didn't say a word as she rose to her feet, carried her bowl to the sink, dropped it in with a loud crash, and stomped from the apartment.

"Okay, good talk!" I yelled after her. "We should do that more often."

Savannah was immediately at my side, helping me unload groceries. "I'll talk to her tonight. She'll come around. I promise."

I barked a laugh and put the milk in the fridge. "I'm not sure *you* need to be talking to anyone."

She extended two cans of peas my way and glared, a perfectly penciled in auburn eyebrow arched with familiar attitude. "What's that supposed to mean?"

I continued unloading the cold stuff. "It means *we* haven't even talked about the other day."

"Look, I said I was sorry."

"Sorry isn't going to cut it this time," I replied while hiding the tub of mint chocolate chip behind a bag of frozen broccoli with hopes it might still be there later that night.

She huffed. "What else do you want from me?"

I moved to the pantry and stashed the chocolate chip cookies behind a box of raisin granola that had been there for at least three years. "Well, first, I want you to drop the shitty attitude."

"I don't have a shitty attitude!"

With waning patience, I shot her an incredulous glare and snapped my fingers, motioning for the peas.

She slapped them into my hands one at a time. "I don't know what you want me to say… I didn't think Chrissy would—"

"And that's your problem!" I exclaimed.

Her body locked up tight.

I slammed the cans of peas down—another block-ade around my secret cookie stash—then gave her my full attention.

Her deep-green eyes were wide and uncharacteristically filled with tears. Short of the day she'd witnessed my argument with Marcos, it was the most emotion I'd ever gotten from her.

So I pounced. "Savannah, you haven't thought about anyone but yourself since you moved in here. The sneaking out? The arguments with me? The constant fights with River? It's all been about Savannah."

"That's not true! You blame me for everything. I didn't want to come here in the first place."

"And you think I did?" I opened my arms out wide and spun in a circle around the tiny kitchen, my fingertips trailing against the counter on either side. "Do you think for a single second that I *want* to be here? We made choices, Savannah. Maybe not the specific choice to come here, but choices that led us to this moment all the same." I stabbed a finger in her direction. "You forget I've been where you are. The day you got in that car with Dante, a lot of choices were made for you. They were the same choices Nic made for me. And I'm standing here telling you they suck in the worst way. But I am not Dante. I'm not Marcos. I'm not your fucked-up parents. And most of all…I am *not* your enemy."

Stepping forward, I palmed either side of her face and lowered my voice. "None of us want this bullshit life, babe. But this is what we have. And as much as I hate to admit it, this is all *I'm* probably ever going to have. But you? You're *sixteen*."

She opened her mouth to object, but I didn't give her a chance.

"And I'm not saying that like it's a bad thing. You have time. You can still get out of here. And I swear on my life I will take care of you until that day comes, but I need you to work with me. You *can't* be out on the street. You can't be getting drunk or smoking weed with the other girls." I grabbed her arms and motioned to the scarred track marks. "It's going to lead you back down that road to addiction. All it would take is—"

The rest of my lecture died on my tongue as our front door slammed shut.

"Cora!" River's arms were stretched out to the sides and her back was against the door as if she were trying to prevent a pack of wild animals from clawing through the wood.

And, with her next statement, I realized that was exactly what she was trying to do.

"They're...here," she breathed.

She didn't have to elaborate. I knew the *who* from her palpable fear alone. Moving from the door, she allowed me to pass.

I went straight to the railing that overlooked the parking lot.

Two men I didn't recognize were climbing out of a beat-up, red extended-cab pickup truck.

Then there was Marcos in his black Mercedes.

And...

"Fuck," I hissed.

Dante.

His visits were rare, especially during the day, but not

unheard of.

Racing back into the apartment, I barked at both girls, "Go. Now."

Neither of them delayed in taking off down the hall. They knew what to do. We'd discussed it at length the day Savannah had moved in.

Squeezing my eyes shut, I clutched the silver star that hung around my neck. Nic had given it to me what felt like a million years earlier. "You gotta help me here, baby," I begged to the heavens. "I really need you right now, Nic."

As to be expected, my dead husband didn't reply. And after a few deep breaths, I did what I always did: I pulled up my big-girl panties and went right back to unloading groceries, cool and calm, as if the devil himself weren't about to knock on my door.

"Dante," I greeted minutes later with a bright and entirely fake smile.

From behind his aviators, his sickening gaze traced over me. As far as he was concerned, since I had large breasts, a flat stomach, a round ass, and a functioning vagina, I was his for the taking. He didn't care that I was Nic's. He never had. Not the day after he'd found out Nic and I had gotten married and ripped my shirt off then sent me to the streets where he thought I belonged. Not the day he'd cornered me at the funeral home and kneed me so hard in the stomach that I'd thrown up. And definitely not on the five-year anniversary of Nic's death, when he'd wandered into my bedroom, high on whatever the hell his drug of choice for the week had been, and beat the hell out of me. It was my punishment for getting his brother killed, or so he'd

THE TRUTH ABOUT LIES

said as he'd stumbled out a few hours later.

Dante Guerrero owned my world. And every so often, he liked to pop up to make sure I couldn't forget it.

I remained statue-still as he reached up and caught the end of one of my curls.

"Cora. It's been a while," he said, his gaze aimed at my chest. His lips were curled in what would have been a breathtaking smile on any other man.

I fought the urge to gag. Waving a hand out, I stepped away, my hair slipping through his fingers. "It has. Come on in."

As he walked in, he shoved a hand into the pocket of his black slacks and pushed his Ray-Bans to the top of his head. "Where's River?"

Every muscle in my body became taut as I shot my gaze over his shoulder to Marcos.

His lips were in a thin line that didn't bode well for me. Neither did the almost imperceptible jerk of his chin ordering me to answer Dante.

It took two attempts before I could finally say the words. "She's in her room."

Dante winked as he strolled away.

Fear consumed me, but I didn't let it show as I followed after him. "She's probably sleeping."

He ignored me, and when he reached her door, twisted the handle, and swung it open—not a single lock in place—I wanted to die.

But it was safer this way; the locks only pissed him off.

"Oh, hey, Dante," River chirped, pulling one of her neon-green earbuds out.

Just as we'd planned, she'd dragged on a baggy hoodie and gathered her hair into a messy knot on the top of her head. A sigh of relief breezed from my lips when I saw Savannah's bed blissfully empty.

"You look like shit," he growled.

She crossed her legs at the ankle and wiggled her dirty sock-covered feet at him. "Well, when you live in a mansion like this, there's not much need for a prom dress. Besides, not *looking like shit*," she said, throwing him a pair of air quotes—yes…fucking *air quotes*, "costs money. And when you're thirteen and your only potential income is from pedophiles, you learn real quick to be okay with *looking like shit*."

I physically braced as Dante's body swelled with anger.

"You little fucking—"

"Hey," Marcos called, shoving me out of the way. "Leave the kid alone." He reached into his back pocket, pulled his wallet out, and then threw a fistful of bills at River's feet. "Get some goddamn clothes. And for fuck's sake, take a shower."

She cocked her head to the side and sniped, "Does that mean you're gonna do something about fixing the water? Or should I use the cash to buy some new threads *and* a bucket to bathe in?"

Marcos glared.

Dante let out a string of expletives.

And I clenched my teeth, mentally locking her in that room the rest of her life.

Completely unfazed, she flashed them a smile, leaned forward to collect the money, tucked it in the front pocket of her hoodie, and then put her earbud back in. Yelling over the music, she said, "Great to see you again! Don't be a stranger!"

"That little bitch!" Dante snarled as Marcos herded him out of the room.

My shoulders sagged as I hurried back down the hall to the living room, hoping like hell they'd follow after me.

Away from her.

Away from *them*.

I came to a screeching halt when I saw the two new men standing on the peeling linoleum of what was supposed to have been a foyer.

The taller of the two looked like every thirty-something white guy to walk the Earth. Plain brown hair. Plain brown eyes. He had a nose, lips, even ears, but not a single noteworthy feature on his entire plain face. He was wearing a plain white T-shirt. Plain jeans. And—yep, you guessed it—plain brown work boots. He was simple, unassuming, and completely nonthreatening. I immediately didn't trust him.

The guy beside him was a different story altogether. While he was an inch or two shorter than his counterpart, his powerful presence cast his shadow far and wide. His skin was tan and his short, brown hair was rich with natural flecks of mahogany and chestnut as though he worked in the sun. His eyes were blue, but not like the indigo of mine. His were...well, *heavy* blue—deep and hollow. He had the nose of a Roman gladiator, distinguished and slightly crooked from battle, while his jaw was composed of sharp, regal angles masked by a thick layer of scruff. He was made of a million counterpoints that somehow formed a brilliant whole. He was wearing a similar thirty-something white-guy uniform, but there was nothing simple about the way it hugged his thick muscles or covered the intricate black tattoos that traveled down his arms to the backs of his hands.

He was entirely gorgeous. Slightly terrifying. And most likely known as Inmate 401.

But the most interesting part of all was that neither of these men was a Guerrero.

Men were *not* allowed inside our building. This was one of the few rules I agreed with and strictly enforced. All it would take was one call to the cops—the real ones, not the crooked badges Dante had under his thumb—for the majority of the building to be hauled away in a set of cuffs—myself included. And for me, I was on my third strike. I'd never breathe outside of a prison cell again.

"Um…" I mumbled. "Who are you?"

Marcos stopped beside me while Dante moved to the couch and started cutting lines of coke he'd retrieved from his pocket.

Marcos stared at him in disgust, but he didn't utter a single admonishment. Clearing his throat, he shook his head. "Meet your new maintenance men. Drew Walker and his brother, Penn."

I turned my head to look at him. "I'm sorry. Was there a plague that wiped out the entirety of the Guerrero family that I somehow missed?"

"Order came straight from Pop. Seems he became close with Drew while they were cellmates."

Ah, yes. I was correct: Inmate 401.

Marcos flipped his dark gaze on me. "Apparently, the Walkers used to work construction. When Pop heard about Hugo's…unfortunate accident, he sent word for me to assign them here." He paused, his jaw ticking with an intensity that made me fear for his teeth. "Said he trusts Drew like a son."

Which really meant Manuel Guerrero, Inmate 402, trusted this Drew guy more than he did his own dumbass sons. Something I did *not* find shocking, but something I found abundantly amusing. I did everything I could to hide my smile, including looking back at Drew and Penn just in case a lip twitch squeaked out—and it totally did.

"Show them your problem," Marcos ordered.

"My problem?" I parroted because, seriously, he was going to have to be more specific with that. I had more problems than not.

A loud snnnnft came from the couch before Dante elaborated. "Your fucking water leak or whatever's got this goddamn place smelling like a landfill." He snapped his fingers at the men and pointed down the hall. "Do your goddamn job and figure it the fuck out."

Like good little minions, they both started toward the hall with the same foot.

"It's in the kitchen," I told their backs.

The tall one, who I assumed was Penn, replied, "The way that wall looks, it's probably leaking through from a bathroom."

Oh, shit! Oh, shit.

Oh. Fucking. *Shit.*

Savannah.

Things I was good at: math, the Dewey Decimal system, and time management.

Things I was not good at: hiding sixteen-year old girls from psychopaths.

I'd planned for that day the best I could. Any time Dante

had shown up, he'd always go into River's room. And he'd come into my room more times than I'd ever care to admit—or remember. There were no doors on any of the closets, and all of our mattresses sat on the floor. There were only so many places she could hide.

However, in all the years I'd lived in that apartment, Dante had never once stopped by for a shower.

With these two assholes convinced that my problem was in the bathroom, my good friend Panic blasted through me.

Jogging after them, I called, "The bathroom's fine."

They kept going.

I kept freaking the hell out.

"Seriously, it's fine." I glanced over my shoulder. Marcos thankfully hadn't followed.

As we reached the bathroom, my heart was beating so fast that it probably could have been read on the Richter scale. They entered before me: Penn and his lanky body then Drew and his brickhouse frame.

The three of us would barely fit in that tiny bathroom, but I forced my way in and strategically wedged myself between Drew's tattooed bulk and the shower.

"Could be leaking from behind the sink, running down the wall into the second and first floor," Penn guessed.

His brother's only acknowledgment was a grunt.

"The sink!" I repeated a little too loudly for such a small space. "Good idea!" Whatever. Just as long as they didn't think it was the shower.

"Could be coming from the line to the shower," one of them suggested, though I was too busy cursing Murphy's Law to notice which one.

"It's not the shower!" I exclaimed.

They both turned to look at me. Penn's eyes were wide with surprise. Drew's narrowed with suspicion.

I laughed awkwardly. "Look, um… Any chance you guys could come back in say, an hour? I really have to use the, um… No!"

Drew snatched the curtain open, revealing Savannah curled into a ball in the tub. Her knees were tucked to her chest and her eyes were filled with terror as they slid from him to me.

"Jesus, fuck," Penn mumbled.

Drew remained stoically quiet.

Suddenly, Dante's voice floated down the hall along with his footsteps. "The fuck are you yelling about, woman?"

With shaking hands, I yanked the curtain shut and whispered, "Please don't tell him about her." I grabbed his tattooed forearm and peered up into his hollow blues. "I will do *anything* you want if you just don't mention her." I could sell myself to the devil. One time wouldn't kill me. At least not physically.

Especially not if it saved her.

When he didn't reply, I stepped closer until my breasts brushed his arm. "Drew, *please*."

As if I'd punched him, his whole muscular body recoiled.

Glancing to the curtain hiding Savannah and then back to me, he silently waited for an explanation. But I had none to give. At least not any that I could convey in the seconds it would take for Dante to reach us.

"Drew," I hissed urgently.

His gaze never drifted to my breasts the way I'd expected.

45

Nor did he seem to have any interest in my promise of *any-thing*. He just stared at me, the massive weight of his gaze alone anchoring me in place. And then, finally, in a jagged voice that was equally as intriguing as it was intimidating, he rumbled, "I'm Penn."

My mouth fell open. No. Freaking. Way. That would make Mr. Plain cellmates with Old Man Guerrero?

I blinked.

The "alleged" Penn Walker blinked back, and then, just as Dante rounded the corner, he jerked his arm from my grasp and marched from the bathroom, calling over his shoulder, "Leak's in the kitchen."

Goose bumps pebbled my skin as relief exploded inside me. I was positive my hands were shaking as Dante pinned me with a vicious glare before following after Penn, but I didn't care.

No one, not since the day Nic had used his body to shield me from a wall of bullets, had anyone done anything to actually *help* me.

Not without a price.

Not without a punishment.

Not until now.

CHAPTER FIVE

Penn

"She was a fucking kid," I growled, sliding the toolbox from the bed of my old Ford before slamming the tailgate.

Drew lowered the cigarette from his lips and taunted, "But you said you *needed* this, remember?"

"And you said we were working at a whore house. Not a fucking pedophile's haven."

"It's not too late for you to leave." He flicked his gaze to the tattoos on my hands. "They might not let you join the country club, but I'm sure you could make other friends."

"Fuck off."

"Then shut your mouth. The chick was obviously hiding her in the shower for a reason. Maybe the kid's only in training or something."

"In training? Because that's better?"

The sound of dirt and rocks crunching behind us caught our attention. Drew straightened as Marcos and Dante approached, but my focus was pulled up to the third floor. The blonde was standing there with her small hands wrapped around the railing as if it were the only thing supporting her.

As soon as her eyes found mine, she mouthed the one word that had the power to demolish me. "*Please.*"

One in. One out.

I immediately looked away, that hot knife twisting in my stomach.

"Drew," Marcos greeted.

"You two heading out?" He tucked the cigarette between his lips and extended his hand for a shake.

Marcos spared it only a glance before sliding his hands into his pockets. "I take it you remember the rules?"

Drew inhaled deeply and then blew it up to the sky. "Fix broken shit. Keep my hands off Guerrero property. And not one goddamn thing else." He smirked and dropped the cigarette to the ground, stubbing it out with the toe of his boot. "Though, just to clarify, it's cool if I jerk my dick, right? Technically, I know it will be in a Guerrero shower, but don't worry. I'll clean it up real nice."

Dante lurched forward, his chest colliding with Drew's.

I didn't move, but I was ready, every muscle I possessed coiled for action.

The brothers had been on the edge of explosion since we'd met up with them that morning. Marcos and Dante had been none too thrilled their dear old daddy had assigned two strangers to work for them. But they'd both managed to keep it in check—well, almost.

"Outstanding," Marcos groaned as if he'd been inconvenienced.

"Listen up, motherfucker," Dante snarled. "You're in my house now." He slid his drug-induced, glassy eyes to me. "I dug both your graves last night. Nice quiet little spot where the vultures can feast for days."

Drew had always been an arrogant smartass. Swear to God, he came out of the womb with his hands raised loud and proud, flipping the doctor off. But he used to at least realize there was a time and a place for his stupidity. Clearly, prison had changed that.

"So, not underground, then?" He covered his heart with his hand. "Whew! Thank God. Few years in lockup and suddenly I'm claustrophobic as fuck."

Dante did not seem amused—a fact he made known when, less than a second later, a gun was retrieved from the back of his pants and pressed between Drew's eyes.

Just as fast, I dropped the toolbox and caught Marcos around the neck. If anything happened to Drew, I was ready to crack his spine without a single hesitation.

In a blink, Marcos produced his own weapon and stabbed it under the hinge of my jaw. I tightened my hold around his neck.

"Whoa. Whoa. Whoa!" Drew exclaimed. "Everyone just relax." He laughed. "This is nothing more than a little spat among family."

Yes, with a gun to his head and another under my chin, the idiot laughed.

Suddenly, I was the one who wanted to kill him.

But that could wait…

"We are *not* family," Dante seethed.

Drew lifted his arms out to his sides. It would have looked like a surrender if he hadn't stepped closer to the gun, pressing the tip deeper into his flesh. "My last name isn't Guerrero, but your father made me one." Another step forward forced Dante to take one back. "Go ahead. Let word get out that you put a bullet in my skull. You'll be begging for the birds to pick the flesh from your bones." He dropped his hands. "You can't touch me any more than I can touch you. So how about you get your tweaked-out ass in your car, drive away, and let me do my goddamn job."

Jesus fucking Christ.

My lungs burned as I held my breath. This was not exactly the new start I'd been looking for that morning. It was perilously close to an end instead.

Dante stared, his trigger finger twitching each time he sniffled.

And Drew stared back, a huge shit-eating grin splitting his face, all the confidence in the world damn near suffocating me.

Finally, it was Marcos, still in my hold, who broke the tension. "We have shit to do and that does *not* include listening to Pop's line of bullshit if you do something stupid, Dante. Leave them be and let's get the fuck out of here."

Dante didn't immediately move, and as the seconds wore on, I feared he wasn't going to. But then, with a quick burst of laughter, he lowered the gun.

And promptly head-butted Drew in the nose.

"Motherfucker!" Drew boomed.

My vision flashed red, and on pure instinct, I slung Marcos to the side and bolted toward Dante.

Drew threw up a hand to stop me. "Stay out of it, Penn."

I couldn't do that. He knew that better than anyone. He was all I had left.

However, the decision was made for me when Dante

simply tucked the gun into the waist of his pants, threw one last glare at Drew, turned on a toe, and then strolled away. Marcos fell into step at his side, straightening his suit coat as they leisurely walked to the black Mercedes.

What. The. Fuck.

As their car disappeared around the corner, Drew sidled up next to me, blood pouring from his nose and soaking the front of his shirt. "I think that went well."

I clenched my jaw. "Are you insane?"

Tilting his head back in a useless attempt to stop the bleeding, he waved me off. "Please. That guy was a pussycat. You should meet their old man. Manuel's a beast. They go against anything he says—son or not—and he'll snatch the spine from their bodies Mortal Combat style."

Incredulous, I scowled at him. It only made him start laughing like the dumbass he truly was.

"That was impressive," a woman called, joining the conversation. "I get it now." The blonde from earlier jogged over, a towel thrown over her shoulder. She stopped in front of us and peered up at me.

Christ, she was beaut—Whatever. It didn't matter.

I crossed my arms over my chest and aimed my gaze at nothingness over her shoulder. "Get what?"

"I had you pegged all wrong." She used her hand to shield the sun from her eyes. "You're the brother." She offered Drew the towel. "And *you're* Inmate Four-Oh-One— Manuel's new *son*."

Drew chuffed and took the rag. Holding it to his nose, he mumbled around it, "Guilty."

"I'm Cora." She dropped her voice before finishing

with, "Guerrero."

Oh, fucking fuck me.

Of course she was.

Of. Fucking. *Course.* She was.

It was hot for Chicago in early May, but a cold chill erupted across my skin.

I blinked at the empty parking lot, and before I could stop it, my gaze flicked back to her.

I regretted it immediately.

She was staring up at me through thick, painted-black lashes, the strangest mixture of curiosity and confusion dancing in her haunting, blue eyes. "Why didn't you tell them about her?"

Unable to take her scrutiny, I bent to pick up the tool-box. "None of my business you keep a kid in your shower." I walked to the truck, dropped the tools in the bed, and called out to Drew, "We need to hit the hardware store." *A.K.A. I need an escape.*

I started to open the door, but her hand—complete with perfectly painted red nails—came from behind me and slapped on the glass to hold it shut. "I don't *keep* her in the shower."

I did everything I could to stare through her reflection in the window—desperately trying not to see her. But my vision refused to focus on anything else.

Those fucking eyes.

Forging ahead, I tugged at the door. "Like I said, none of my business."

Her heat landed on my back. Cora was small, maybe five-two, whereas I was six-one. So her soft curves hit me in all the right—and completely wrong—places.

"Back up," I ordered.

She didn't move the first muscle—except for her mouth. "Dante found her after he put an ad online for models," she said, careful to keep her voice low. "It's how he gets new girls. He pulls them in, gives them drugs, flashes cash, fucks them, tells them he loves them, tells them he hates them, beats them, or whatever the hell it takes to get in their head and make them dependent on him. After that, he turns them out on the street to work for him." She swayed impossibly closer and my breath turned to ice in my lungs. "That girl back there is a sixteen-year-old runaway with nowhere to go who learned the hard way—and, Penn, it was Dante, so I'm talking the *real* hard way—not to trust a man. A feeling she and I unfortunately share."

My body turned to stone and my grip on the handle became murderous. Oh, but she wasn't done with her little fairytale from hell.

"I found her half dead on the floor, needle still in her arm, at Dante's house a month or so ago. I was there to pick up a new girl, but while he was passed out in bed, I took Savannah too. If he ever finds out she's here, there is no telling what he would do to her." Determination filled her voice. "I will *not* let that happen. So hear me now. I don't know what kind of men you and your brother are. I'll be honest: I don't give the first damn as long as you keep your hands off my girls. But I appreciate what you did back there. More than I can ever express. So..." She paused, her gaze finding mine in the reflection, those fucking eyes boring into me like she was pillaging through my head. And then she finished with, "Thank you."

I was mere seconds from peeling out of my skin just to get the hell away from her when she backed off.

She looked to Drew, who was still standing at the tailgate. "And...thank you, too, I guess."

He moved the towel from his face to reveal his mouth hanging open. "Oh, I'm sorry. Do I exist again? Because I swear, for a minute there, I disappeared."

Curiously, she tipped her head to the side. "You were seriously cellmates with Manuel?"

"Yep."

"And he liked you?"

Drew grinned and hooked his thumb in the direction Dante and Marcos had left. "A hell of a lot more than he likes those two jackasses."

And that was when the sky opened, the light of the Lord shined down, and he finally told me what I'd known for years: *Penn, I fucking hate you.*

Because she smiled.

And not like that ridiculous fake one she was wearing when she opened the door. Not even like the lip twitch when Marcos had told her that Manuel thought of Drew as his son.

This smile was different.

It was the kind of smile that could have shredded the darkest soul.

And I knew—because it was the exact moment I felt the first slice through mine.

CHAPTER SIX

Penn

"So this is it," Cora said in what sounded like an apology. And, as I glanced around our new shithole apartment, I understood why.

Hugo's crap was everywhere. Dirty clothes, dishes, and empty pizza boxes were strewn across the half-linoleum, half-concrete flooring.

But at least it wasn't carpet.

Drew spun in a circle. "Home sweet home."

"It's only one bedroom," she said—another apology.

I felt her gaze land on me: soft as a feather, harsh as an interrogation. I didn't dare look in her direction. We'd shared enough contact earlier in the day to last me a lifetime.

Switching the black duffel that held my limited clothing and toiletries to my other hand, I escaped down the hall, the sound of Drew's motor-mouth filling the space I left empty.

"Ignore him," he told her.

Yes. Please ignore me.

"What's his deal?" she asked.

There wasn't enough time in all of eternity for Drew to explain that one. Not that he would.

I continued to listen to them talk as I took in the filthy bedroom, complete with a stained mattress and a tower of beer cans.

"He was born without a personality. You'll get used to it," Drew replied.

There were several beats of silence where I could only assume they were exchanging knowing looks. But, again, I wasn't willing to turn around and see for myself.

"All right. I guess I'll let you guys settle in. The bathrooms in the front of the building still work. I've shifted the girls around so one-oh-two is open. The door has three locks. If you're inside…*use them*. On the flip side, if they're locked, it means one of the girls is taking a shower." Her voice took on a hard tone. "In which case, don't even *think* about going inside."

Drew barked a laugh. "Cora, babe, we're not here for your girls."

"Yeah, well, supposedly, neither was Hugo."

According to the half-empty economy box of condoms in the corner of his room, she was wrong. I didn't inform her of this. I kept listening.

"Okay, how about this. Penn or I get the taste to take a woman to bed, we'll head into town, hit one of the bars, lie about how much money we make, take 'em back to their place, and then sneak out the next morning before they wake up."

"Wow. How very chivalrous of you," she deadpanned, and as much as I wanted to deny it, her being a smartass made my lips twitch.

"We do what we can," Drew replied.

"Right. As long as you're *doing it* somewhere else, we'll be just fine."

Drew laughed and then both of their voices grew distant. But I didn't turn around. I just stood there, my knuckles turning white on the handle of my duffel bag as I stared at that bedroom, dread and impatience settling in my stomach.

Jesus Christ. How had I ended up there?

My lids fell closed, twenty-nine minutes of memories bombarding me.

"No, please!" she screamed as she fell to the foot of the bed, crimson blood seeping through her pale-pink shirt.

One in. One out.

The stale, stagnant air that filled my nostrils did nothing to tame my demons, but it did wonders to remind me where I was—and, most importantly, where I wasn't.

Her perfume didn't linger in that apartment.

Her clothes didn't fill the closet.

Her herb garden she loved so much didn't sit dead and overrun by weeds on the back deck.

Her smiling, carefree face didn't hang in images on the walls, tormenting me.

No. That rancid, stomach-churning apartment was exactly where I needed to be.

One in. One out.

I startled when Drew's hand came down on my shoulder.

"Jesus, man. You going deaf?"

Swallowing hard, I packed down four years of regrets and turned to face him. "Sorry. She gone?"

His thick eyebrows furrowed. "Yeah…she's gone."

"Good." I walked back down the hall, settled my bag on

the counter, and parked my ass on a wooden barstool—the only surface I was willing to touch.

"How the hell do you think you're going to get shit done around here when you're acting like the boss lady is Medusa's evil twin?"

"I'll manage."

"Right." He shook his head and wandered around the counter to a small galley kitchen that had seen better days—like, say, the seventies. "Though, after today, I might need you to continue acting like a mentally unstable asshole to level the playing field for me." He let out a low whistle. "Did you see her ass?"

"Don't be a dick."

A loud, condescending laugh bubbled from his throat. "I'll take that as Penn the Priest noticed her ass too?"

Actually, I'd noticed a lot of things about Cora Guerrero.

Things like the way that simple turquoise tank top had hugged her, tracing and accentuating curves no woman that small should have possessed. And how her bra had been too thin because, as she gave us a tour of the building, it was her peaked nipples that gave the real show. And the fact that she'd been wearing a pair of tight ripped-at-the-knees jeans that rode so low on her hips that, as she walked up the stairs, the tan skin of her lower back peeked out, teasing a starving man—and maybe Drew too.

That woman was a natural disaster waiting to happen, and if I didn't watch myself, I was at risk of being victim number one.

"I didn't sign up for that shit," I muttered.

"Relax. I already told you I'd take care of Cora." He

scrubbed a hand over his cheek. "No way she can resist a face like this."

But it wasn't his face that Cora would fall for. Drew was good with people, even better with women. All that wit and charm that had gotten him in so much trouble over the years was finally working in our favor.

What was not working in our favor was the way Cora had been staring at me all day.

Or the way my pulse spiked each time she came near me.

But that was a different story. One that would never matter.

"Though she seems rather fond of the ink. Either you need to invest in some long-sleeved shirts or I'm going to need to hit a tattoo joint."

Desperate to change the subject, I barked a humorless laugh. "Is this before or after you get yourself killed?"

"What the hell are you talking about?"

"You acted like a child today, pulling that shit with Dante." I moved around the bar, bumping my chest with his. "I've buried one too many goddamn people in my life. Don't make me do it again."

All humor left his face as he suddenly paled. "Penn, man. I had that shit under control. It wasn't a big deal."

"It was to me. He put that gun between your eyes…" I shook my head. "We're here to *work*, Drew. Not to pick a fight with a cracked-out pimp with a God complex." I paused and locked my gaze on his, pleading just as much as I was demanding. "You have a job. I have a job. *That's it.* Got it?"

He stared at me for several beats, a darkness brewing in his eyes. "You *know* I fucking got it, *brother*." He went straight to the cheap fridge, which was a few inches shorter than he was. Sucking in a deep breath, he opened the door, and then, in true Drew fashion, the tension melted away.

"God bless your fat, perverted ass, Hugo," he exclaimed, revealing a six-pack of horse-piss beer.

After tossing one my way, he cracked a can open and moaned when it hit his lips. He was on beer number two before I was on the second sip.

The hum of the fridge droned in the background until he finally broke the silence. "You gotta admit she's a firecracker."

Outstanding. We were back to Cora. Not that I'd forgotten.

"She's crazy," I mumbled.

"Oh, I don't know. There's something special about a woman brave enough to pin you to a truck just to say thank you."

I became enthralled with my boots and tried to think of anything except for how soft her breasts had felt pressed against my back. And then I struggled to forget the desperation and fear in her deep-blue eyes as she promised me *anything* to protect that young girl hiding in the bathtub. When, truth be told, the minute Cora had whispered the word *please*, all I'd really wanted to do was protect *her*.

Lisa had been dead for four years and I could still hear her pleas echoing in my ears, every day and every night. I didn't need to add Cora's to that never-ending symphony of my failures. Yet I feared I already had.

Clearing my throat, I gave my attention back to Drew. "Any other man, that stunt could have gotten her killed."

"I'm not thinking the woman's real concerned with her

safety. Did you see that bruise on her face?"

I had. And it'd lit me on fire. "Whatever. I just need you to keep her off my ass."

"Apparently, after today, you mean that literally."

"I mean that in *every* way possible. She keeps that shit up, it's not going to be good for anyone."

He tipped the beer to his lips, smirking around it. "I gotta admit, Penn. That *shit* being a smoking-hot woman getting all up in your space, plastering her fine body against your back? I'm not particularly feeling sympathetic for you right now." He smirked. "But I'll take care of it. In the meantime, you can take the bedroom. After two years in a cell, I'm not real eager to spend the night in another."

I glanced down the hall. I hadn't been behind bars for the last few years, but I'd been living in a prison all the same. That dingy eight-by-eight bedroom barely big enough to hold a nasty mattress wasn't exactly the escape I'd been hoping for.

But it was better than going home.

CHAPTER SEVEN

Penn

J ust as I'd suspected, rest was nowhere to be found that night. Though I'd often heard that sleep required a flat surface that didn't make a person fight the urge to gag, which was exactly what had happened each time I'd so much as thought about Hugo's disgusting mattress. No amount of sheets, blankets, or plastic wrap could convince me otherwise. So, after I'd spent hours cleaning, sweeping, and mopping, I'd stood the mattress up against the wall, retrieved the sleeping bag that lived under the seat in my truck, changed into a pair of sweats, switched the lights off, and settled in for some heavy-duty staring at the ceiling. It was midnight and I'd made it a solid five minutes without losing my mind before Drew came knocking at my door.

"Hey, Penn? You up?"

I propped myself up on my elbows. "Yeah."

The door swung open, light flooding in around his dark silhouette. Leaning his shoulder against the doorjamb, he crossed his arms over his chest. "You think there's anywhere around here that sells full-body condoms?"

Squinting, I put a hand up to block the blinding light.

"This neighborhood? Probably."

He chuckled. "That couch is a nightmare. I swear something's dead inside it. I'm gonna see if I can find a place open that sells an air mattress. We should probably start thinking about buying some new stuff."

"We gonna be here long enough to warrant furnishing the place?"

He shrugged. "Maybe we should hold off on hiring an interior decorator and the custom addition of a second bedroom, but a futon that's not covered in another man's cum stains and a TV that turns on don't seem like too much to ask."

Shaking my head, I aimed a grin at the floor. "You always were a diva."

"You know it. Wait until tomorrow morning. I'm gonna start demanding shit like coffee that doesn't taste like asphalt."

Drew was crazy, but I'd missed him so damn much over the last few years. Losing him during such a traumatic time in my life had only made my anger and isolation that much more devastating. He got on my nerves to no end, but he was also the only person who made me feel human.

After Lisa, there weren't a lot of people left in my life. My parents had passed away shortly after I'd graduated college, and the few friends I'd had who didn't remind me of her had wisely hit the road when I'd transformed into a miserable bastard. There had been a lot of dark days for me.

Dark weeks.

Dark months.

Dark years.

But Drew? He hadn't judged me when I'd shut down,

nor had he attempted to force me to move on when I could barely breathe through the rage. He understood my pain on levels no else could. And I loved him beyond measure for that alone.

"Any chance I can get the keys to my truck?" he asked. "I'm not feeling up to getting mugged tonight."

"Your truck?"

"Uhhh, did you not sell it to me? Because I distinctly remember handing you a dollar and you writing me a bill of sale."

"You dick, it's still mine. We only put it in your name because if something happens to me you wouldn't have been able to buy a new one."

He squinted one eye. "See, I hear what you're saying, but I'm pretty sure no matter how you spin this, it all ends with the truck being mine." He grinned.

I rolled my eyes, snagging the keys from my bag and then throwing them his way. "Whatever. Be careful with her. You break it, you buy it. For real this time."

He caught them in one hand, a wicked smile splitting his mouth. "I'll get a twenty-five-dollar IOU ready."

His footsteps disappeared down the hall, and then, with the slam of the front door, I was alone and trapped inside my own head again. It was a terrible place. One filled with blood and despair, built on a foundation of helplessness and failure.

It was where I'd lived every night for the last four years. And where I was so desperately hoping to escape.

"Please!"

One in. One out.

At some point, I must have dozed off, my body finally

trumping my mind, because when I rolled over, the clock read three and I'd yet to hear Drew come home. Obviously, he'd gone in search for more than just an air mattress. Like a warm bed that included the bonus accessory of a naked woman.

I couldn't blame him. My life had never been the revolving door of women that his had been, but there had been a few drunken nights when I'd found myself with a woman in my bed since I'd lost Lisa. They were usually hollow, meaningless one-night stands dictated by biology. But I was no saint. They'd happened. And I understood why Drew would be out searching for that. When a mind was so consumed with hate and pain, even a single second of distraction felt like a monumental reprieve.

And, God, did I need a reprieve from the chaos in my head right about then.

The curve of Cora's ass flashed into my mind.

"Shit," I breathed, scrubbing my hands over my face as if I could erase the thoughts.

Giving up on sleep, I sat up, my back screaming in protest. At thirty-seven, my body wasn't nearly as forgiving as it had once been. I ate right, worked out, all that shit that would supposedly extend my fruitful journey on this wonderful planet. *Cough. Bullshit.* Mentally and emotionally, I felt like I was at least two hundred—and dead.

I tugged a shirt on and wandered down the hall to the kitchen. Hugo's crap was still everywhere. Obviously, Drew had *not* been doing the Mr. Clean routine the way I had in the bedroom. I was digging through the bag of food we'd brought, in search of my protein powder, when I heard footsteps pounding on the stairs. I froze, trying to figure out if they were coming or going, and then the pounding hit my door.

"Hey hey hey! Open up!" a female voice shouted. The panic in her tone spiked my own.

I dropped the bag and hurried over to the door, snatching it open.

The young girl Cora had introduced as *Don't even look at her* the day before shoved past me, demanding, "Bolt cutters."

"What?" I asked.

She was in pajamas, and her dark hair was in a pile on the top of her head. I'd known she was young when I'd briefly met her, even younger than the one we'd found in the shower. But with terror in her eyes and fear etched on her pale face as she turned in a circle, scanning my apartment, she looked like a baby.

When she saw my toolbox on the counter, she sprinted over, flipped the lid open, and then began frantically rifling through it. "I need bolt cutters."

"For what?"

Before she had the chance to answer, Cora yelled from somewhere in the distance. "River, hurry up!" Her tangible fear sliced through me from all angles as it echoed off the walls.

"I'm trying!" she replied, her voice cracking as she continued picking up and dropping tools in her frenzied search.

"What the hell is going on?" I asked her.

"I don't know. But she's gonna die if we don't get that damn door open."

A blast of adrenaline rocked me back a step. "Who?"

With tears in her eyes, she paused long enough to level me with her brown stare. "Does it matter?"

No. It didn't. Not even a little. And, finally, my confusion transformed into purpose.

"Move," I ordered, reaching around her. The best I had was a pair of cable cutters, but they would have to do. After snatching them up, I took off.

"First floor!" she yelled, running behind me. I barely heard her over the thundering in my ears.

With the all-too-familiar sour in my gut fueling me forward, I took the steps three at a time, launching myself down to the landing. Then again with another flight. The minute my foot hit the first floor, I saw Cora still wearing the same jeans and tank top she'd been wearing earlier, standing outside one of the apartments. Her face was shoved into a two-inch opening, a chain at the top of the door preventing her entry.

"Oh God, Angela. Please hang on! I'm coming, sweetheart. I'm right here."

"Get out of the way," I rumbled.

Her back collided with my chest as I leaned over her and clamped onto the chain. The damn thing didn't budge.

"Hurry!" she cried, squeezing out from in front of me.

"I'm fucking trying," I snapped as if my inability were her fault.

Using my thigh, I leaned my weight against the door to keep the chain taut and brought both hands up for extra leverage. My arms shook and my muscles screamed as I gave it everything I had. Just as I thought my tool was going to crack before that damn chain, the door flew open, sending me stumbling inside.

But I didn't just stumble into an apartment.

I stumbled through time.

Four years, three months, two weeks, and four days to be exact.

On the floor, covered by shitty, gray commercial carpet, a woman lay face down, pools and pools of blood forming all around her.

Her skin was pale.

Her hair was brown.

And I couldn't fucking move.

Pain and memories, past and present, agony and regret all rained down over me like a million rusty razor blades slicing through the numbness.

As if it were in slow motion, Cora raced past me and dropped to her knees at the woman's side.

I'd spent a lot of years trying to change the outcome of the night I'd lost Lisa. Playing the what-if game so often and so intensely that I barely knew what was real anymore. In most of my scenarios, I'd saved her. A few, I'd lain down next to her and died too. But, in all of them, I'd actually fucking done something.

Yet there I stood.

Bare feet to that goddamn carpet. Unmoving. Completely unable to process the all-too-familiar massacre in front of me.

"Help me!" Cora yelled.

Like an involuntary reaction, my eyes slid to hers.

And then, like a bullet from a gun, she said the only word that could have destroyed me any deeper. "Please!"

My mind splintered. Time collapsing upon itself. Reality warring with What-if.

And then all at once, I exploded forward. "Lisa!"

Cora

The boom of his voice rattled the walls, but it was nothing compared to the screaming inside my skull. My heart raced at a marathon pace, and my lungs were more than following suit.

With wide eyes, Penn stormed over, bent, shoved one arm under her shoulders and one under her legs, and then lifted her off the floor.

"No!" I yelled.

She dangled in his arms, her long, dark hair brushing his thigh. But he just stood there, his gaze bouncing around the room without actually focusing on anything.

"Not on the carpet," he rumbled. He didn't spare me the first glance as he marched to the sofa, deposited her flat on her back, and repeated on a mumble, "Not on the fucking carpet."

The carpet. Right. Because, to a dying woman, that mattered. I didn't have time to question him.

Penn became a man on a mission.

Shoving me out of the way, he tugged his shirt over his head, and then, ripping it at the seam, he tore it into two long strips. With fast but precise movements, he tightly tied off the exposed slash on her wrist. Then he moved to her other arm, doing the same.

With nothing to distract my mind, reality crashed over me. Tears stung my eyes as I watched him check for a pulse and then listen to see if she was breathing, but I refused them their dire escape.

"What did you do?" I whispered to the beautiful woman dying on the couch. As messed up as it was, I was angry at her.

For not talking to me sooner.

For not letting me help.

For...leaving me there.

Angela was a first-floor girl through and through. She had little to no ambition to go back to school or get out of the life. She told me often how much she liked her job. Easy money, she'd said. It wasn't my favorite rationale, but it was one most of the lifers shared. But Angela—she was one of true good eggs in this business. She should have been some middle-aged man's trophy wife, sitting on a yacht, drinking a martini, not lying on that dingy couch, life seeping from her veins.

I told myself that it wasn't my fault, yet I still felt undeniably responsible.

Just like when I'd lost Nic.

The pain cut through me so deep that it threatened to take out my knees.

"Cora!" Penn called, snapping my attention up to his. "Lift her arm. Hold it above her heart. And pressure. Lots of fucking pressure." His face was tight with the same desperation that was shredding me. Even in the throes of such heartbreaking chaos, it honestly puzzled me.

To some, a man helping a dying woman was the

obvious expectation.

But that wasn't the way our lives worked.

To most, we were nothing but trash.

A body to use.

A soul to control.

An object to ruin.

But that wasn't the way *he* was looking at her.

Or treating her.

Or treating *me*.

Rather, he was holding her arms above her head as blood covered his hands and smeared over his chest, regarding her like a person and not just a random prostitute who had finally gotten what she deserved.

I could have cried from that small generosity alone.

I didn't. I got to work.

Clutching one wrist to my chest, I leaned forward, wrapping my hand around the fabric he'd tied, and pinned it against the back of the sofa.

Penn started CPR, but if she had any hopes of making it, she needed more help than we could ever give her.

"River!" I yelled. "Call Marcos!"

She gasped in the distance.

"It's okay," I soothed. I looked at her over my shoulder. "He knows what to do. He'll call Larry just like last time. It's gonna be okay."

She stared at me, pleading and begging with tears streaming down her pink cheeks.

God, she was scared.

But so was I.

"I'll deal with Marcos," I assured.

She shook her head and begged, "Cora, no."

"River. *Please.* I can't let her die." I swallowed hard. "*We* can't let her die. This is Angela, sweetie. We owe her this much."

Her face crumbled, and I wished like hell I could take it all away, but I could only help one person at a time.

"Now. Go," I clipped.

Thankfully, she took off.

For what felt like a century, Penn relentlessly worked on Angela. Sweat poured from his forehead as he alternated between rescue breathing and chest compressions.

He never slowed.

He never gave up.

As far as I could tell, he never even considered it.

Thirty minutes later, an ambulance arrived.

Angela was already dead.

CHAPTER EIGHT

Cora

She wasn't the first person I'd lost.

But Angela? She was the first one I'd ever watched die.

That is if you didn't include Nic.

But as I sat in my bedroom with the door locked, a pillow held to my face, blood crusted on my skin, dry heaves acting as the welcoming committee for my sobs, he was all I could think of.

"Cora," River called from the other side of the door. "The cops want to talk to you. Oh…and, uh, Drew and Penn are here too."

I blew out a controlled breath and willed away the tremors in my voice. "I'll be right out. I'm just"—I glanced at my blood-soaked shirt and gagged—"Changing clothes."

"Okay. I'll tell 'em."

She couldn't see me, but she was still too close for me to reveal any weakness. I waited until her footsteps disappeared down the hall before I stood up on newborn-giraffe legs.

"You can do this," I whispered to myself. It wasn't a pep talk. It was a direct order from my mind to my nervous system. "Get it together," I murmured, peeling my bra off and then stepping out of my pants. I wasn't sure what to put on. Whatever it was, I'd have to burn the very next day.

River and Savannah had tried to force me into one of the showers when the paramedics left, but I'd been too close to breaking down for that.

I couldn't escape that building—or the life it represented.

All I'd been able to do was race up the stairs, lock myself in my bedroom, and then cry tears for a woman who would never be able to again. It was disgusting, and the guilt I felt afterward was overpowering, but somewhere in those tears was a selfish pang of jealousy that she had gotten to leave.

And I had to stay.

I found my ruined turquoise robe hanging over the back of my rocking chair. The sleeve was already covered in blood from my nose the day Chrissy had left; a little more would seal its fate at the bottom of a burn can.

Using a towel and a bottle of water next to my bed, I cleaned myself up as much as I could, all the while compartmentalizing my emotions.

There was a place for everything.

Anger. Sadness. Resentment. Guilt. Dread. Remorse.

And once they were all tucked away in their filthy little drawers in my head, I tied my robe as tight as I could get it, drew in a breath, and set forth on ending my latest nightmare.

As I entered the living room, my gaze landed on Penn first. He was standing beside the door, still mostly covered in blood, though he was wearing a clean T-shirt. His weight shifted subtly at first. Then he lurched toward me, only making it a step before throwing the brakes on. His Adam's apple bobbed as he scanned me from head to toe. And then his sad, desolate eyes came back to mine.

"I'm sorry," he whispered. "Fuck. I'm so sorry."

My chest squeezed. "It's not your fault."

"I don't know if that's true anymore."

I watched him intently as if I were memorizing his features. He was a stranger, but after everything we'd been through that night, it seemed like I'd somehow known him longer than a day.

A lot longer. Like, say, a million years longer.

It didn't make sense, but I had to physically restrain myself from running into his arms, burying my face in his chest, and letting him hold me while I cried for at least a week. I couldn't remember the last time I'd had someone to lean on. And, while Penn couldn't possibly realize what he'd done for me just by being there that night, he'd given me something huge.

He'd given me faith in humanity again.

His dense, blue eyes tracked me as I moved deeper into the room, but it was Drew who rose from his seat on the couch and met me in the middle.

"Jesus, Cora," he murmured as he made it to me in three strides. "How ya doing?"

"I'm…fine." I flicked my gaze back to Penn. His body was rigid, and his face was nothing more than a cold mask.

Drew gave my arm a squeeze.

Curiously, I watched Penn follow the movement of his brother's hand.

Even more curiously, I immediately stepped away from Drew despite the fact that his offer of comfort felt nice. But not as nice as Penn's would have been.

"I'd love to tell you two that stuff like this doesn't happen often." I cleared my throat to keep the emotion at bay. "But, well, I… All I can really tell you is that I'm sorry and I hope like hell it doesn't happen again."

Drew bent at the knee, bringing us to eye level. "Are you kidding? Don't apologize." It was soft and sweet, everything a woman in my position should have wanted to hear, but once again, I looked at Penn.

"Thank you. For, ya know…*trying.*"

His eyes closed and his chin jerked to the side like I'd wounded him rather than praised his efforts. "Yeah. No prob," he replied on a pained chuff.

A suffocating amount of awkward silence ensued until I finally gave us all a break by turning my attention to the badge-wearing elephant in the room.

"Hey, Larry," I said, offering him a weak smile.

His salacious gaze raked over my bare legs up to my breasts. "Cora."

Larry was as crooked as cops came. And despite the wedding ring on his left hand and the fact that he was old enough to be my grandfather, he was also as fucked up as johns came. This was most likely why he found himself at the beck and call of the Guerreros.

I noticed the familiar coffee mug in his hand and turned to arch an eyebrow at River. She shrugged. She'd no doubt been doing the hostess-with-the-mostess bit to buy me time to collect myself. But, now, it was time for her to do the get-the-hell-out-of-here bit.

"Can you do me a favor and go check on Libby?" We

didn't have a Libby.

Dipping her head, she focused on her feet. "Do I have to? I'd rather just go back to bed. It's been a long night."

I narrowed my eyes, trying to figure out what she was playing at, when it suddenly dawned on me that Savannah was nowhere in sight.

God, my girls were smart.

"Yeah. Go ahead," I said and then watched her head down the hall. Before Larry could hear River's soft knock or Savannah opening the locks, I got to talking. "What can I do for you?"

A wolfish grin split his mouth. "Oh, I could think of a lot of things you could do for me."

Crossing my arms over my chest, I shot him a bored glare. "Yeah, well. I don't have enough time, energy, or Viagra to make that happen. So let's try this again: Why are you still here?"

Drew coughed to cover his laugh, but the only thing that came from Penn's quadrant of the room was a whole lot of pissed-off energy and a death glare.

Larry sucked through his teeth and rested his palm on his gun at his hip. "Woman, you got a record a mile long. I put you in cuffs in the back of my car, you'll die in a cell. One of these days, you're going to learn to watch your mouth."

He was full of shit. I had a record exactly two sentences long: two drug charges. Fun story—I'd never so much as smoked a joint in my life. The real story was I spent three years in jail for pissing off Marcos and Dante. It was a pure power play for them. And seeing as I was riding the wave of thirteen years under their control, it had worked. Now, though, I was on the wonderful list of what the State of Illinois called *Habitual Offenders*. Three-strikes-you're-out kind of deal.

"I'll be sure to start working on that." Snapping my fingers, I motioned for the return of my coffee mug. "She's dead, Larry." God, that burned, but I tucked it away in its own little disgusting drawer in my subconscious and powered through. "You can fill me in later on the details about how and where you claim to have found her in case any of your buddies start asking questions. But, right now, you have to get the hell out of my apartment. I need a shower, a metric ton of coffee, and then I have a building full of grieving girls to check in on."

Passing my mug back, he held my stare. "Watch yourself, Cora."

I gave him the most honest answer I'd ever spoken. "I always do."

His lips formed a thin line as he scowled at me for several beats longer.

Jerking my chin to the door, I prompted, "Have a good night, officer."

On a muttered curse, he turned on a toe and walked out, leaving the door wide open like a surly teenager.

Once he was gone, I blew out a ragged breath and reached up to pinch the bridge of my nose, jerking it away when I saw the blood caked under my nails. My stomach rolled.

"Oh God, I really need a shower." I glanced up at Penn. "You do too. Let me just grab my shampoo and I'll make sure none of the girls are in the other bathroom for you. It's the least I can—"

"You got this?" he clipped at his brother.

"Yeah," Drew replied on a sigh.

Before I had the chance to inquire with the obvious, *Does he have what?*—the answer clearly being *me*—Penn all but sprinted out the open door, slamming it behind himself, also not unlike a surly teenager.

Confused—and a tad insulted—I peered up at Drew. "Did I say..."

He shook his head and hooked his arm around my shoulders, pulling me into a side hug. "Don't worry about Penn. You've got enough shit on your plate without adding his to it. He'll be fine."

I immediately shifted out of his hold. "What kind of shit does he have?"

"The kind that no one can fix. So wipe that look off your face."

Challenge accepted!

"Who's Lisa?" I asked.

Drew's gentle face morphed into stone-cold fury, and his voice turned to gravel. "What did you say?"

I squared my shoulders. "Lisa. That's what Penn called Angela when he saw her on the floor."

Visible relief sifted through his features until he was back to Mr. Nice Guy. Gripping the back of his neck, he replied, "He probably just got confused. Thought that was her name or something."

Yeah, judging by nothing more than Drew's reaction, that was a load of bullshit. But we all had our secrets. God knew I had a mountain of my own. So I let it go.

For now.

"Yeah, that had to be it," I mumbled.

He offered me a gentle smile. "Now, for real, you gonna be okay?"

I shrugged. "It's kinda my only option."

CHAPTER NINE

Penn

I fell to my knees as I violently threw up in the trash can.

I couldn't breathe. And the pain was relentless—not even my numbness could block it out.

Lisa's face.

Lisa's blood.

Lisa's cries.

And then…

Cora's face.

Cora's desperation.

Cora's pleas.

My failures.

My failures.

My failures.

Just as another wave of nausea tore through me, I heard the door crack open and then quickly close. Seconds later, I felt a towel being draped around my shoulders. His knees cracked as he dropped into a squat beside me.

"It wasn't her."

"I know," I choked out, using the back of my arm to wipe the sweat off my forehead.

"Do you? Cora said you called her Lisa."

Fuck.

Bile rose in my throat, and I leaned deeper into the trash can, ready for another seizure in my stomach. "Yeah. Sorry 'bout that."

His hand landed on the back of my neck in what I assumed was supposed to be comfort, but it felt as though it singed my skin. "Penn, man. It *wasn't her.*"

When my gut ended its revolt, I settled on my ass with my back to the wall. "I fucking know it wasn't her. I was actually there for the woman tonight. Lot of good that did."

His jaw snapped shut, which was quite possibly the smartest thing Drew could have done. I'd listened to the *it wasn't your fault* bullshit too many times. The last had been the day before he'd gone to jail. It had ended in blows.

Using the edge of the towel, I wiped my mouth. "What the hell is wrong with this place?"

"I warned you it was a different world," he replied, dropping beside me to his ass.

"A different world?" I scoffed. "This is a whole other planet." I raked a hand through my hair. "For fuck's sake, we've not even been here twenty-four hours and we've got teenage addicts hiding from pimps who sexually abused them, women slicing their wrists, corrupt cops trying to get their dicks sucked. Don't even get me started on those EMTs. If I wasn't a hundred percent positive that the girl was already dead, I'd have killed them both on the spot. Swear to god, Drew, one of them winked at Cora when he strolled in with all the urgency of a slug."

With a sigh, he lowered his chin to his chest. "That's

another thing. We need to talk about Cora."

"Oh, no. We are *not* fucking talking about her."

He gave a low whistle and shook his head. "The way she looks at you?"

Oh, I'd seen it. And I'd give anything to be able to forget it.

She looked at me like I was a hero.

Like I was some sort of savior sent from above.

Like I could possibly drag her from the pits of hell.

I couldn't even save myself and she thought I could save her?

And, fucking worse, I wanted to.

But I wasn't that man.

At least not for her.

"I don't care how she looks at me," I lied.

"You should. Because after you pulled the damaged-white-knight routine tonight, I don't have a shot in hell at getting in there."

I blinked at him, in an honest-to-God stupor. "You're kidding me, right? I ruined your game by trying to help that dying woman?"

"I didn't say that. I'm just sayin—"

I shot to my feet. "Nothing. You're saying *nothing*."

I was marching down the hall, desperate for space, when he stopped me in my tracks.

"She's under your skin and it's freaking you out."

It was the most shockingly accurate thing he had ever said, even if it did confuse the hell out of me. But admitting that I was copping a case of the feels for the broken, brave, and beautiful Cora fucking Guerrero was a whole lot like accepting it. And that just *wasn't* going to happen.

Planting my hands on my hips, I wheeled around. "Fuck off, Dr. Phil. You have no idea what you're talking about."

"That why you were hovering all around her when I showed up tonight? Standing guard at her door like some kind of sentinel? For fuck's sake, Penn. You're covered in blood, but I couldn't drag you out of there until you knew she was okay."

"Excuse me for being a decent guy."

His face took on the strangest expression. "You know it would be okay if you did want her."

A searing blaze of pain hit me in the chest. "The hell it would be okay!"

"Lisa's been gone for four years."

"Yeah, I'm well aware of that."

He shrugged. "Who knows. Cora seems to have the Mother Teresa thing down pat. Maybe she could rub a little of that on you."

Rage built within me. "And then what? She and I just ride into the sunset while Lisa sits buried six feet under? Have you forgotten everything we've worked for?"

"I've forgotten nothing!" he boomed. His body became taut as he let out a frustrated growl, yanking at the top of his short hair. "Fuck. Fucking fuck."

I stood there with my chest heaving, watching his meltdown. God knew he'd watched enough of mine. He paced a path in the floor, kicking anything he came into contact with. The couch. The stool. His duffel of clothes. Everything was fair game.

Finally, he stopped his assault on inanimate objects and

shot me a glare. "I need you to do this."

I needed a lobotomy. "I can't and you know it."

And then, as though he were flicking a match into a puddle of gasoline, he announced, "Word is Marcos usually stops by a day or two after shit goes down. Roughs her up. Little reminder to keep her girls in check."

Visceral fury ignited inside me.

She'd been sporting a bruised cheek. This should not have been a shocker.

But try telling that to my roaring body.

My heart thundered.

My lungs seized.

My mind screamed.

And, this time, it was Cora's voice begging, *"Penn, please."*

One in. One out.

One in. One... "No one touches her."

Drew's lips lifted into a sinister smile. "Now you're talking. We'll switch shifts keeping an eye on her."

I nodded.

And, goddamn it, fuck me seven ways to Sunday—she wasn't even in the room, but as my heart slowed and my anger evaporated, I felt the warm curl of that woman sinking deeper under my skin.

CHAPTER TEN

Cora

"**N**o. Dante, please. It's not her fault!"

I was in a cold sweat when I jolted awake to the sound of my ringing phone. I had no idea what time it was or when I'd fallen asleep, but the overwhelming terror I'd felt in my nightmare while watching Dante drag River away from me had followed me into consciousness.

It had been twenty-four hours since we'd lost Angela. My chest still ached and my mind was still a swirling mess. But, much to my surprise, none of the Guerreros had shown up to issue their personal brand of punishment—yet. They would. Eventually. Of that much I was sure.

I just had to be ready when they did.

"It was a dream," I told myself, blindly slapping around on the nightstand until I found the offending device. "Hello," I croaked.

It was Mindi from the second floor. "Hey, Cor, I'm home."

"Good. What about Jennifer?" I had finally memorized the new girl's name.

The line went silent.

Squeezing my eyes tight, I sent up a prayer that she was just checking Jennifer's room, but when her response never came, I sat up with a groan. "Mindi?"

"I, uh… She didn't text you?"

While the women on the first floor were free to come and go as they pleased, I required the girls on the second and third floors to text me when they got home as long it was before four a.m.. After that, they had to call. They sometimes forgot and I read them the Riot Act. And a mere twenty-four hours after losing Angela, I wasn't cutting them any slack.

"No. She didn't. Is she there?"

"She's…um…in her room."

I exhaled in relief and used my thumb and forefinger to rub my eyes. "Go wake her up and tell her to call me."

"Okay. Give me a minute."

Touching the end button on the screen, I stared up at the glowing stars Nic had once upon a time stuck to the ceiling above our bed. The crooked letters were created from the luminous points. When I'd moved after he died, I'd taken every single one of those stars with me, and when I'd been sentenced to a life in that apartment building, I'd re-adhered them with little balls of putty in the exact same design he'd once created. It wasn't the same—but the sentiment was still there.

I could still hear his voice.

"You want the moon, Cora?" he'd said with a wicked grin, those dark eyes of his dancing in the moonlight. "Just say the word, and it's yours."

I'd smiled, the sweet intoxication of first love making me feel like I'd been floating. "I don't care about the moon, Nic. I just want you…and maybe the stars."

A single tear rolled down my face just as my phone started ringing.

I coughed to clear the emotion. "Hello?"

"Hey, Cor," Jennifer said sadly.

"What's wrong?" I asked, rolling out of bed. I was wearing my usual sleep uniform: panties and a thin camisole. Since my robe was up in smoke, I grabbed the quilt at the foot of the bed and draped it around my body, holding it tight with a hand at my chest.

"Nothing… I'm home. Sorry. I forgot to call."

"Are you sure everything's okay?" I pressed. Using my shoulder to hold the phone against my ear, I unlocked my door and headed down the hall, though I paused on my way out to test River and Savannah's knob. Thankfully, it was locked.

"Yeah, positive. Mindi just woke me up—that's all. Look, I'm going back to bed. I'll see you in the morning." She hung up without so much as a goodbye.

Forget about the morning. She was going to see me in about, oh…one minute.

Three more locks and I swung my front door open…

And then promptly had a heart attack.

My phone went flying from my hand, skittering across the concrete, as a baleful silhouette rose to its feet across the breezeway. Blood roared in my ears as I took in his black sweatshirt, the hood pulled up to cover his head. From shape alone, I knew it wasn't Dante or Marcos, but with only the moon serving as light, I couldn't make out his face.

That is until he tilted his head up, shoved the hood back,

and found my gaze with a tangible weight that nearly crushed me.

"Jesus, Penn." My heart slammed in my chest partially because he had scared the hell out of me. But mainly because he was staring at me.

Hard. Penetrating. Acute. I had not one doubt that he was reading me down to the marrow in my bones, and for the strangest reason, with him, I was okay with that.

A rush of heat pinked my cheeks as I managed to stammer out, "Wh…what are you doing out here?"

"Why aren't you dressed?" he countered, leaving me to question if he actually could see through the quilt.

I glanced down, finding that my trusty quilt had split open, revealing my legs all the way up to my panties. Quickly shifting, I used my other hand to hold the bottom closed as well. "I was just running down to check on Jennifer."

"Naked and in the dark?" He remained eerily still, his hands at his sides, his feet set shoulder-width apart, and his eyes locked on mine to the point that I could barely breathe.

"I'm not naked and…I didn't think anyone else was up."

He blinked and I swear the night dimmed with his lids.

Cocking his head to the side, he repeated more slowly this time. "In…the…dark, Cora?"

"The lights on the third don't work. They haven't in at least a year." Careful not to release my blanket, I used a single finger to point up at the ceiling. "I've changed the bulbs, but I think it's electrical."

"Shit can happen to a woman when they're alone and in the dark." It wasn't a threat; if anything, it sounded like he was trying to offer me a fatherly warning. But I'd lived in that building long enough to know it was bullshit.

"Shit can also happen to a woman when they're in a group and in broad daylight. Company or time of day isn't exactly a factor."

Suddenly, he became unstuck. Long strides carried him toward me. It would have been a *really* good time for nature's fight-or-flight to kick in.

But that was the thing: I wasn't afraid.

I didn't know Penn. Where he had come from? Why he was truly there? What he was capable of? So call me naïve or just plain stupid, but he didn't scare me.

Not after that day in the bathroom with Savannah.

Not after everything he'd done for Angela.

Not after everything he'd done for *me*.

I'd met a lot of bad men in my twenty-nine years, and Penn Walker was not one of them.

He stopped in front of me and rumbled, "Time of day might not be a factor, but this fucking neighborhood is."

He was not wrong. The two other complexes on the street had been broken into so often that it seemed like they were on a weekly rotation. But a Guerrero had owned our building from the very first brick, which made it clear to the criminal population that we were untouchable—at least from the outside world. The monsters we worried about had their own set of keys. They were the same monsters who hated me, beat me, and had me locked away more than once, but they would have murdered an entire city if anyone else had laid a single finger on me. It was the only perk of being Guerrero property.

"Trust me, Penn. No one would be brave enough to

take a stab at me."

Out of nowhere, his face paled and a tortured combination of pure masculine beauty and soul-crushing agony crashed over him.

I knew that look of pain all too well. I usually saw it in the mirror though.

After shuffling over, I placed my palm on his chest. "Jesus, Penn. Are you okay?"

"Don't do that," he choked out as though my hand were wrapped around his throat and not resting over his heart.

I made a move to pull it away, but before I had the chance, his eyes slammed shut, his face drew up tight, and his large palm came down over my hand, pinning it to his heaving chest. "Shit, don't do that, either."

Okay. So no touching. And no *not* touching. Got it.

I searched his face for answers but came up empty. Though, after the last twenty-four hours, one could assume... "Is this about Angela?" I asked, wishing I'd had the courage to ask the real question. *Is this about Lisa? Whoever she may be.*

"No."

"What about—"

He gave my hand a squeeze. "Cora, shhhh."

Ooookay. So no talking, either. Not exactly my forte, but I'd give it a try.

For about thirty seconds.

"You can talk to me. I'm a great listener." When he didn't reply, I tacked on, "Please."

Popping his eyes open, he winced. "You gotta stop sayin' that."

"I'm just trying to help."

"But you're not." Releasing my hand, he flew away as if I'd been holding him hostage. The loss of his warmth was violent, and the cold night's air assaulted me.

He started to pace. "I can't do this," he huffed in pure and utter defeat. "You have to stop this bullshit with me."

I blinked slow and incredulous.

I had to stop *this bullshit* with *him*?

I glanced around the empty hallway as if I could discover the answer to my question before I was forced to ask it. "What exactly is *this bullshit* you think I'm doing?"

He refused me eye contact as he cut two fingers through the air to indicate my body. "That. Right there. You gotta stop."

Curling my lip, I looked down at myself. I was covered—for the most part. "Oh, right. Because I totally planned this. I somehow sensed that you'd be in the breezeway, having a nervous breakdown, so I quickly threw on a blanket, teased my hair into sleep knots, and then raced out here. Damn it. You caught me."

He gripped the back of his neck. "I'm not saying you planned it. I'm just saying you have to *stop*. I'm begging you. Just put on some clothes and stop walking around in the dark. It's not safe."

I wrestled the blanket up. "In my experience, Penn, if a man wants something, a pair of pants and a light bulb won't stop him."

"What?" he snapped in a harsh tone that suggested he had very much heard me. And then he moved with long and heavy strides, advancing on me.

My stomach pitched, and a hum in my veins became deafening.

Gentle as a pillow, he collided with my front. His hand found my hip, firm but without the first hint of pain. Dipping his head low, he brought his mouth to my ear and asked, low and ominous, "In your experience?"

Heat rolled off him in waves, chasing a thrill down my spine and sparking my every nerve ending to life. "Oh, wow," I whispered, closing my eyes. It had been over a decade since I'd felt that spark for a man.

"Answer me, Cora."

Like a wanton fool, I swayed into him. "It's a lesson we all learn."

His hand tensed and he shook his head, his jaw ticking as though he were chewing on a curse. But he said no more.

And I couldn't bring myself to break the static silence.

Not with him looming over me, touching-not touching-impossibly close-but-worlds-apart. And definitely not while I was floating in the most blissful pool of erotic anticipation.

As I was lost in sensation, rational thought wasn't firing in the right direction, but there was nothing logical about the way my body responded to him.

With every inhale, his chest brushed against mine.

And, with every exhale, his breath seductively danced across my skin.

"Unlearn it," he ordered. "*In your experience.*" He bent lower, his lips only fractions of millimeters away from sweeping my ear, and repeated, "*Un*learn it."

"Okay," I panted, unsure of what exactly I was agreeing

to and too entranced to care.

He stared, his eyes ticking back and forth between mine, until he finally spoke in a pained whisper. "How do you do this to me?"

"I guess that depends on what you think I do?" I asked, praying it was the same all-consuming heat he caused in me.

His eyes fluttered closed. "If I could answer that, I'd know how to block you out."

My skin tingled as I pushed the envelope of what I thought he might allow. Cupping his cheek, I whispered, "Or you could just let me in."

He groaned at the contact, a mixture of torture and desire. And then he leaned against my hand, agony etched across his face. "You have no idea what you're asking from me."

"No. I don't. But that's the beauty of getting to know someone."

"And there's our problem," he mumbled before his lids flashed open and the man who had ignited me disappeared. He backed away, the cool air once again parting us, but it was the emptiness blazing from his hollow orbs that carried the chill. "Don't try to get to know me, Cora. I'm not a puzzle you can figure out or a broken lamp you can put back together." He patted hard on his chest. "This thing living inside me. It fucking burns. And if you get too close, I swear to God, it's gonna light you on fire too. I will not be responsible for that." He took a giant step toward me and seethed, "I can*not* be responsible for that."

My head snapped to the side. "Who asked you to be responsible for anything?"

"*You did.* The longer you stand there looking like that. The more you stare at me when you think I'm not looking. The more you smile and laugh. Every single minute that you are around me, *you* are making me responsible for that fire taking over your life too. So I am begging you. Drop this bullshit with me. Because, God's honest truth, I don't know that I'm strong enough to do it for both of us."

I blinked at him, hating that I was so transparent but downright gleeful because… "You feel it too?"

He scoffed, those heavy, blue eyes coming back to mine. "I've known you two days and I'm drowning in it, Cora. So, yeah. It's safe to say I feel it. But, right now, I really need you *not* to."

He was drowning in *it*.

He was drowning in it.

He was *drowning* in it.

I didn't even know what *it* was. But I felt it. And he was drowning in it.

"You're afraid I'll get burned?" I whispered, more than likely smiling.

"No." He shook his head vehemently. "You're a strong woman. You could probably handle the heat. But if this goes anything like my past, what I'm afraid of is that, when that fire inevitably finds you, I'll still be in the ocean, gasping for breath and completely helpless, when all it would take is a single drop of that water to save you."

Oh. My. Gahhhhhhhhhh.

What did that even mean, and why did it awaken my entire body?

I stared at him, a warmth traveling through me.

He stared back, the picture of desperation.

My heart pounded.

His jaw ticked.

The muscles at his neck were taut.

My breathing was labored.

"I don't want you to drown," I whispered.

"And I don't want you to burn. So, please, let's just agree that this goes nowhere. I work here. You work here. End of story."

I swallowed hard, unsure if I could promise him that. Penn was the first man who'd sparked anything inside me since Nic died. I couldn't honestly tell him that I didn't want to explore that.

Maybe it'd fizzle out.

But maybe it wouldn't.

But, in my world, where pain, filth, and fear were a way of life, why waste the possibility of finally feeling something incredible?

So, for that reason alone, I replied, "Lie. Okay. End of story."

He arched an incredulous eyebrow. "Lie?"

I shuffled toward the stairs. "I said okay, didn't I?"

He eyed me with suspicion. Rightly so. But it wasn't my problem that he didn't understand how Truth or Lie worked. I'd clearly stated that I was lying. He could hardly be mad about that.

"If you'll excuse me, I need to check on one of the girls."

His eyes narrowed to slits. "Don't bullshit me. What did you mean by 'lie'?"

I held my blanket tight as I gingerly took the steps one at

a time. "I said okay. What more do you want?"

"Maybe the truth," he said, following me down.

I kept going. "Lie. I told you the truth."

He kept following. "Why the hell do you keep saying 'lie'?"

I ignored his question and carried on to the second floor. Giving him another lie wasn't going to help my case.

Once we got to Jennifer's door, Penn must have realized he wasn't going to get a straight answer, but he didn't turn around and march home the way I'd expected.

For the next five minutes, he silently stood guard at the side of the door while I forced Jennifer out of bed, gave her a once-over, and interrogated her about her night.

When she had convinced me that she truly was fine, Penn walked me back up to the third floor and stopped in the breezeway, much the way I'd found him.

Full circle—only this time, I knew how amazing it felt to be in his arms and that he was drowning in the same *it* that had been consuming me.

My heart lurched as he took long strides toward me. Unfortunately, he veered away from me at the last second, bent at the waist, and retrieved my long-since-forgotten— and more than likely broken—phone before offering it my way. "Go inside. It's cold out here."

It wasn't cold when you were holding me.

As if he'd heard me, he shook his head. "Jesus, you're stubborn."

I grinned. "I don't know what you're talking about."

"Right. Of course not." He cut his eyes over my shoulder, staring blankly at the brick wall. "Can you at least tell me you heard what I said earlier? It's dangerous out here. If I were a different type of man standing in the hall tonight when you came out looking like that, things could have gone bad for you."

If curiosity killed the cat, I'd have been on my ninth life for the day and the sun hadn't come up yet.

"And what kind of man are you, Penn?"

He sighed, planted his hands on his hips, and answered, "Four years ago, I could have answered that no problem. Now? I have no idea anymore."

"Maybe I could help you figure it out."

"Christ. You're not going to let up, are you?"

I shrugged noncommittally and repeated, "I said okay."

"And you also said it was a lie." He blew out a heavy breath. "Just…go inside and lock your door."

I nodded but didn't move.

"Cora," he groaned, but it was definitely a plea.

For a fraction of a second, I felt guilty.

Until I remembered his hand on my hip. His breath on my neck. His chest against mine.

After that, all bets were off.

"You know. Just to be clear. I live in hell, Penn. I'm not scared of the flames."

Out of the corner of my eye, I saw him stiffen, but never one to bask in the suffering of another, I turned, opened my door, and went inside.

When I slid the third lock into place, I heard his door shut.

CHAPTER ELEVEN

Penn

"Oh God," I breathed, putting my back to the door. My skull hit the wood with a dull thump, but pain splintered in my head, ricocheting through my body until I thought I was being divided in two.

And honestly, I feared that was exactly what was happening.

My chest ached and my throat felt like I'd swallowed a bag of sand, but it was the swirling in my gut that I knew would destroy me.

Cora fucking Guerrero.

Screwing my eyes shut, I pinched the bridge of my nose, wishing I hadn't been waiting in the hall on the off chance that Marcos had made his move.

Of course she'd come out half naked, her honey-tanned legs traveling up to bubblegum-pink panties that were damn near invisible.

Of course, when she'd touched me, it'd shredded the numbness I'd purposely constructed to keep the anger locked inside—and people like her out.

Of course I'd felt it all, right down to her fingerprints

branding me through my shirt.

And, of *fucking* course, I'd had to go to war against my body not to take one single taste of her mouth. If she had pushed the issue a second longer, I'd have lost that battle in spectacular fashion.

Sliding down the door, I sank to my ass and whispered, "What the hell am I doing?"

"Good question," Drew replied.

I jerked my head up and found him sprawled out across the couch, his eyes closed and aimed up at the ceiling, but a classic smile tipped his lips.

Grasping at straws, I lied, "I heard something and went to check."

He opened his lids and swiveled his head to face me. "And you just so happened to stop to put on a jacket and boots first?"

"I was already up," I mumbled, rising to my feet and walking away, headed nowhere in particular as long as it was away from him. "Couldn't sleep."

"That might be because you sat in the hall all night, staring at her door."

I ground my molars, cursing myself for not giving him the bedroom.

He knifed up, stretching his arms over his head. "This building is made of construction paper and paperclips. If Marcos had shown up, we'd have heard him."

"I had a bad feeling. Okay? Get off my ass."

"I'm not giving you shit. You're a free man, Penn. Stare at her door for the rest of your natural life if you want. But I will say—you getting into a clench with her is hardly gonna help my case."

Of course he'd seen. I bet his eye had been glued to that goddamn peephole like it was his job. Which…I guessed it kinda was.

"Fuck off."

He put a hand to his chest. "I can keep trying, but we both know she's into you, whether she's ready to admit it or not. We'd be idiots not to capitalize on that. It's been two days and you've accomplished more than I could do in two months. Why are you fighting it?"

"Please, help me. Please."

"Because we had a plan," I said.

He stood and walked over to me. "And plans change. Five years ago, being here was *not* my plan. And it sure as hell wasn't yours." He took my wrist, lifting my tattooed arm up as though it were exhibit A. "Adapt or die, remember?"

God, I hated it when he was right. I'd lived thirty-three years of my life without so much as the first desire to be inked. I'd worn suits to work and driven an Audi. I'd slept in a bed that had been custom made for my maximum comfort. And I'd fallen asleep each night with the sound of waves crashing outside my bedroom window.

That was all before twenty-nine minutes changed my life.

Now, I was nothing.

No one.

I had but one purpose.

And, because of Cora and the fucked-up shit she was doing to my head, I was already failing.

Tugging my arm from his grasp, I groaned and used my

thumb and forefinger to rub my eyes. "I can't adapt to this one."

"Honestly, I don't think you have to. The mystery-man bit seems to be her type."

"Fuck her type." I stabbed a shaky finger at my chest. My voice got loud as I seethed, "That woman is going to kill me."

"I'm not sure if you've touched the decorative ornament hanging between your legs recently, but you're still a man. And she's a good woman who's into you. Of course she's going to kill you. That's what women do." He gripped my shoulder and captured my gaze. "*And that's okay.*"

I shrugged out of his hold and started pacing. "It's not okay. It's going to be another fucking tragedy all over again."

"No, it won't. This time, *we're* in control. Just be nice to her. Figure out what she likes and doesn't like. Talk a little. Listen a lot. And be there when she needs something. Too easy."

I stopped and leveled him with a glare. "And if she gets hurt?"

There was no *if* about it though. *When* she got hurt was more like it. I'd known it would happen coming into this. I just hadn't realized I'd be the man responsible—or that I'd even care.

I'd always been of the thought process that all was fair in love and war.

But two days with that woman had me reconsidering everything.

She wasn't collateral damage. Or a pawn we needed to move.

She was an incredible woman who needed a life raft, not

another shark in the water.

Drew moved back to the couch and sank down. "She's been hurt a lot. A heartbreak is the least of her worries. But… if it comes to that, we'll make it right." He threw his legs up and resumed his position with his head on the armrest, his eyes closed and aimed at the ceiling.

"How exactly are we going to do that if we're both dead or in prison?"

"One day at a time, Penn." He turned his head, bringing his gaze to mine. His façade was gone, all the bravado he usually carried going with it. In its place was the cold, malicious darkness that, years earlier, had become the true Drew Walker.

It was the same vile black that stained my soul. I barely survived with it eating me away like acid from the inside out, eagerly waiting until the day it would finally devour me.

But not Drew. I hadn't seen that side of him since he'd gotten out of prison, but there it was, front and center, staring back at me with all the gentleness of a dagger.

"You having second thoughts?"

"No," I answered definitively. "But this does *not* blow back on Cora. No matter the cost."

He arched a menacing eyebrow. "Those are some dangerous words, *brother*."

"No matter the cost."

An approving grin pulled at his lips. "Then I guess we're going to have to make sure there's no one left to blow anything back."

CHAPTER TWELVE

Cora

The very next night after my run-in with Penn, the lights on the third-floor breezeway miraculously started working.

Penn, however, turned into a ghost.

Drew showed up every morning bright and early and worked long hours ripping out walls in my apartment, trying to find the source of our water leak, but Penn drifted in and out throughout the day. He didn't speak. He didn't linger. He was just there, like a figment of my imagination. But for the way my chest tightened and my body tingled each time he so much as walked into the room, I knew he was very, *very* real.

I tried to distract myself from harping on Penn's phantom routine by dealing with the aftermath of Angela's suicide. However, that only brought me back full circle—Penn working relentlessly to save her.

The majority of the girls had been adjusting well. They were good at that. But the ones who had been close to her were struggling. Some secretly—and some not so secretly.

I was in the secretly category. I couldn't stop racking my brain for all the signs I'd missed. She'd seemed happy.

But was happiness really possible for women like us?

Sure, we laughed.

And smiled.

And made the best of the shitty hand we'd been dealt.

But happiness? Maybe that should have been my first clue. Prisoners were never truly happy.

It took two solid days for me to find the courage to go back down to Angela's apartment. Armed with a bucket of bleach, a face mask, rubber gloves that went up to my elbow, and an onslaught of paralyzing memories, I made my way down the stairs with dread rolling in my stomach. As soon as I swung the door open, I suffered a minor cardiac arrest.

Her apartment had been cleaned: the carpet torn out, brand-new linoleum glued in its place. The bloodied couch was gone, and the fresh scent of Lysol danced in the air.

With a lump in my throat and tears stinging the backs of my lids, I spun in disbelief.

There were two possible suspects in the whodunit: Drew and Penn. Only one of those men caused the somersaults in my stomach.

Whoever it had been had known I wouldn't have survived cleaning that room. At least not in one piece.

"I've known you two days and I'm drowning in it, Cora."

There were no words as I looked around that spotless apartment. Quite honestly, I found it hard to process.

In my experience, people didn't just do things out of the kindness of their hearts.

Everyone had a motive. And, suddenly, I was desperate to know Penn's.

So I played a card I'd been hiding up my sleeve for well

over a year.

I called our good old perverted pal, Larry the cop. He was a dick, as usual, and hung up on me. But when I texted him a snippet of a video one of the girls had secretly shot during an unfortunate night with him, I immediately received a call back.

If I'd learned anything over the years, it was that leverage was never a bad thing to have.

Larry was none too happy to be doing me favors. Though he was pretty eager to keep that video from landing in his wife's email.

An hour later, I got a more informative call back.

Surprisingly—and excitingly—enough, Penn was squeaky clean. Not so much as a parking ticket on his record.

And Drew, well… He'd stolen a car. And then, a few days after he'd been released with nothing more than a slap on the wrist and two years of probation, he'd stolen another one. *Dumbass.* But it wasn't a violent crime or related to drugs, and he wasn't on the sex offender's registry. In my eyes, that was a total win.

Hope had whispered inside me when I'd seen Angela's apartment. But, by the time I hung up with Larry, it was a deafening roar.

Maybe decent men still existed.

And maybe, just maybe, Penn Walker was one of them.

With Penn dodging me, I approached Drew about the cleanup job. He denied having anything to do with it. Though he quickly accepted my invitation to come over for dinner and promised to bring his brother.

I spent the better part of the day cooking, cleaning, doing

my hair and makeup, and then agonizing over what to wear. It was ridiculous. Especially when Drew showed up *alone*.

It was probably stupid, but I was crushed.

Drew stayed for several hours, ate half a pan of lasagna, drank three beers, and laughed and talked with Savannah and River.

I spent those hours warming an untouched beer while staring holes in the door as though I could have willed Penn to appear on the other side.

He didn't. And the weight of my disappointment was stifling.

That very same night around midnight, I was tidying up the living room before making my way to bed when a sound outside caught my attention. A quick peek out the peephole revealed Penn parked in the hall, wearing that same black hoodie from days earlier, while watching my door like it was his favorite movie.

My stomach dipped, and that spark that only he ignited inside me turned into a raging inferno. I convinced myself that he was waiting for me out there.

Spoiler alert: He wasn't.

The first night, I made an excuse to go out there by setting the trash outside my door as I so often did. He didn't acknowledge my fun-and-flirty hello, and after a full minute of awkwardly rocking on my toes, waiting for him to reply, I rushed back inside and called it a night. It stung. A lot. But my trash was in the dumpster the next morning.

When he was out there again on the second night, it started to unnerve me. Never one to beat around the bush, I decided to ask why he was sitting alone in the dark.

Maybe Drew snored. Maybe he liked the fresh air. Maybe he was a serial killer. Really, it was anyone's guess.

His only answer was a grunted, "I like the quiet. It's easier to think." Then he stood up and went into his apartment without another word spoken. Thirty minutes later, he had resumed his position. I did not.

The third night, I couldn't handle anymore rejection, so I casually drank a beer while standing at my peephole and stared at him staring at me. He was beautiful. I was a weirdo. I went to bed.

Night four, I was still a weirdo.

Night five, I forced myself to stop the insanity and instead sat on my couch, watching the same door he was watching, just from the other side. Then I decided that wasn't any less ridiculous, so I gave up and went to bed.

Wash, rinse, and repeat on nights six and seven.

Each night, I fell asleep staring at Nic's stars on the ceiling.

But each morning, I woke up with Penn's piercing, blue eyes invading my dreams.

I couldn't explain my draw to him. With the way I grew up, with a father who had thrown me to the wolves, then dealing with Marcos and Dante, it wasn't exactly a mystery why I hadn't been keen on the Y chromosome throughout the years.

But, when it came to Penn, my body overruled my mind every time.

Too many nights, I'd lain in bed, my overactive (and surprisingly descriptive) imagination as my only company. Those little daydreams had started off innocent enough.

In my head, we'd sit in that hallway, talking and laughing. He'd eventually reach over and take my hand or drape his arm around my shoulders. Quiet comfort. Nothing more. Nothing less.

But, as the days rolled on, those daydreams spiraled into something else altogether.

My skin igniting under his callused hands.

His mouth gliding from breast to breast and then down between my legs—giving rather than taking the way I knew only Penn would.

The earth-shattering sensation of being coaxed to abandon, the rest of the world slipping into nothingness, leaving only him, me, and our merciless mouths behind.

Yeah. It had been a rough week filled with cold showers and sleepless nights.

This wasn't exactly a terrible thing though, because on day number eight, I was tired, annoyed, and all around *done*.

Done waiting. Done feeling like a stalker. Done with… well, everything except getting to know the real Penn Walker.

So, on that particular morning, with both of the guys clanging around in my bathroom, I decided I was done letting him call the shots.

"How's it coming?" I asked, leaning against the doorjamb of my deconstructed bathroom. The toilet and sink were sitting in my living room, and all of the moldy drywall had been ripped out, revealing a maze of rusty pipes.

Drew popped out from the inside of what had once been my linen closet. "It's coming along about as well as you can expect from a building that was constructed by the Pilgrims."

"I doubt the Pilgrims would be happy with you insulting

them like that. Is any of it salvageable?"

His lips curled into a slow grin. "It's going to have to be."

I tipped my chin at the only remaining wall that divided my bedroom from the bathroom. "Any chance you can tear that down and put a door in to make it an en suite for me?"

"Any chance you could say that in English, Fancy Pants?"

I laughed. "Like an adjoining bathroom to my room?"

"Ahh. I think that stud might be structural, but I could probably put in a doggy door." He dropped his gaze, giving me a flirty once-over. "You're small enough to fit."

"I'll pass, but thanks." Lifting my coffee mug to my lips, I cut my gaze to Penn.

He was on his knees, a wrench in his hand, doing something with the pipes where my sink should have been.

"So, Penn, how's the apartment working out?" I asked his back.

He remained silent.

Drew answered though. "It's good. Penn finally Herculesed the old couch and mattress down the stairs last night. Fingers crossed he took all of Hugo's DNA with him."

"Oh, gross!"

He tapped the tip of his nose. "Exactly. Now, if we can get the water back on so we can take a shower or actually use the bathroom without hoofing it down two flights of stairs only to wait in line at three a.m., we'll be better than good."

I slapped a hand over my chest and breathed, "Dear

God, what is this utopia you speak of?"

Drew chuckled. Penn didn't.

"Can I get you two some coffee?" I asked.

"Nah," Drew answered. "I had some black sludge courtesy of the Stop and Shop."

I faked a gag. "Ew! That place is disgusting. I wouldn't walk through the door without a hazmat suit."

He twisted his lips adorably. (Okay, fine. Mr. Plain wasn't so plain anymore.) "So what you're saying is I probably shouldn't have eaten one of the little rolling hot dogs for breakfast?"

My mouth gaped open. "Oh God, no!"

He raked his teeth over his bottom lip. (Yeah, not even close to plain.) "Then definitely not two?"

"Oh sweet Jesus, Mary, and Joseph. I hate to be the one to tell you this…but there is a good chance you're dead right now."

He used two dirty fingers to check the pulse at his neck. "Nope, still ticking. Looks like you're stuck with me until at least tomorrow."

"Tomorrow?"

He shrugged. "They were really good hot dogs."

I laughed, and he joined me—because that was what Drew did.

And through it all, Penn never so much as glanced in our direction—because that was what Penn did.

"You mind if I take a smoke break?" Drew asked.

"Not as long as you take it outside."

He offered me a salute, and I turned sideways to allow him space to exit—which left me alone with Penn.

River and Savannah were at school, and my schedule for the day was packed.

Yet I stood there, staring at Penn's back, determined to make him talk. "Any estimate on when you'll get the water back on?"

The muscles beneath his shirt rippled and his wrench stilled, but he made no verbal response.

"I mean…a rough estimate would be fine."

More silence.

"I'm sure you're doing everything you can. I'm just curious. Are we talking days or weeks?" I shifted uncomfortably, twirling a curl around my finger. "Please don't say months. I'm not sure how much longer I can deal with this. The girls have been at each others' throats sharing two bathrooms. I gave them all little plastic baskets I got from the Dollar Shop to carry their toiletries, but if I hear one more argument about someone using someone else's shampoo or toothpaste, I'm going to have to be checked into a padded room."

He sighed, allowing his head to sag forward, but his posture remained tense. "You're not going to let this go, are you?"

My eyes flashed wide, and a victorious smile split my lips. "I have let it go. But that doesn't mean we can't talk to each other."

"Bullshit," he told the floor. "You think I don't see you standing at your door every night? Your lights come on and off. Your feet shadow the crack at the bottom. And, worse than that…I feel you. Watching me." He slowly turned his dark, hollow gaze over his shoulder. "I know you're there,

Cora. Because I feel it when you leave."

On one hand: *Busted!*

On the other hand: Oh my gahhhhhhhh. He felt me.

I cleared my throat and straightened my back. "Okay. So...maybe I haven't exactly let *it* go. But you're sitting outside, *staring* at *my* door, Penn. You're not at the railing that overlooks the parking lot. Or the stairs out back that nobody uses. Not even the roof, where you could actually see the stars. You are sitting in the breezeway, staring at *my door*. If you ask me, that feels a lot like you haven't let it go, either."

He shook his head and once again faced forward, muttering, "Why are you so fucking stubborn?"

"Me? Are you going to stop boring holes into my door each night?" *Please say no. Please say no. Please say no.*

"Fuck. Me," he grumbled.

But it wasn't a no!

Unwilling to crowd him, I remained in the doorway and continued talking to his back. "We don't even know what this thing is, Penn. I'm relatively sure a conversation is not going to kill either of us. Who knows? Maybe you like mustard and it will be a total wash from the get-go."

He blew a hard breath out, which I thought *might* have been in the same sound family as a laugh, but since I couldn't get a read on his face, I couldn't be sure. It quickened my pulse all the same though.

"Think about—"

We both jumped when a shrieked, "Cora!" came from my front door.

"Ugh," I groaned, cursing the evil gods of bad timing.

Another day.

Another drama.

And right in the middle of my own personal drama with Penn.

"Hold that thought," I told him, shoving off the doorjamb. When I reached the front door, I snatched it open and snapped, "What?"

Guilt slammed into me like a freight train when I saw Brittany standing there with a bloody towel pressed to her shoulder and sporting a grimace.

"What the hell happened?" *And why is everyone suddenly bleeding all the time!*

I pulled at her wrist, revealing a gash at least six inches long on her collarbone.

"The fucking ceiling fan fell on me."

My head snapped back. "How is that possible?"

She wrenched her arm away. "Because we live in a death trap! The whole goddamn building is going to collapse on us one of these days."

"It's not a death trap... We're just...going through a few hard times right now."

Yeah, okay. It was totally a death trap.

"Well, it's about to become a whole hell of a lot harder for me now. How am I supposed to go to work tonight with this?" She huffed. "'Sorry, dude. I know you're paying for a hand job, but the good one's out of commission. How do you feel about a lefty? Oh, don't worry about that blood pouring from my shoulder. Fetish is free of charge tonight.'" She tipped her head to the side and shot me a murderous scowl.

I rolled my eyes. "How about you put the dramatics aside

114

and let me bandage you up?"

She laughed without humor. "Oh, right. *I'm* dramatic. I could have been killed. Meanwhile, your highness is up here having her bathroom renovated."

I hooked my thumb over my shoulder. "I'd hardly call this a renovation. I couldn't get the diamond-crusted floors or *anything*. Call the Enquirer. I'm being forced to make do with…" I leaned forward and partitioned off my mouth before whispering, "Running water."

"Okay, while you get that, I'll try not to let Meredith and Jewels cave in on me." Turning on a toe, she stomped away.

Drew rounded the corner, jumping out of the way to escape being run over. "Everything okay?"

"A ceiling fan fell on one of the girls downstairs and she's convinced that the building is crumbling, and I'll be honest: I'm not sure she's wrong." I sifted my fingers through the top of my hair. "Aren't ceiling fans connected to a stud or something? They can't just fall from the sky, can they?"

He quirked his lips. "The sky? No. The ceiling?" He shrugged. "Depending on who installed it, and given that I've seen Hugo's handiwork, anything is possible."

I huffed, "Fan-fucking-tastic."

"Pun intended?" he asked on his way over to me. He stopped, teetering on the edge of too close, but it wasn't uncomfortable. It was just…Drew.

"Hardly," I replied.

He smiled, his brown eyes warming like smooth chocolate. (So beyond *not* plain.)

"I have to go down there and patch her up. You guys okay up here while I'm gone?"

His eyebrows perked. "You want me to come with and take a look at the fan?"

"That would be…" The words died on my tongue when movement at the mouth of the hall caught my attention.

His lips were thin and his jaw was hard, but his eyes… They were molten.

Penn. And not the guy who had told me to stay away.

This was the Penn who had held me close and told me to unlearn it.

My whole body roared to life, the fine hairs on my arms standing on end as his penetrating stare drilled into me. That beautiful hum in my veins returned.

"Amazing," I finished breathily.

Drew gave my shoulder a squeeze. "Don't worry—"

"I'll go," Penn announced so roughly that it was jarring—and mesmerizing. His molten eyes had turned to ash, the pupils so large that I could barely see the blue around them. He was staring at his brother's hand—but there was no love in that glare.

He looked to me. "You good with that?"

"Absolutely," I replied immediately.

Drew flicked his gaze back and forth between us in what I assumed was bewilderment, but I couldn't tear my eyes away from Penn long enough to confirm.

"You sure about that?" Drew asked.

I had no idea which one of us he was talking to, so I whispered, "Yeah," at the same time Penn declared, "I'll take it from here."

Drew chuckled, but Penn didn't say anything else.

CHAPTER THIRTEEN

Penn

I. Was. Fucked.

Plain and simple.

My plan was fucked.

My head was fucked.

Worst of all, I feared Cora was fucked too.

Because this was not going to end well for any of us.

But, God, I was sick of fighting to stay away from her.

So there I was, alone in an apartment with her, feeling like I'd just bet my entire life on red and was waiting on bated breath to see where the roulette wheel would land.

"So, how old are you?" Cora asked as she swirled around the apartment, wearing a pair of ridiculous hot-pink dish gloves. She had a spray bottle of bleach that was burning my nostrils in one hand and a rag so dirty that it registered on the black spectrum in the other.

I readjusted my footing on the ladder and kept working to correct Hugo's unbelievably novice attempt at hanging a ceiling fan. There had been exactly one screw mounting it to the stud in the ceiling—a screw that was too short. The rest were only anchored into the sheetrock, which made each spin of the blades a literal game of Russian roulette for anyone unlucky enough to be standing beneath it.

It was a miracle Brittany and Ava hadn't been killed at least a dozen times. Or so I'd been told as Cora paced the room, furiously doing the calculations. Out loud. Explaining every single solitary variable as she solved for X. I didn't figure she had much of an education, but when she started prattling off formulas and crunching the numbers in her head, I'd never been more intrigued by a woman in my life.

During my time avoiding her, which wasn't really avoiding her at all—it was more like a lion watching over his lamb—I'd learned a lot about Cora.

She never walked anywhere. If her feet weren't at least trotting, she wasn't moving at all.

And she made amazing sandwiches. Soft white bread, deli-sliced ham, mayo, and the perfect dash of salt and pepper. She didn't use any of the fanfare like lettuce or tomato. It was just a sandwich. But, damn, it was good. I hated that she made Drew and me lunch, catering to us like we were doing her a goddamn favor. Yet she did. Every day. Whether I was speaking to her or not.

She didn't have the time—or the money—for crap like that.

I'd witnessed her going door-to-door twice, holding an empty coffee mug to collect cash to help one of the other girls buy whatever the hell they needed.

Meanwhile, Cora's phone remained cracked, her car was rolling on three bald tires and a donut, and the strap on her purse was knotted to hold it together.

But if she cared about any of those things, she'd never let on.

Cora didn't bitch or complain. Nor was she angry or bitter. Actually, she laughed—a lot.

And she kept doing, and doing, and doing for everyone else until she was dead on her feet. I'd caught her dozed off on the couch once. It made me an absolute creep, but I'd stood there, watching how peaceful she was. Her lips curled up even in slumber.

Her life wasn't easy, but that fucking woman *smiled* while she slept.

Who did that?

In the understatement of the decade, it was safe to say that I was not emotionally equipped for going toe-to-toe with the likes of Cora Guerrero. But for no good reasons—and a lot of bad ones—I couldn't stop myself.

"Thirty-seven," I answered.

Her back shot straight, her head tipped back, and she aimed those dark-blue eyes, the ones that I feared would be my undoing, up at me. With two simple words, you would have thought I'd given her the world.

Her mouth split, revealing a brilliant, white smile that crushed my chest.

"He speaks," she teased.

"Occasionally." I turned my attention back to the ceiling fan.

"Thirty-seven, huh? Well, you don't look that old."

"She lies," I mocked.

She giggled, soft and sweet, like I was learning everything about Cora was. She went back to trying to scrub the finish off the countertop. "So you know how to rip out walls, fix pipes, and hang ceiling fans. There has to be a job market for that out there? I get Drew. He's fresh out of jail, and he was tight with Manuel, but why are *you* here?"

"To work."

"You owe Manuel any favors?"

"No."

"Does he have any dirt on you?"

"No."

"On the run from a woman?"

My chest locked up tight. She had no fucking idea.

"No," I semi-lied.

"Have you ever been to rehab? If so, for what drugs? Or was it alcohol? Any twelve-step programs in your past?"

"No. No. No. And No."

She remained eerily quiet as I twisted the last screw in. When my peripheral vision told me it was safe, I glanced to see what had suddenly bought me the silence.

She had her head stuck inside the fridge. After a loud sniff, she shuddered and her long blond curls shook. "Holy shit. I think that milk was produced by the very first cow God created."

I bit the inside of my cheek to hide my smile. It did not help my case when she was cute.

Without warning—thus without giving me time to prepare—she peeked over her shoulder and caught me looking.

"Are you smiling?"

So, apparently, biting my cheek didn't help.

I forced my lips flat. "No."

She crinkled her nose.

So. Fucking. Cute.

"Holy shit, the ever-stoic Penn Walker has facial muscles!"

I'll be damned if I didn't smile again.

She gasped, dramatically bringing her hand to her chest. "Dear Lord, he gives me an encore."

I chuffed. "Jesus, you really are crazy." Desperate for an escape—and a way to hide my growing grin—I shoved the screwdriver into my pocket, my head down like a moron, and turned away... "Fuck!" I boomed, my elbow landing hard on the floor.

The screwdriver stabbed through my pocket and into my thigh, causing a blast of pain to radiate through my entire lower body.

"Oh my God!" She jogged over and dropped into a squat beside me.

I pushed up onto my good elbow and grumbled, "I'm fine."

"Did you slip?"

No, I was gawking at you and forgot I was standing four rungs up on a ladder.

"Yeah," I replied instead of sharing that fun little tidbit.

She used the fingers of her gloves to pull them off. "Are you okay?"

With her that close? Not even a little bit. "Course."

Cora was all kinds of beautiful. Any man with two eyes could recognize that from across a football field. But, with only inches between us, she was a different kind of beautiful.

She was real.

Not a job.

Not a plan.

She was just…

"Penn, roll over. Let me look at your leg. Shit, you're bleeding." She angled her body forward until she was all I could see.

I should have closed my eyes. Done the whole one-in-one-out thing.

I *should* have focused on the past. I'd been all too good at fixating on that for the last four years.

Instead, I stared.

Faint pink painted the skin beneath a light peppering of freckles on her cheeks. She had this tiny mole just below her bottom lip. Being that she was a woman, she probably hated it. And for that assumption alone, I fucking loved it.

A soft floral scent ever so slightly tainted by bleach wafted off her. It was a cheap store-brand lotion. I'd seen it in her bathroom once. But, on Cora, it was better than any high-price perfume I'd ever smelled.

Her silky, blond curls trailed over my forearm, causing the hollow ache in my chest to travel below the belt.

And when she looked up at me, her blue eyes sparkled in a way that made me wonder how spectacular they would look fluttering shut as I drove inside—

"Take your pants off," she ordered.

"Excuse me?" I scrambled away, the damn screwdriver stabbing me all over again. Rolling to the side, I dug the bastard from my pocket and dropped it to the floor.

"I can't see anything with your pants on."

Wincing, I tried to stand. "You can see more than enough."

In a real stinger to the ego, she grabbed my arm and helped me to my feet. "Stop being a baby. I've seen men's underwear before."

"Not mine," I defended.

Bringing a hand to her mouth, she tried to hide her humor. It was useless in muffling her laugh.

"I'm serious," I told her. "I'm not taking my damn pants off."

She moved her hand, revealing an earth-shattering smile. "You know, I think this is the most you've spoken me to in a week and it's because you're afraid I'll see you in your boxers?"

"No, I'm afraid you'll see me *not* in my boxers. Who wears underwear anymore?"

She arched an eyebrow. "Like, ninety percent of the population."

"Women maybe."

"It's been a while since I had any firsthand experience, but I'm pretty sure men wear underwear too."

It made me an asshole, but I felt every word of that little "it's been a while" confession ghost over my skin like heat licking off a bonfire.

"Well, not this one," I replied, heading to the door before I had a chance to do something stupid. Like… actually drop my fucking pants.

Because she was stubborn as hell—a trait I couldn't decide if I loved or hated—she followed after me. "I'm a nurse, Penn. And you need someone to look at your leg."

Things I knew about Cora Guerrero:

She was twenty-nine.

Gorgeous—not important.

She mothered thirty-ish prostitutes like the biggest, grizzliest mama bear out there.

Each morning, she drank coffee like it was the only thing keeping her alive.

And while tearing out the wall between her bathroom and pantry, I'd found no less than ten boxes of cookies she'd hidden. And I knew they were hers because, when Drew had tried to relocate them to the kitchen counter, she'd come through denying they were hers but then carried them to her bedroom for "safe keeping."

But a nurse?

"You're not a nurse."

She waved her hand dismissively. "Not like with a degree or anything. However, I'm currently the only other person standing in this room and you're injured. It's the law of default."

"I'm not sure that's the way it works."

She tsked, her tongue making a spectacular appearance against her teeth. "Hate to break it to you, but around here? *It is.* I'm a nurse when people are hurt. Security when fights break out. A chef when people need to eat. A therapist when they need to talk. A chauffeur when they need to get to a job. And just a heads-up, if a nuke suddenly appeared that needed to be disarmed, I'd magically become a nuclear engineer too. So, speaking as a professional whatever-the-hell-I have-to-be-at-the-moment, I'll get you a blanket to cover your manly bits, but you're dropping your damn pants."

Not at all how I'd thought this day was going to go when I'd rolled out of my sleeping bag that morning. But I had to admit, in the history of days I'd had, a beautiful woman ordering me to drop trou wasn't even close to being one of the worst. In an alternate dimension, where she wasn't her and I wasn't me, my pants would have been on the floor along with hers the first time she'd touched me.

But here? Now?

"I'm fine," I grumbled, once again making a break for the door. I had my hand on the knob when she caught my forearm.

"Okay, okay. Can I at least give you some gauze and antibiotic cream so it doesn't get infected? I can't risk you coming down with gangrene. It's been a while since I've had to be a surgeon."

Incredulous, I glanced at her over my shoulder. "Tell me you're kidding."

She winked. "I'm kidding. But!" She lifted a finger in the air. "Not about the gauze or cream."

I may or may not have stared at her ass as she walked over to the first aid kit she'd used to patch up our sleeping ceiling fan victim.

"I'm almost out of gauze though. Between my nose and Brittany's shoulder—"

Ice hit my veins and the words were out of my mouth before my brain had fully processed them. "What the hell happened to your nose?"

"I had a little run in with—"

I took a long step toward her. "Marcos?"

Her wide eyes snapped to mine. "What? No!"

125

Another step. "Dante, then?"

Her hand went to that tiny silver star she always wore around her neck. "No. Why? Are they planning to stop by?"

"I have no clue."

She blinked at me, her hand dragging that star back and forth across the chain as though she were trying to start a fire. "Would you tell me if they were?"

"Absolutely. Would you tell me if they hit you again?"

Her face paled, and the movement at her neck stopped. "How do you know about that?"

"You had a bruise the day we got here. Wasn't hard to put two and two together. If they come back—"

"You can't do anything," she rushed out, closing the distance between us. "If a*nd when* they come back, stay out of it. Okay?"

I crossed my arms over my chest. "Not gonna happen."

She lifted her hand toward my forearm before thinking better of it and dropping it to her side.

I wished like hell that she'd have followed through.

Her voice softened. "Penn, I'm serious."

"So am I. So we're making a deal. I'll tell you if I hear anything about them heading this way. And, if they do, you come find me." I leaned toward her. "Immediately."

Her eyes searched mine, the most beautiful disbelief crinkling the corners. "Why would you care?"

Because you hold the answers to end my miserable existence once and for all.

And because no woman deserves to live in fear—but especially not you.

"I just do." I extended a hand in her direction. "Now,

tell me we have a deal."

The confusion on her face slayed me. Christ, this woman was so far gone that she couldn't fathom why someone would want to protect her.

But I did—fiercely.

I pushed my hand out farther. "Say it."

She tipped her head to the side and eyed me warily. "Not until you tell me why you care?"

I wanted to tell her. She deserved at least that much. But neither of us was ready for that venomous snake.

So I told her a different truth. "The world is an ugly place, Cora. It's filled with more sinners than saints. More hate than love. More chaos than kindness. And that's not because the world is filled with bad people. It's because the good ones stay silent."

Her whole incredible body jerked in surprise. "Is that why you sit outside my door?" She lifted a shaking hand to her mouth. "Are you trying to...*protect* me?"

"I won't keep quiet. I won't turn a blind eye. And I won't stay out of it. No man should ever put his hands on you. Please tell me you know that?"

Her breath hitched. "Who are you?"

"I have no fucking idea."

She held my unwavering gaze.

And I held hers, making silent promises I prayed I would be able to keep.

After several beats, she squared her shoulders, straightened her back, took my hand, looked me straight in the eye, and lied, "I think I liked it better when you were avoiding me."

"Bullshit."

"Okay, okay, fine. You've got a deal." She gave my hand a sharp pull, tugging me closer. Not that I fought her or anything. "Under one condition: You actually accept my invitation to dinner this time so I can properly thank you for cleaning up Angela's apartment."

She'd been lucky I only cleaned it. My original instinct had been to burn the place to the ground. Had it not been filled with sleeping women, I'd have done just that.

"It was nothing."

"Fine. Then it can be a nothing-thank-you dinner. And for the love of all that's holy, bring Drew. I figure the only thing that can counteract the formaldehyde he consumed in those nasty hot dogs he ate for breakfast is, like, broccoli or carrots or… Shit, I may need to bring out the big guns. How do you feel about Brussels sprouts?" She paused, her gaze dipping to my mouth. "Shit, you're smiling again."

I was. And it was radiating throughout my entire body.

I pointed to my mouth. "This? Nah. It's a medical condition that flares up every now and again. I'm sure you learned about it in nursing school."

She laughed, and I felt that too, deep down in places I'd long since forgotten about. Places she had no business being.

"So, is that a yes to dinner?" She peered up at me, batting her lashes and smiling huge.

Alarms screamed in my head, dread planting roots in my stomach.

It was wrong to touch her. To steal her warmth when I'd never be able to offer it to her in return—not honestly, anyway. But I couldn't stop myself. Finding the curve of her hips, I pulled her off-balance until she stumbled into my arms.

I couldn't see her face, but her body melted against me as if I'd answered her one and only prayer.

If only I still believed in God.

"I'll be there, Cora," I whispered into the top of her hair.

CHAPTER FOURTEEN

Cora

"Please tell me we don't have to eat this?" Savannah complained, carrying a baby-spinach salad to the table.

I swallowed a sip of beer and set the bottle on the counter beside the pan sizzling hand-molded turkey burgers. "Vegetables are not the devil. And your thirty-year-old metabolism will thank me for teaching you that."

River walked by, snagging a piece of bacon off a plate and popping it into her mouth. "Doesn't bacon defeat the point of making turkey burgers?"

"Probably. But I like to think they cancel each other out."

Crunching on another strip, she propped her hip against the counter and gave me a once-over. "You look nice tonight."

Twisting my lips, I gave her the side-eye. "It's jeans and a tank top. Practically my uniform."

"Nooo," she drawled. "It's jeans that have been ironed, a silky tank top with spaghetti straps. *And* you're wearing wedges and"—she reached up and gave my silver chandelier earring a jingle—"jewelry."

I swatted her hand away. "We have company coming over."

She shot me a who-you-trying-to-lie-to glare. "Penn gonna show this time?"

I looked away to hide my smile. "He said he was."

"Ah, so he's finally speaking to you? Makes the whole obsessing thing a lot easier."

I turned to fully face her, my spatula hovering over the pan. "I haven't been obsessing about him."

"Pssshhh." She rolled her eyes so hard that I thought they might roll out of her head. "I think Drew might be the only one in the building who doesn't realize you've been obsessing about Penn."

My mouth fell open. "What?"

Savannah came up and stood behind River, reaching over her shoulder to grab a piece of bacon too. "Oh, come on, Cora. Don't play dumb. Drew's got it for you *bad*." She took a bite and spoke around it. "Only problem is you've got it bad for his brother. Dun. Dun. Dun." She grinned as she finished chewing.

"Okay, first of all—"

"Truth or lie?" River interrupted.

My mouth clamped shut. We'd been playing this game for years. It was simultaneously the best and worst thing I'd ever thought up.

On one hand, it gave us a way to communicate about the hard stuff. On the other, it gave us a way to hide the even harder stuff.

In our lives, lies were sometimes necessary. She was just

a kid; she didn't need to know all the horrors that happened on a daily basis. But our little game made discussions safe for us. If you told someone you were lying, was it really a lie?

I swallowed hard. "What do you want?"

"Truth."

I sucked in a sharp breath. "I wouldn't say I've been obsessing about Penn. But…I have certain…well, feelings about him that… Fine. He's…piqued my interest."

Savannah grabbed another piece of bacon. "It's because he's hot."

I turned back to the stove, catching River's smirk on the way around. "No. It's because he's nice."

River barked a laugh. "And hot."

"Hey! You are not old enough to be calling anyone hot. Unless it's a twelve-year-old boy from school who makes straight A's and has plans to become a priest but just so happens to have a giant trust fund but he needs a wife to inherit it when he turns twenty-one."

"I see you've given this some thought." She scoffed and moved past me to the pantry. "And I'm thirteen, Cora."

"Yeah, but I liked you better when you were twelve."

She laughed. "Do we have any cookies?"

"You know I don't keep that junk in the house."

Savannah assumed River's position and leaned her hip against the counter. "Is that the truth or a lie?"

See, it was times like these—when my precious sweets were in jeopardy—that our little game backfired on me. But that was the thing about games: When you made them up, you got to make all the rules.

"Hey, hey, hey. You have to have good grades before

you're allowed to play." I arched my eyebrow. "I saw that C in your bookbag."

She looked away sheepishly. "I'm not good at math."

"That's crap and you know it."

She opened her mouth to object, but a knock at the door silenced us all.

Nerves rumbled in my stomach as I stared at the locked door. He was right on time.

"You want me to get that?" Savannah whispered.

"No," I whispered back, but I kept staring at the door.

River sauntered through the small kitchen, a bag of my prized chocolate chip cookies in her hand. "Right. This is you, totally *not* obsessing."

Coming unstuck, I plucked the cookies from her hand and tossed them onto the counter. "I swear to God, if either one of you embarrasses me in front of Penn, I will wash all of your white clothes with red socks. Got it?"

They glanced at each other and grinned. Savannah made a zipper motion across her mouth.

Blowing out a calming breath, which coincidentally wasn't calming at all, I smoothed out my shirt and did a quick pat-down of my hair. I was being silly. It was just Drew and Penn. They'd been in my apartment every day for going on two weeks. This was no different.

Except, when I pulled the door open, finding Penn standing completely alone on the other side, wearing a pale-blue button-up that made his eyes so bright that they might as well have been glowing, the sleeves rolled up to his elbows, showing off thick muscles covered by black ink, a six-pack of beer, and a store-bought tin of brownies in his hands, I knew

I wasn't overreacting.

I was seriously, seriously underreacting.

"Wh...where's Drew?"

His brows pinched together. "Couldn't make it. That okay?"

"Yeah, of course!" I exclaimed—entirely too loudly.

And we stood there. Me a statue. Him waiting to be invited inside, but, again, I was a statue so...

In the awkward lull, his gaze dipped from my head to my toes and then back again. And, as if he'd reached out and touched me, I felt it from my nipples to my toes—and everywhere in between. My skin exploded with chills, and my mouth ran dry, rendering me unable to speak. Not that I had any words. A crazy combination of anxiety, fear, excitement, and maybe even a touch of desire bloomed within me as I continued to stare at the beautiful man standing in my doorway.

"Hey, Penn," River chirped, sidling up beside me, no doubt running to my rescue. And God bless her because I seriously needed it. "Come on in," she said, pulling me out of the way.

I teetered on my wedges as I shuffled to the side.

Penn tipped his chin in gratitude as he walked inside. "I noticed you liked chocolate the other day, so I grabbed this from the grocery store."

"It's perfect. She loves chocolate," Savannah said, pulling up the rear in mission Rescue Cora. "Good choice in beer, too." She winked, taking them both from his hands and carrying them to the kitchen.

Okay, I was acting like a madwoman. I'd invited him to

dinner. He was drowning in it. He felt me. He'd been losing sleep while sitting outside my door and protecting me from the inevitable.

Also, I felt him. He caused sparks to flare inside me. And, according to him, I was risking being burned.

This was what was supposed to happen!

But he was bearing gifts of brownies and beer like he had truly read my soul, and he'd dressed up like he was trying to impress me.

"Why are you just standing there?" River hissed in my ear.

"Why is he dressed like that?" I hissed right back, watching him as he followed Savannah toward the kitchen. Which, given the size of my apartment, wasn't far.

River twisted her lip and then turned to look at him, offering him an uncomfortable smile when he caught her.

"He's wearing jeans and a shirt."

"Yes, but it's a *nice* shirt. He always wears plain white T-shirts."

"And?"

"And he looks like he's going on a date."

She leaned away to catch my eyes and whispered, "Uh... he *is* on a date. *With you.* So stop acting like a nut job before he jumps ship."

Oh, shit!

She shook her head as if I were insane. And the longer I stood there, the more I thought she might have been right.

"I haven't been on a real date in a hundred years."

She slapped my arm. "Well, then you've aged nicely, Granny."

135

I shot her a glare.

Suddenly, Penn cleared his throat. "Is everything okay?"

I peeked up, finding his handsome face filled with a healthy dose of concern—and amusement.

Damn it! Savannah was right. He was incredibly hot. Not exactly a revelation, but still worth noting.

Abandoning my hysteria in lieu of annoyance, I snipped, "It's rude to eavesdrop, Penn."

He smirked, all sexy and crooked. "You're standing three feet away. It's hard *not* to eavesdrop."

Double damn it! He had a point.

"Right." I ran my fingers through the underneath of my hair, stopping before I caused any tangles. "I'll just…finish up with the burgers." Finally remembering how to walk, I started past him.

But he gently caught my arm. Bending at the hip, he aimed his lips at my ear and rumbled, "Relax. You don't want this to be a date, it's not a date." Then his voice grew husky as he finished with, "Though, if at any point you change your mind, you won't hear the first complaint from me."

My lungs seized as I slanted my head so I could see him. He was no longer smirking, but his heated gaze locked to mine like a missile finding its target.

"Okay?" he pressed.

Hypnotized, I nodded an embarrassing amount of times before breathing, "Okay."

Releasing my arm, he drew a deep inhale in through his nose. "It smells great in here. I'm starved."

He grinned down at me, cool, calm and flirty, like he and Drew had experienced some Freaky Friday personality transplants before he'd come over.

Staring at his mouth, I asked, "Is that medical condition of yours flaring up again?"

His smile grew. "It seems to happen a lot around you."

God. This. Man.

"So, did I hear something about burgers?" he asked.

"Turkey burgers, actually."

"Oh," he said, sounding rather let down.

"With bacon," I amended.

This got me a much more upbeat, "Ohhh!"

At least he had good taste.

And, with that, I put one foot in front of the other and focused on dinner—but only so I didn't have to admit that I was one hundred percent, totally, utterly, and absolutely obsessing about Penn Walker. Again, not a revelation, and this time, probably not even worth noting.

e

Over dinner, we all loosened up. Penn didn't quite talk as much as his brother, but he was still far chattier than I'd ever seen him. His eyes never strayed far from me, not even as the girls gave him a meet-the-parents-style interrogation.

He was thirty-seven. (This I knew.)

Grew up in Florida. (This I did not know.)

The tattoos on his arms and hands did not travel any farther south and he had no piercings. (Thank you, Savannah.)

He loved football—mainly pro rather than college. (I had no interest in either.)

And he had shut down completely for a solid five minutes after River asked if he'd ever been married. (Interesting!

Though it kind of answered the burning Lisa question.)

Much like Drew, he ate a ton. Two turkey bacon burgers, two sweet potatoes complete with butter and cinnamon, and over half the spinach salad later, there were no leftovers for me to put away. As he leaned back in his chair, a satisfied expression pulling at his lips, my only regret was not cooking more.

"I can't remember the last time I ate that well. Thank you."

"I'm glad you liked it," I murmured, wiping my mouth before discarding my napkin onto my plate.

"Truth or lie," River announced out of the blue, her dark eyes and wicked grin landing on me. "If me and Savannah give you guys some privacy for the rest of the night, you won't force us to wash the dishes?"

"That sounds great," Penn answered for me. "You ladies cooked. I'll handle the cleanup."

"You don't have to do that." I rose to stop him, but he was already on his feet, collecting plates. "Penn, really. Tonight was my way of saying thank you. To *you*."

"It's okay. I got it." He winked before adding, "Wouldn't be much of a date if I made you do everything."

The girls started laughing and I shot them a glare that probably left burn marks on the wall behind them. Though, much to my dismay, it didn't faze them. Savannah even had the audacity to waggle her eyebrows.

Lord, raising teenage girls was the second ring of hell.

Penn continued gathering plates and cups as the girls fled down the hall. Their door shut, followed by the click, tick, and slide of their locks.

"Sorry about that," I said as soon as we were alone.

He breezed past me to do another round of Molly Maids on the table. "Don't be. They seem like good kids."

"Good might be an overstatement. But kids is definitely accurate."

He chuckled, carrying four glasses sandwiched between his large hands.

I stopped at the edge of the kitchen without entering, the space suddenly feeling too small for the two of us.

"Truth or lie?" he asked, depositing the dishes into the sink.

"Lie," I answered instinctively, too afraid of what he was going ask.

His head popped up, his mouth splitting beautifully. God, I loved it when he smiled.

"No, I was asking what it means… Truth or lie? River said it."

"Oh!" Out of habit, I toyed with the star around my neck. "It's a game we play."

"You want to teach me?"

There was only one answer. "Lie. And yes."

His mouth fell open. "So that was what your lie bullshit was about when I asked you to stay away from me."

"Lie. I have no idea what you're talking about."

He laughed. "Now, you gotta tell me."

"No. I really don't." Cursing my luck, I nabbed the laundry basket off the floor and set it on the counter. "Put the dishes in here. I'll carry them down to the first floor and wash 'em in the morning. No water, remember?"

His handsome face filled with apology. "Shit. I'm sorry."

"Not your fault." I slid the basket in his direction. "Last I checked, you didn't take a magical wand of rust to my pipes."

"No. But I'll get it working again this week. I promise."

"No pressure."

"Cora, look at me."

My gaze snapped to his and then my body locked tight.

He was only a few steps away, but as he moved closer, there was no mistaking his prowl. "I'm gonna take care of it."

"Okay," I breathed as he stopped, his large chest filling my vision. I had no choice but to crane my head back to see his face.

Just like he did so often, his hands found my hips.

And, just like it always did, it set me ablaze.

"I'm gonna take care of a lot of things from here on out. You just gotta trust me."

Unable to stop myself, I rested my hands on his firm biceps and shuffled closer. "I appreciate it, but, Penn, you have no idea what you're talking about."

He searched my face. Then his gaze lingered on my mouth as he whispered, "I know enough."

With a fluid movement, he slid his other hand around to my lower back, two of my fingers slipping under the hem of my shirt to tease my skin.

Oh wow. A soft gasp escaped my mouth as the most delectable chill rolled through me. God, how did something so simple feel so incredible?

"Penn," I breathed.

He shifted me deeper, our fronts becoming flush. "Say you understand me, Cora."

I honestly didn't. I didn't even know what he was so faithfully promising. Or, better yet, why he was promising it to me.

"You've known me for just over a week."

"Irrelevant."

"Is it?"

His hand slipped higher up my back until his whole palm was warming my skin—and scrambling my thoughts. "It's gonna be okay, Cora. From here on out, I swear on my life, you're gonna be okay."

I wanted to believe him. That was the dream, right? A white knight riding into town, saving the damsel in distress. But I didn't live in a fairytale. I lived in a world where good people died, got arrested, or just flat-out disappeared. And I couldn't live with myself if I added Penn to that list. However, I had a sneaking suspicion that keeping him off it wasn't going to be all that easy, either.

And, for that reason alone, I looked him straight in the eye and told him a lie. "I trust you."

He breathed an audible sigh of relief, a ghost of a smile pulling at his lips.

Until I added, "But I need you to trust me too."

That smile vanished. "Cora."

I lifted a hand to silence him. "I was there the day you and Drew got here. It was obvious that there wasn't a whole lot of family love between you two and Marcos and Dante. But what you don't understand is I can handle them. I've been doing it for over half of my life."

His jaw went hard, and his eyes narrowed.

"Yeah. Do the math on that. I was sixteen when I married

Nic, Penn. Six*teen* when I became a Guerrero, and sixteen when I buried a Guerrero. This isn't my first rodeo. Marcos and Dante are terrible, disgusting assholes. But they won't kill me. They will, however, kill *you*. You gotta trust *me* on *that*."

His face got dark. "Fuck that. Manuel—"

"Is in jail because his own daughter flipped on him. And you know what? He, Dante, and Marcos have been hunting her ever since. So don't for a second think that the Guerreros aren't capable of killing the people who cross them. Enemies, friends, and family alike. Do you understand me?"

His jaw ticked as he scowled down at me. I prayed I was actually getting through to him. Clearly, though, I wasn't.

"Where's the girl?" he asked.

My head snapped back in surprise. "What girl?"

He licked his lips and then cut his gaze over my shoulder, but he never loosened his increasingly tight hold on me. "The girl... Manuel's daughter."

"Catalina?"

"Yeah. Her." His gaze came back to mine. "Drew and I, we know some people. We could get someone on her. Keep her safe. Just give me an address."

A knot of unease suddenly twisted in my stomach as alarm bells started a distant ringing in my ears.

Before Cat had testified against Manuel, she and I had been close. She was the only Guerrero who didn't treat me like a waste of oxygen or trash who had purposely robbed them of a brother. She believed in me. She couldn't do much to help me, considering that the whole family acted like she was nothing more than an imposition too, but she tried. Nic and I had been there the day her daughter, Isabel, was born. I'd held Cat as she cried in her hospital bed, trying to figure out how the hell she was going to keep a sweet baby girl away from her brothers and her father. And I guessed, ten years later, when she'd disappeared into the night, she'd finally figured it out.

They'd never stopped looking for her. And not because they were missing their little sister. If and when Catalina was found, it would be the last day of her life.

I was good at lying, but it'd taken a full month of constant abuse at the hands of Marcos and Dante to convince them I had no idea where she'd gone. And that didn't include the time I'd been cornered by Isabel's biological father in the grocery store parking lot. He'd been furious that Catalina had taken off on him too. I guessed I was the closest thing he could get to beating her again. Thomas Lyons was worse than any of the Guerreros though. He didn't have to hide from the law. As the District Attorney and the man responsible for locking Manuel away, he *was* the law.

It was true. I didn't know where Cat had gone. Yes, she contacted me fairly frequently. Yes, we met up at a hotel once a year on the anniversary of Nic's death. Yes, I'd funded her escape with Guerrero money right under their noses. And yes, I would go to my grave if they ever found out. But if I was going to break free of that life too, I needed someone on the outside to help me.

At that moment, though, with a strong and mysterious man staring down at me, asking questions about a woman who shouldn't have been a blip on his radar, I had the strangest fear that maybe she was the *only* blip on his radar. "I…I

143

have no idea where Catalina is. From what I can tell she took her daughter and ran off right after the trial. Thomas reported her missing years ago. It got some national coverage, but no one has ever heard from her again."

"If she's in danger, you can tell me, Cora. I'll take care of them, just like I'm gonna take care of you."

"Just like I'm gonna take care of you."

I'd begged the universe more times than I could count to send me someone to say those words to me. And there he stood, gorgeous, compassionate, kind—everything I could have wished for—saying them to my face in the biggest lie I'd ever heard.

It felt like a punch to the stomach, tearing the breath from my throat.

I shouldn't have been surprised. I'd survived a lot in my life at the hands of the Guerreros.

A lot of pain.

A lot of suffering.

A lot of…fighting.

But this? This was a whole new level of emotional terrorism.

Pushing on his chest, I fought to get free. "Let me go."

His hands instantly fell away. "Cora?"

Bile rose in my throat, causing me to swallow back the urge to puke. Racing out of the kitchen, I went straight to the front door. With frantic hands, I snatched open each and every lock keeping the world out—or, in this case, me trapped inside.

I swung a pointed finger into the breezeway and ordered, "Get out."

"What the hell?" he grumbled, planting his hands on his hips, the defined muscles of his forearms making an appearance.

Of course I'd been attracted to him. The Guerreros had custom chosen him for me.

And hook, line, and sinker, I'd taken the bait.

God, I was such a fucking fool.

Barely able to get the words out around the lump of emotion, I spoke with an increasing intensity. "Get out. Get out. *Get the fuck out!*"

"What just happened?" he asked while *not* getting the fuck out of my apartment. "Talk to me."

My hands shook as I reached up and caught my necklace.

I would not cry.

I would not cry.

I would not...

Shit. Why did this hurt so much?

Oh, that's right. Because I'd dared to dream that maybe I hadn't lost the only decent man left the day Nic died.

I'd dared to hope that I could actually have a genuine connection with another human being.

I'd dared to feel, because when Penn touched me, no matter how chaste, I had no other choice.

And, now, it was over. Before it had even gotten started.

"How much are they paying you?" I asked.

His brows sank. "To work here? Like two-fifty a week. Free rent."

I crossed my arms over my chest to hide the trembles. "And if I give up any information on Cat, how much, then?"

His eyes darkened and his already large body swelled

until it was daunting, but I'd faced far bigger men than Penn. And while I wouldn't say I'd come out of those interactions unscathed, I'd come out alive all the same.

"How much!" I exploded.

He lifted his hands in surrender. "I have no idea what you're accusing me of right now."

"Liar!" I yelled, my traitorous voice cracking at the end. "I don't know where Catalina is, okay? Go. Run back to Manuel and let him know. And then take your brother and get out of my building." I gasped for breath, but according to my burning lungs, there was no oxygen in that room anymore.

And then the strangest thing happened. His face softened. His eyes lit. And his entire body slacked.

Taking a cautious step toward me, he kept his voice low and even as he said, "You've got the wrong idea. Hear me out. I've never met Manuel. I sure as hell am not here to relay information to him."

I was something of an expert with lies, and I'll be damned if it didn't look like he was telling the truth. But my gut had been wrong for over a week.

"Bullshit."

He took another step toward me. When I instinctively backed away, he threw the brakes on. My back T-boned on the corner of the doorjamb, but I locked down the wince.

"I'm not going to touch you." He lowered his hand. "I just want to talk."

I shook my head and whispered, "Please leave."

He folded his hands in prayer, bringing them up to tap his lips. "I'm not here because of Manuel. I only offered help because you told me she's a woman with a kid on the run from her fucked-up family. You don't know much about me, but I have some pretty strong opinions about a man putting his hands on a woman. It's the reason I'm so hell-bent on making sure Marcos and Dante steer clear of you. And it's the reason why I'd be willing to put my ass on the line for this Catalina chick, who I've never even met. Just stop, take a deep breath, and think about it. I've spent the last week trying to make you stay away from me, not pumping you for information. This doesn't make sense."

I blinked, all the gears in my head spinning in different directions. God, why did it look like he was telling me the truth? Not the first flicker of deception was showing on his face.

Or maybe I just couldn't see it. Hope could blind the strongest of radars.

"Why are you here, then?"

"Currently? Because a beautiful woman asked me over for dinner."

"And a week ago? What about then? Don't bullshit me. You've got marketable skills, you don't have a record, and you say you owe nothing to the Guerrero family. So explain to me what the hell you're doing here."

His eyes flared, and he shook his head. "Cora, don't."

"This is a simple question." I bent at the hip, bringing us closer without ever moving my feet, and demanded, "Why... are...you...here?"

The air in the room took on an icy chill, and his face filled with dread. "Don't make me do this."

"I'm not making you do anything. You don't want to explain to me why I should trust a single word that comes out of your mouth, then we're done here."

I stared at him.

Challenging him to lie.

Begging him to tell the truth.

Praying he wasn't the type of man I feared he was.

And hoping beyond all reason that he was the type of man I so desperately needed him to be.

It was that part of me that whispered, "Please, Penn."

His whole body jerked, his forehead crinkling as he swayed his head from side to side before looking down at the floor. His powerful shoulders rounded forward and he raked a hand through the top of his short, brown hair.

And then Penn told me a truth I never wanted to hear.

"I watched her die," he rumbled. His head came up, his gaze as heavy as the day I'd met him, but it was no longer hollow and empty. His eyes were filled to the brim with every emotion under the sun, and each one of them was slicing him to the core. "Lisa. My wife. I watched her die."

My lungs seized, and my hand came up to cover my mouth. I'd had my suspicions, but confirmation still felt like a blindside.

"She was a freelance journalist away on a job. I use the term 'freelance' lightly. She really just loved to travel and to meet new people. I swear we spent the majority of our marriage on Skype or FaceTime. I'd asked her to quit a million times, but she couldn't. The adventure of it all was a part of her." He almost smiled at the memory—until it devoured him. His hands began to tremble as though the emotions were seeking a way out, frenzied to find a breach. "We were talking on a video call when…" He paused to clear his throat.

"I watched two men break into her hotel room and slit her throat, but not before they spent twenty-nine minutes beating and stabbing her like a twisted game." A rabid snarl contorted his face, but his anger was aimed inward. "And I could do *nothing* to stop them."

"The drop of water to put out her fire," I breathed with an aching chest when I remembered his words from that night in the hall.

He nodded. "If I could have gotten to her, I could have saved her, Cora. I was just too far away. She was begging for help. Crying, pleading, choking on blood, and I didn't even know what hotel she was at. What kind of husband doesn't know where his wife is staying for the night? One question and I could have stopped it. I had her on my cell phone while on the landline, feeding the cops the tiny bits and pieces I could see about the room. It took thirty minutes for them to find her. But it's that one fucking minute that they were too late that haunts me." He stabbed a violent finger at his chest. "And that's on me. For the rest of my life. That failure is on *me*."

I reached out as if I could perform the impossible task of soothing the gaping hole in his heart. I knew that feeling. The helplessness. The anger. The pain. I remembered it all clear as the day I'd watched my husband take his dying breath, riddled with bullets, while sprawled out on top of me, his final words asking if I was okay. Even in death, his first priority was my safety.

Catching my hand, he tugged me toward him and rested my palm over his chest before covering it with his own. "That's why I'm here, Cora. I've spent four years trying to outrun the memories of that night. And when Drew got out of jail, I pounced on the opportunity to start over." He leaned into me, pressing my hand hard against his chest as though he could make me feel the truth in his confession.

To a degree, it worked; the rhythm of his heart was not one that could have been faked. It was the same staccato that played beneath my ribs every night as Nic's dark, dead eyes strobed on the backs of my lids with every blink.

"Did they catch the guys?" I whispered.

Penn nodded. "The cops killed 'em."

"Good."

We stood in silence, his heart gradually slowing along with my fears. It made sense. I'd have done anything to start my life over after losing Nic. I'd tried, only to be dragged back into the pits of hell. And then I'd tried again.

And again.

And again.

And again.

Each time ending in a different variation of the first.

And then I stopped trying—and made a plan.

"I lost my husband, too," I admitted for some ridiculous reason. However, at the time, it didn't feel ridiculous at all.

The two of us shared different, yet tragically similar experiences few people could understand. And we were forced to carry them, like a five-hundred-pound backpack cementing our feet to the Earth far more than gravity ever could. Suddenly, the heaviness in his eyes made sense. It was the same burden that had settled in my chest.

I understood Penn in ways I didn't want to. And, suddenly, for the first time since Nic died, I wanted someone to understand me too.

"We were just walking down the street when he was gunned down. God, Penn. The blood was everywhere, covering me from head to toe, seeping into the cracks in the sidewalk. He asked if I was okay, and then…he died right on top of me. But it was my life that ended on that sidewalk too. Nothing was ever the same after that."

"Jesus, Cora," he breathed, slipping his arms around my waist and pulling me into the curve of his large body.

He was offering comfort in his arms, and I was taking it without question.

"In a way, Nic saved me twice. My dad was crazy religious. Emphasis on crazy. As far as he was concerned, my only place in life was barefoot in a kitchen, serving the Lord and whatever man would take me. Meanwhile, from the time I was old enough to look out the window, I wanted to see the world." I laughed sadly. "I was going to be famous, with plenty of money, and gallivant around the globe. I just knew it. Instead, I found a star in Nic and then fell into an even bigger black hole than my father ever could have created. The entire Guerrero family tried to stop us from getting married. We were kids. Sixteen and eighteen. But there was no arguing with Nic when he got his mind stuck on something. And, for some reason, from the day we met, he was stuck on me—a troubled girl on the run who counted on him for everything."

"That why you took in Savannah?" he whispered, rubbing a hand up and down my back. "She remind you of yourself at that age?"

Fighting back tears, I turned my head and planted the side of my face against his chest so he couldn't see my eyes.

"Yeah. And River too. A few more years and that child is going to land me in a padded room, I just know it."

"That's why you take care of all the girls here."

I shrugged. "Somebody has to."

"Shit, Cora." He rested his chin on the top of my head. "So Nic took care of you, and then he was gone."

"Pretty much. I've been on my own a lot. And then you… This thing. You don't know me, and technically, I don't know you, but just standing here while you hold me, somebody having my back… Well, it's more than I've had in over thirteen years."

Penn gathered me tighter, and I thought I felt his lips press against the top of my head, causing the most beautiful calm to wash over me.

This part of me, very few knew about. I kept it close to my chest. It was safer that way. But telling Penn didn't feel like I was exposing myself.

With him, they didn't feel like secrets at all.

"It's stupid. I know. And I'm sorry I've been pushing you to make something happen here. But I needed this. Whatever it is. For however long it lasts. I needed it." My voice broke at the end.

"Shhhh… Maybe I needed to be pushed."

There was no denying that I felt his lips on the top of my head that time. I would have recognized it even if the shiver hadn't traveled down my spine.

"And, Cora, being with you isn't exactly torture. So no apologies needed, okay?"

I was definitely right about Penn. He was a *really* good guy.

He sucked in a deep breath. "However, at the risk of pissing you off again, I want to be honest and let you know I've heard all about Nic. Drew told me."

I turned to stone in his arms.

Right. No doubt Manuel had rambled for hours about the devil I was and the curse I'd brought onto his family.

Straightening, I tried to wiggle out of his grasp, but Penn didn't budge.

"Say the word, Cora, and I'll let you go, but I'd really like it if you didn't."

I stilled, my heart aching. "Did he tell Drew that it was my fault? Nic dying?"

He shook his head, the five-o'clock stubble on his jaw scratching my cheek. "I don't know what Manuel told Drew about that. But I can promise you, after meeting Marcos and Dante, neither of us think a Guerrero getting killed was *your* fault."

He was not wrong about that. However...

"Nic wasn't like them. He was a really good guy. One of the best."

"And knowing he was *your man*, neither of us would doubt that, either."

God, why did that feel so good? Someone assuming the best about me rather than the worst?

I melted deeper into his arms.

"If you knew about what happened to Nic, is that why you cleaned Angela's apartment?"

He sighed and his arms loosened for a fraction of a second. "Partially. Ripping out the carpet was completely selfish. I couldn't live in a building knowing the bloodstains were

153

there. It was too much like… Yeah. Anyway. Laying the lino-leum and getting rid of the couch was for you. I didn't know that woman, but you did. And I didn't want you to have to go down there and let her go all over again."

A silent sob reverberated in my chest. "Thank you. Truly. I'm not sure turkey bacon burgers and screaming at you to get out of my apartment was the appropriate way to say it, but…thanks."

He leaned away to flash me a weak smile, and then he dipped low to rest his forehead on mine. "I don't like talking about Lisa, but if you ever want to talk about your man, I'll listen."

Great. I'd been an ass and he was being sweet and under-standing. Guilt soured in my stomach. "I'm sorry I accused you of working for Manuel."

His nose brushed mine. "I'm sorry I gave you reason to think I was. But I swear to you, I have no fond feelings or sense of obligation toward *any* of the Guerreros." He paused. "Present company excluded. Because, even though she's stubborn as hell and refused to let this thing go between us, I happen to have quite a few fond feelings for this one."

My cheeks heated, and I bit my lip.

He groaned. "Christ, you're fucking cute."

I'd prefer stunning, irresistible, or sexy. But, from Penn, I'd take cute any day of the week.

"So, truth or lie?" I blurted.

His mouth stretched, so obviously recognizing my redi-rection. "You gonna explain it now?"

"It's a game I made up so that I can tell lies."

"Oh, well, that's reassuring."

Rolling my eyes—and probably grinning like a maniac—I took advantage of our continued embrace and traced his biceps up to his shoulders. "If someone asks a question and you don't want to answer it, you can lie, but you have to announce that it's a lie. That way, you don't break trust and there are no hurt feelings, but the truth remains a secret."

His hand traveled up my back, stopping between my shoulder blades. "Makes sense."

"You can also ask for a lie if you're not ready or don't want to hear something."

"And what if I want the truth?"

I shrugged. "Well, you can ask for it. But I'm under no obligation to give it to you. That's the purpose of the game. So, truth or lie? Which one do you want?"

His smile fell. "From you? I always want the truth. You don't have to hide with me, Cora. I'm not somebody else you have to protect."

My breath caught. Sweet baby Jesus. He was not allowed to say things like that anymore. Because I liked them. A lot.

I cleared my throat and then stated, "Okay, then. Truth. Despite me turning into a statue when you arrived, then morphing into a crazy woman after dinner, and then spending a solid five minutes telling you all about my ex, this wasn't the worst date-slash-non-date in the history of all date-slash-non-dates."

His hand came up to my face, sweeping my jaw up to my cheek before tucking my hair behind my ear. "It did end pretty okay, didn't it?"

"Is it already over?" My disappointment was laughable.

"Well, considering that River and Savannah are standing

in the hall behind me, I'd say the date part is over, but I'd be happy to hang around for the non-date portion of the evening."

I pushed up onto my toes to peer over his shoulder, and just as he'd stated, both girls were peeking their heads out, watching us intently.

"What happened to you two staying in your room all night?"

"We heard you yell," Savannah defended, River's pale face confirming it.

Reluctantly, I released Penn, hating the loss immediately. After walking over to them, I patted Savannah on the cheek and then threw my arm around River for a side hug. "All the more reason you should have stayed in your room. You both know better than to come out during something like that. But relax, okay? Everything's fine. Penn and I just had a little misunderstanding. The good news is he's offered to hang around and watch *Moulin Rouge* with us."

Penn put his palms up in defense. "Whoa, whoa, whoa! I did *not* agree to that!"

The girls both laughed.

Penn grinned.

And I beamed at him.

Definitely, definitely not the worst first date.

CHAPTER FIFTEEN

Penn

All three of them were asleep. The home screen on the DVD player illuminated the room. Savannah was stretched out on the ugly, brown loveseat. River was curled into a ball on the opposite end of the couch. And Cora was in the middle, her legs pulled up, her heels to the cushion, her head resting on my chest, and her hand on my abs.

My body was still amped from her confessions about her family and her ex. I wanted to slay the entire universe for having abandoned her in a life like that. If there was ever a woman who deserved more, it was her.

I tightened my arm around her and she briefly stirred only to fall back asleep with a sigh.

Cora was a cuddler.

And I was whatever the hell she wanted me to be.

Now, with her secured to my chest and lost in what I hoped were dreams for her future, I hated that I had to wake her up.

I hated that I had to leave.

I *hated* the life that awaited me outside that apartment.

This wasn't supposed to be a part of it. The warmth in my chest. The overwhelming contentment with her in my arms. The singe of desire.

But, for some fucked-up reason, it was all there, rising to the surface like a pot of boiling water.

Sweeping my fingers around the curve of her face, I whispered, "Cora. Baby."

She hummed, but her eyes didn't open.

"I gotta get going. I need you to lock the door behind me."

With closed eyes, she tilted her head up. "What time is it?"

Resting my palm on the side of her face, I lazily traced her cheekbone with my thumb. "One."

She groaned, stretching her legs out like a cat. "Shit. I need to make sure all the girls got out on time." She pried one eye open and peered up at me like an adorable weirdo. "Hi."

I smiled, feeling it radiate over my entire body. "Hi."

"Sorry I fell asleep."

"Don't be. I thoroughly enjoyed watching you do it."

"Not creepy at all," she teased.

"Nah, creepy was when I held your nose to make you stop snoring. For the record, it didn't work."

Her mouth fell open and a brilliant laugh bubbled from her throat. "You liar."

"All right, fine. You caught me. It actually worked like a charm."

She slapped my chest and softly giggled. "You know, I like this guy. He's a lot more entertaining than Mr. Broody."

I quirked an eyebrow. "You better be talking about me,

or *Mr. Broody* and I are going to have words."

This earned me another giggle, only she didn't slap me. She glided her hand up my chest and around my neck, all the while staring at my mouth.

Or at least I think she was staring at my mouth. Because I sure as hell was staring at hers. With the way she'd been watching me all night, it was a miracle of epic proportions that I hadn't kissed her already. I'd snuck a few in on the top of her head while she had been pouring her heart out, but I hadn't been brave enough to take her mouth yet.

Snapping my attention away from her pink, crescent-shaped lips before I had the chance to do something seriously stupid—and more than likely seriously amazing—I said, "I gotta go. Can you lock the door?"

"Yeah," she groaned, sitting up. Dragging her messy hair up into a ponytail, securing it with a rubber band from around her wrist, she glanced at River and Savannah. "Jeez, we all passed out."

I stood. "Obviously, it was a very stimulating movie."

"Hush, I saw you mouthing along to 'Roxanne.'"

"It was a cover of The Police. But, being that you were barely a fetus in the eighties, I don't expect you to understand." I extended a hand down to help her up.

Her round ass swayed as she led me outside. I closed the door behind myself so as not to wake the girls. The cool, early morning temperature was only hours from giving way to the heat of the sun, but for now, it swirled all around us.

"I had fun tonight." Crossing her arms, she rubbed her shoulders for warmth.

I needed to walk away. Go back into my apartment.

Remember who I was and why I was there. Instead…

"Come here," I said, opening my arms.

She didn't delay in moving into them.

I wrapped her in a hug, warding off the chill in the air—and in my chest. "That better?"

"Much," she whispered, snuggling in close. "Thanks for tonight. I had a lot of fun. Even if I did snore on you."

I chuckled. "Me too, Cor. Also, I should probably tell you while I've got you wrapped up so tight you could never escape that I do in fact like mustard. But I should warn you it is by far not my worst quality."

She gasped dramatically. "You leave the toilet seat up, don't you? Re-wear socks? Dear God, don't tell me you wear a Speedo."

"I don't wear underwear, Cora. You think I'm tucking into a Speedo?"

She giggled. And I fucking loved it.

My stomach wrenched, and the words were out of my mouth before I could stop them. "Why do you live in a world like this?"

Her body tensed, but she made no attempt to step out of my hold. I ran a hand up and down her spine until she relaxed again.

"Lie," she whispered. "I like it here."

Careful to contain my anger at how amazingly screwed up that answer was, I murmured, "Fair enough."

Her head tipped back, her chin resting on my chest as she gazed up at me. "So I guess I'll see you in the morning?"

"Bright and early." After one last squeeze, I won the war

with my arms and reluctantly let her go.

I watched as she turned to the door, the most incredible high coursing through my veins.

"Hey, Cora?" I called, stopping her just before she went inside. "How do half-truths work in your game?"

She slanted her head to the side and shrugged. "Well, I guess they'd have to be two separate statements. One truth. One lie."

"In that case, I feel the need to tell you that I *haven't* thought about kissing you at least a dozen times tonight." I forced a smile through the storm brewing in my chest. "And yeah. That was a lie."

Her breath hitched and her lips parted, the most beautiful surprise covering her more beautiful face. "That's not fair," she whispered, bringing a hand up to her mouth to touch her lips. I felt it as though she were stroking my own. "No one should be that good the first time playing."

"Beginner's luck?"

Her face lit as she cut her gaze to the ground. Instinctively, I bent at the knee as though I could keep her in my sights. I hated that I was missing her smile.

"A dozen times, huh?" she asked.

"Give or take a three-percent margin of error."

She looked back up at me with eyes so bright that they made my stomach knot. "Only three percent?"

"That may have been another lie." I shot her a wink, but on the inside, I was cursing the universe.

She rocked on her toes. "Maybe we could test the margin of error another night? You know, for research and all."

"That sounds like a date."

"It does, doesn't it?" Her excitement paired with the blush of her cheeks punched me in the gut. "Okay, then. Thanks for…ya know. Everything, Penn."

I nodded. "Night, Cora."

"Night."

I watched her until she shut the door. And I stood there until I heard all three locks click into place.

Only then did I suck in a deep breath and prepare to face my destiny.

The moment I got inside, Drew sat straight up on the couch. "How'd it go?"

"You were right. She knows where Catalina is."

CHAPTER SIXTEEN

Cora

After Penn had left, I hadn't been able to fall asleep. I'd stared at the ceiling smiling like crazy until everyone had checked in, the sun had risen on the horizon, and I'd been forced to get up and get to work.

Throughout the day, I'd seen Penn twice. The first time we'd passed in the hall, he'd smiled, cordial and distant.

It'd sucked—hard and a lot.

However, the next time as he'd squeezed past me in the hall of my apartment, going as I was coming, he'd trailed the tip of his finger across the back of my hand and tossed me a sexy wink that had nearly made me trip.

I'd been mentally replaying that one at around six thirty that afternoon, when I'd sat on the couch for the briefest of seconds.

Some hours later, I woke from a dead sleep because of a hard knock at my door. Disoriented, I leapt to my feet and searched the room, relieved to find it empty when another knock sounded.

"Shit," I mumbled, trying to get my bearings. "Um… who is it?"

"It's Penn. I was wondering if maybe I could give it another go with the pipes in your bathroom?"

I glanced at the clock. It was after nine. The guys worked long hours, but that was a bit much. Though it's not like I was going to tell him no. I'd been dying to talk to him all day.

"Yeah. Sure." I looked down at myself. Old, stained yoga pants and a white tank top, sans bra. Shit. "Can you hang on for a second?"

I didn't wait for his response before I raced to my bedroom. Okay…my options were get fully dressed and try not to look like a woman who was just comatose on the couch, though the wild hair and the seams imprinted on the side of my face would have been hard to hide…

Or I could pull on a pair of not-hideous sleep shorts and a bra, drag my hair up, and pop a piece of gum to combat my middle-of-the-night morning breath.

I hated both options. But I went with door number two.

Finger-combing the curls at the ends of my ponytail, I hurried back to the door, pausing to toss the gum out—ya know, just in case.

"Sorry about that," I greeted.

His smile fell as he gave me a quick head-to-toe. "Shit. Were you asleep?"

Stepping to the side, I motioned for him to come in. "Kinda. I passed out on the couch."

He remained in the hall, his large red toolbox at his side. "Damn it. I should have called. I didn't mean to wake you up."

"It's okay. I needed to get up anyway."

His smile returned. "Truth?"

I rolled my eyes, regretting that I'd ever taught him that

damn game. "Fine, no. That was a lie."

He finally took a step over the threshold. "Whatever. I'll take it." I watched his back as he headed to the…kitchen? He set his toolbox on the counter. And then things got even more confusing.

After flipping the thing open, he revealed two white takeout containers. "How do you feel about Thai?"

"From a restaurant? I don't know. I've never had it. Out of your toolbox? I'll pass."

Humor danced on his face. "It's from a restaurant, crazy. I just didn't want anyone to see me carrying it in here. I didn't figure you'd want word to get out about our non-dating status."

My back shot straight. "We have a status?"

He smirked. "No. Currently we have a non-status. Though I was hoping Thai food"—he retrieved a bakery box—"and six cupcakes might help me change that."

My mouth fell open, and I clutched my chest. "Dear God, you're like Mary Poppins with muscles and a toolbox."

He laughed in a short burst. "One, I like that you've noticed the muscles. Two, it's Maury Poppins, actually. Mary's a distant cousin."

Giggling, I took the bakery box from his hand, cracked it open, and then moaned. Dear sweet, sweet baby Jesus. They were chocolate with mounds of chocolate icing and even more chocolate shaved on top. These were *not* your average grocery store cupcakes. These snack-sized cakes from heaven had come from Delilah's—my absolute favorite hole-in-the-wall bakery in the world. Well, maybe just Chicago; I hadn't really traveled anywhere else to shop comparisons.

Delilah's was a good twenty minutes away, but one bite of that melt-in-your-mouth icing and it was well worth the trip. Every year on my birthday, I made the trek, paid thirty freaking dollars for six of those orgasm-inducing confections, and then spent the next few days treating myself for breakfast, lunch, and dinner. Very few people knew that though.

As in *one* other person knew that. Only because I would get her six on her birthday as well.

Lifting them to my nose, I inhaled deeply and then spoke on the exhale. "Maury, what did you do?"

One side of his mouth curled up. "I *may* have enlisted River's help in exchange for these." He withdrew more cupcakes from his magical box.

"Ohhhh," I breathed, trading packages with him.

Three of them were vanilla with vanilla frosting and colorful sprinkles: River's absolute favorite. But the other three were all different. One was red velvet. One appeared to be something lemony. And the last, judging by the smell, was peanut butter—River's arch nemesis of cupcakes.

"She picked peanut butter?"

He scratched the back of his neck. "I, uh, didn't know what kind to get Savannah, so I just took a guess."

I blinked. Then blinked again. And then, suddenly, I couldn't stop blinking.

It started in my fingertips. Faint, like a million pin pricks. I stood frozen as it traveled up my arms and over my chest, stealing my breath.

He'd bought them cupcakes.

Thirty-dollar, roughly nine percent of his weekly salary, cupcakes. And he didn't want to leave Savannah out, so he'd just guessed on fifteen dollars' worth of freaking cupcakes.

Panic hit me as I felt my throat get thick. I softly gasped, trying to collect as much oxygen as I could before it closed.

And then I felt it. The stinging at my nose followed by the burning in my eyes.

Oh shit. I was going to cry.

Oh shitty shit shit shit. I was going to cry *and* I wasn't alone, hidden by the walls of my room.

"No," I croaked. Dropping the box on the counter, I was ready to sprint when his hand curled around the back of my neck, rendering me motionless.

"Cora?" he rasped, the question of what the hell was wrong with me being clear.

I shook my head repeatedly, trying and failing to fight it back.

Do not let him see you cry, I told myself. Unfortunately, my tear ducts missed the memo. A droplet slipped from the corner of my eye, and with no other choice, I face-planted against his chest. He wasted no time before folding his arms around me. One went around my shoulders, the other going around my waist, plastering me to his front.

"Talk to me," he rumbled.

"I…uh…think I'm having some kind of emotional allergic reaction to you buying cupcakes," I told his shirt.

He didn't immediately respond. However, when he did, it was not at all what I had been expecting.

A deep, rich laugh sprang from his throat. It was bold and carefree. The antithesis of everything I knew about Penn. I'd heard him chuckle. I'd heard him attempt to muffle a laugh. But this was…different.

This was beautiful.

Slowly, and without concern for any tears that might still be showing, I tilted my head back to enjoy what would surely be a spectacular show.

At the movement, he looked down at me, a wide smile splitting his lips. "You're crying over cupcakes?"

"I wasn't crying. I was just…having a moment."

Using his thumb, he wiped under my eye and then lifted it so I could see it. "Then I should probably warn you that you've sprung a leak."

I huffed with mock frustration. "*Fine.* Consider it a medical condition like that thing with your mouth. Which I'd like to note seems to have developed a new, much noisier symptom."

He winked. "I'll keep your secret if you keep mine."

"Deal." I started to push out of his arms, but he shook his head and gathered me tighter.

"Nuh-uh. We need to talk."

Those words usually struck fear into me. Conversation meant questions. And, more often than not, questions meant I had to lie. But, considering he was still smiling and I was utterly content to stand in his arms for however long he wanted to hold me, I didn't put up a fight.

"About what?"

He glanced down the hall. "Where are the girls?"

"They're watching movies on the second floor with—" I paused when a thought dawned on me. "Wait…did that cost you cupcakes too?"

"No. That cost me cash."

"Penn!"

"What?" He laughed again and I'd been absolutely right, it

was spectacular to witness. "I couldn't risk getting roped into another non-date musical. Don't think I didn't see *Chicago* on your shelf last night."

I circled my arms around his neck. "Wow. All that to avoid seeing Catherine Zeta-Jones naked."

"She gets naked?"

I shrugged. "I guess you'll never know."

Burying his face against my neck, he burst into laughter all over again.

I let myself go and started laughing too. I used him for balance, and he more than took my weight.

And then he *really* took my weight.

I squeaked when he lifted me off my feet and carried me into the kitchen.

"What are you doing?" I asked, still lost in hilarity when he sat me on the counter next to the sink.

My legs opened and he didn't delay in moving between them like it was the most natural thing in the world. And maybe it was. Though the nerves in my stomach were fluttering at full tilt. I kept my hold around his neck while he bent, put his hands on the counter on either side of my hips, and leaned in close. As in *super* close. Like we were breathing the same air. Not that I was actually breathing or anything.

My mouth dried as those blue eyes of his, which were no longer carrying the weight of the world, met mine. They were bright and sparkling with excitement even in the dull florescent lighting. "I have a surprise."

"What kind of surprise?" I whispered. "Is it better than cupcakes?"

"I thought so, but then you cried. So, now, I'm not sure."

I pinched his shoulder. "Hey! Secrets, remember?"

"Right. Sorry." He looked down, but it was impossible to hide a grin that big.

I loved every second of knowing that I was the one to put that on his face.

"Close your eyes," he ordered.

"How about I keep them open?"

His large hand cupped the back of my neck, and his nose brushed mine. "Eyes closed or no surprise."

Forget the butterflies—a stampede of elephants took up residence in my belly. Licking my lips, I followed his direction and dropped my lids.

And then, much to my dismay, he disappeared.

My shoulders sagged. "Uh…Penn?"

"Nope. Keep 'em closed," he said from somewhere nearby. In the background, there was a metal squeaking like he was twisting a screw.

"Can I at least have a clue?"

"Well," he murmured as he blessedly resumed his position between my legs. "It's wet and warm." His voice grew husky as his hands landed just above my knees and then coasted up my thighs. I gasped when they stopped at the hem of my shorts, but not before his thumb slipped under the fabric, gently teasing in circles. "I've wanted to give you this since the moment we met. To rain it over every inch of your smooth skin and dampen your perfect lips."

Chills exploded across my body, and my heart picked up a marathon pace. My throat closed as I waited for his mouth to find mine. His tongue to sneak out, urging my lips to part before starting a slow and dizzying rhythm.

Unfortunately, he only continued with the verbal seduction. "And some nights, I've done nothing but lay in bed, my mind spinning, trying to figure out when I was finally going to have the chance to do it."

A soft moan escaped my throat. Then, in the miracle of all miracles, his lips ghosted across mine. It wasn't exactly a kiss. But it wasn't exactly not a kiss, either.

"Penn," I breathed, gripping his strong shoulders, my nails biting into the hard muscle.

"You ready, Cora?"

I nodded multiple times before finally finding the word, "Yes."

"Give me your hand."

Hypnotized and teetering on the edge of anticipation, I obeyed immediately.

His callused fingers folded around the back of mine, and, palm up, he extended my arm out to the side.

And that's when I felt it.

Everything he'd described.

Everything I'd been asking for.

Yet, in that moment, nothing I wanted.

"Penn!" I exclaimed as water from my kitchen faucet rushed over our joined hands. My eyes flicked open and I found him standing in front of me, a shit-eating grin splitting his mouth.

He feigned innocence. "What?"

I gave his chest a shove that did nothing to move him. "That was mean."

"Wait, what'd you think I was talking about?"

I glared. "Oh, I don't know. Wet. Warm. Laying in bed

dreaming of *giving it to me*."

His eyebrows shot up and his mouth fell open, but he was still joking as he said, "Oh wow. I did *not* realize how filthy your mind was."

I barked a laugh and flicked droplets of water off the tips of my fingers, splashing him in the face. "I didn't mean sex!"

He wiped his cheek on his shoulder. "So, what, then? A kiss? Like on the forehead? Farther south? I'm gonna need specifics here."

I rolled my eyes, feeling my face go up in flames. "Sweet Lord. Let's just talk about the water. You actually fixed it?"

His only answer was to hook his arm around my hips, forcing me to the edge of the counter.

I cursed, fisting my hands in the front of his shirt when my core met his zipper.

His smile grew knowingly. Rough as velvet, he murmured, "We could try a forehead kiss, you know?"

"Oh, goodie," I smarted, pushing at his chest, desperate for an escape. "Is the bathroom working too? I want to see."

"No. I need to connect a few pipes. But, first, close your eyes again."

Forging ahead on my escape plans, I shimmied, trying to get down while mumbling, "I think we've had enough surprises tonight."

With a hand in the back of my hair, he stilled my retreat and tipped my head back until our eyes met. His face had drained of humor, but the flicker of desire remained. "Have you unlearned the *In my experience* yet?"

I swallowed hard and shook my head.

"You been with anyone since your ex?"

My eyes flared. "Not before and not after."

"Right. So this is going to work a little differently for me and you." Sliding his free hand down my calf, he wrapped my leg around his hip. "Say the word, Cora, and I'll kiss you breathless. But that's where we start and stop tonight. We take this slow. Get to know each other. Gain some trust. Ease into things." His voice became jagged. "Don't look so disappointed, baby. There's a lot of fun to be had with our mouths. You just gotta ask."

The herd of elephants resumed their stampede, and my throat got tight. "What word exactly?"

"Any of them."

"And you'll kiss me breathless?"

His mouth twitched. "That's what I said."

I licked my lips as I tried to formulate a witty retort that hopefully included *The Word*. When I came up with nothing, I smarted, "That doesn't sound like a forehead kiss."

Grinning, he nuzzled his nose with mine, whispering on an exhale, "You'll have to ask and find out."

The magnificent sound of water running played in the background as I stared into his eyes.

On one hand, I wasn't particularly eager to beg a man to kiss me.

On the other hand, he was giving me control and thus the safety that came with it.

I hated that he knew I needed that.

But I adored that he used what little he knew about me to make me comfortable rather than using it against me.

And, for that reason alone, I felt not one bit of shame as I whispered, "Kiss me, Penn."

CHAPTER SEVENTEEN

Penn

D rew had told me that I didn't have to fall in love with her or even sleep with her.

But there were no two ways around it. I *had* to kiss her.

I had no concept of why Cora Guerrero wanted me.

I'd tried to push her away. Tried guiding her in Drew's direction, despite it feeling like acid in my veins. He could have taken care of her. He had an end game.

I had a grave waiting for me.

But if this was what she wanted from me, I wasn't going to deny her.

God knew I was attracted to Cora more than reason or logic could ever explain. So I stopped trying to rationalize it.

I'd picked up Thai food and cupcakes she loved, bribed River and Savannah to get gone, and opened myself up for whatever the hell made her happiest.

As it turned out, we'd wanted a lot of the same things.

Like my mouth sealed over hers.

And, eventually, my body driving between her legs.

For fuck's sake, someone had to win in this entirely

messed-up situation.

Why couldn't it be her?

I could spend my days making her happy and my nights making love to her until we were both too sated to remember the past. Who knew? Maybe that was all she truly wanted from me.

A distraction from reality.

A warm body to make her forget.

A man to worship her.

I could do all of it.

What came after, I had no idea.

But I could make this easy for her.

And, selfishly, it would give me time to gather up a few million memories to torture myself with when I was gone.

"Kiss me, Penn."

She didn't have to repeat herself.

I kept my eyes open, drinking her in as I angled forward, slanted my head, and then took her mouth without a single regret. Her long lashes fell, and with one more stolen glance, I let mine follow.

Palming either side of her face, I relished in the way the ache in my chest disappeared.

Her lips were just as soft as I'd feared. Warm and pliant, her mouth opened, welcoming me in.

I groaned when her tongue touched mine. I'd thought about how she'd taste more times than I'd ever admit. Turned out, it was mint, soft and smooth. Just like her.

She set the pace of desperation, and I more than followed her.

Her tongue rolled with mine, her fingers slid into my

hair, and her legs locked around my hips, holding me as though she thought I was trying to get away.

But, in that moment, the world could have fallen off its axis and I was going *nowhere*.

I glided my hands down her sides, allowing my thumbs to sweep over the curve of her breasts. Her mouth fell slack, a soft moan escaping, and I swallowed it like a man on the brink of starvation.

I wanted more of those.

I wanted to *give* her more of those.

She released my mouth and started shoving the front of my shirt up. A curse tore from my throat as she latched on to my neck, her teeth raking deliciously across my skin. I sucked in a sharp breath when her nails traveled down the ridges of my abs, teasing at the waistband of my jeans.

"Take this off," she ordered.

I'd told her we'd go slow.

I'd fucking lied.

Panting, my cock thick and ready behind the denim, I stilled. "Jeans or shirt?"

She giggled, peppering kisses up my neck before nipping at my ear. "Have you reconsidered your stance on boxers?"

"Nope."

"Then maybe we should start with the shirt."

It was gone in the next heartbeat, and then my mouth once again sealed over hers.

We both moaned that time.

Our upper bodies were flush, her large breasts pillowed between us. But she was wearing entirely too much clothing.

"Tell me what's off-limits," I murmured.

"Nothing."

"Cora," I pressed.

"Shut up and touch me, Penn."

That I could do.

Her shirt joined mine on the floor, revealing a simple white bra that did nothing to hide her peaked nipples. My mouth watered as I dove between her cleavage. Licking and sucking, I made my way up to her delicate collarbone before heading south again.

"Oh God," she breathed, throwing her head back and using the top of my hair for balance.

I could have handled that. The erotic sting on my scalp. Her breathless urgency and sultry mews.

But what I could *not* handle was the roll of her hips, searching for friction against my zipper.

"Shit. Slow down," I groaned.

Get naked, my mind screamed.

She leaned forward, forcing me upright. One of her hands snaked into the back of my pants. I couldn't help but smile when she gripped my ass and bit my shoulder, mumbling, "Speed up."

"Any faster and I'm gonna be inside you."

She suddenly stilled, her head popping up, some unreadable emotion blazing in her wide eyes.

In my experience, Penn...

"Fuck," I muttered, regret dousing me like a bucket of ice water. I started to back away, but she refused me my space.

"That's not where this is going," I said. "I'll kiss you any way you want. But that's as far as we go."

She shook her head. "Wait, Penn, I—"

"I don't need an explanation. We got ground rules. Pants stay on. Everything above the waist is fair game."

She opened her mouth, but I silenced her with another kiss.

"No more talking." With both hands on her ass, I scooped her off the counter.

Her legs once again encircled my hips, and our mouths reconnected. Our tongues danced and dueled as I carried her from the kitchen, blindly bumping into walls.

The couch seemed to be approximately seven miles away, but with our mouths fused together, I was content to take the scenic route.

We lay on that couch, making out for somewhere between ten seconds and a hundred years.

I catalogued her every curve, and she explored my back from ass to shoulders.

My pants stayed on.

Her bra remained in place.

But there was nothing innocent about the way our bodies rolled together, like waves unable to find a shore. And I was a delirious man lost at sea who never wanted to be found.

When the frenzy finally ebbed from our bodies, I was lying on my side, my back against the couch, her front pressed to mine, our noses only inches apart as her head rested on my arm, and my fingers teased at her lower back.

Our breathing was labored.

Our skin was damp.

And I had no doubt the drumming of our hearts could be heard on the first floor.

"Wow," she breathed, her eyes still closed.

"Agreed," I rasped, ghosting one last kiss over her lips. "That was by far the hottest forehead kiss I've ever given."

She giggled and cuddled closer, nuzzling her face against my chest. "I'm pretty sure you missed my forehead completely."

"Did I? I've always been shit at anatomy."

"That explains why I'm still wearing pants."

"Smartass." I tickled her side, causing a brilliant laugh to spring from her throat. I couldn't have stopped my smile if I'd tried. Not that I was trying anymore.

She wiggled in protest as I folded her in my arms and held her tight. My fingers played up and down her sides like she was a grand piano, her laugh being my first—and greatest—symphony.

"Penn!" she screamed, writhing against me.

"Cora!" I mocked.

And then, like a poacher, I closed my eyes and absorbed every ounce of warmth Cora was offering.

Because, soon enough, it would be gone.

Just like me.

CHAPTER EIGHTEEN

Cora

"**O**h God!" I cried, falling over to the side, barely able to save my beer. I was in my hallway and thankfully already sitting down, so it was a short trip to the wood floor.

Penn was in the bathroom, his position mirroring mine except, rather than being dead from embarrassment, he had a wrench in his hand and was doubled over in laughter.

"Stop laughing!" Two words I'd never thought I'd say to him. A river of beer later, I had to repeat myself. "Stop laughing!"

That night, I'd eaten Thai food for the very first time. This being after Penn and I had put our shirts back on—a sight I'd seriously lamented as the fabric stole my favorite view. The man was gorgeous in clothes. But shirtless? His cut pecs covered in a light smattering of hair and a six-pack trailing down to meet a mouthwatering V that disappeared below the low-hanging denim at his trim waist? He was downright edible.

And while the Toolbox Thai had actually been delicious, I would have way rather feasted on Penn.

That damn second of hesitation had foiled it all. It was a gut reaction that had been programmed into me over the years. For the women in the building, sex was a paycheck. A means to an end. A way of life.

But, for me, sex was nothing more than a weapon in my arsenal.

A bargaining chip.

A last-ditch resource to stay alive.

But one kiss and I wanted it to be different again.

However, despite the fact that I'd thrown every please-God-get-me-naked signal I knew, including a few I made up on the fly, Penn had stuck to his guns and kissed me senseless in a very PG-13 version of what I truly wanted.

Not that I was complaining or anything. He was talented in the mouth department.

After Thai food and a sizable amount of self-reflection, I'd taken a step outside of my comfort zone and offered Penn one of my coveted cupcakes. It had been hard, but my manners had finally won out. I'd never been so relieved or genuinely puzzled in my life when he'd refused, stating that he wasn't big on sweets. I should have known after seeing the thick muscles hugging his frame, but come on. Who hated sweets? The disgust on my face must have been obvious, because he'd chuckled, shaking his head before planting a kiss on my lips and saying, "But I'd love to watch you eat a cupcake, Cora."

I'd retorted, "I didn't know you could get creepier, Penn." But I'd said it while peeling the wrapper off three layers of chocolate and then shoving it into my mouth, bordering between ladylike and a lion attacking a gazelle on The Discovery Channel.

ALY MARTINEZ

After the cupcake massacre and a lot of laughs, we'd broken into the beer.

Penn creeped hard during this time, his hip leaning against the counter, his legs crossed at the ankle, his arms over his chest, his eyes sparkling with mischief as the tiniest of smirks pulled at his lips.

We talked for over an hour. Eventually, the conversation moved to the hall (me) and the bathroom (him), where he'd started the monumental task of putting my bathroom back together, but he didn't stop creeping.

More than once, I'd caught his hooded gaze glued to my legs, my breasts, or my throat. *Gorgeous.*

I decided right then and there that Penn Walker could creep on me any day of the week.

And I would creep on him while he creeped on me, and together, we could be the creepiest creeping couple who ever creeped. I believe those had been my exact words to him while I was sitting on the floor when, suddenly, I'd laughed so hard I'd snorted.

Thus taking us back to me folding over on the wood floor, rescuing my beer, and dying of embarrassment.

Penn's laughter got louder as he approached. I rolled flat to my back and opened my eyes in time to see him crawling on his hands and knees to hover above me. He plucked the beer from my grip and set it somewhere nearby, and then his weight settled on top of me.

Head to toe.

Chest to chest.

His mouth was gloriously close as he asked, "Are you drunk?"

I scoffed. "Lie. And *no*."

"You laugh so hard you snort often?"

"Lie. And yes."

He grinned, wide and toothy. It was by far the least attractive smile I had ever seen him wear and it still made my pulse spike.

"I love when you laugh," he whispered before sweeping his lips across mine.

I lifted my head to keep contact, but he was gone. "I love that you actually know how to laugh. I was worried for a while there. All the stoic silences were really throwing me off."

I got another kiss.

"It's getting late. I should probably get going."

"Noooo," I whined, the heat from my flush, drunk cheeks spreading across the rest of my body. Arching my back, I pressed my breasts against his chest. "You could stay. The girls should be back soon, but they won't bother us if we're in my room. And if you're just going to sit in the hall all night, watching me, you might as well do it up close and personal."

"That would make it easier."

I slid my hand around his back and under his shirt. "I promise to wear pants."

"I can't make that same promise, Cora."

I nipped at his bottom lip. "Okay, so pants optional. We'll see how it goes."

"I can tell you how it's gonna go." He returned my nip. "It's not."

I exaggerated a pout.

He kissed it away. "Stop giving me hell, woman. I'm

pretending to be a gentleman here."

I huffed and rolled my eyes. "Fine, but if you ask me, this seems like a gross misuse of your cold, hard cash. The girls aren't even back yet."

Smooth and completely unhindered by the alcohol, he climbed to his feet. I attempted to follow him, but I did it fully affected by the alcohol and without a graceful bone in my body.

"Whoa!" He caught my arm when the floor started to rise toward me. "How much did you drink?"

I clung to his strong arm only partially for balance. "Apparently, more than I should have. Though this totally explains the snort."

"Come here," he mumbled, scooping me off my feet with an arm under my knees.

"Wow," I breathed. "You weren't lying about the gentleman bit."

He walked the short distance to my bedroom door and jutted his chin at it. "Open it. I'll hang until the girls get back. But it's probably safest for your skull if we get you horizontal again."

I beamed up at him. "Really?"

"Yeah. You're drunk on, like, two tablespoons of beer. Someone's got to keep an eye on you until your parents get back."

I slapped his chest. "I meant about you staying. But, for the record, I had four *full* beers, thank you very much."

"*Four beers* isn't helping your case. But yeah, Cora, I'll stay for a little while longer."

Victory sang in my veins.

I was nowhere near ready for it to be over.

For one night, everything outside of my apartment had disappeared.

Marcos.

Dante.

Manuel.

Even Nic.

My whole wretched life faded into the background.

For one night, I'd talked and laughed with a gorgeous, kind, and thoughtful man.

For one night, responsibility hadn't been suffocating me.

For one freaking night, I had been *free*.

Tracing the curve of his lip, I whispered, "Truth or lie?"

"Truth."

"I could get used to doing this with you."

His eyes flashed dark and a shadow passed over his face. "Please don't."

I frowned, alarm bells screaming in the back of my mind.

But before I had the chance to question his odd answer, he ordered, "Get the door, baby."

Baby. Le sigh.

I was smiling all over again.

I twisted the lock and pushed it open. Penn didn't make it one step over the threshold before he fired off a string of muttered expletives.

"This is your room?"

"No, this is the Taj Mahal. My room is the twenty-seventh door on the left."

He glared down at me, completely unimpressed by my joke, but I was drunk and hadn't slurred a single word. I was crazy impressed and burst into a loud fit of laughter.

"It's carpet," he announced as if I hadn't lived there for over a decade.

"Excellent observation." More giggling.

More glaring. "Why?"

I wiggled in his arms, and he caught the hint and set me on my feet. "Why what?"

"Your entire house has wood. Why the hell do you have carpet in here?"

Very aware that his eyes were following me, I put some extra sway in my step as I sauntered to the bed and promptly collapsed.

"And she sleeps on a fucking mattress on the floor," he bit out. "Jesus, fucking, Christ."

With a curled lip, I lifted my head off the pillow and slowly glanced over my shoulder, a mouthful of attitude ready to go. It died on my tongue when I found him still standing on the wrong side of the doorway, a haunted pallor coloring his face.

I sat up. "Penn?"

He drew in a pained breath, the muscles in his neck straining, his hands opening and closing at his sides as though he were about to go into battle, but his gaze was locked on the floor. "I'm ripping up this goddamn carpet."

My chest tightened as memories of him telling me why'd he torn up the carpet in Angela's apartment flashed through my drunken mind. "Shit."

I ached for him. It had been thirteen years, and if I could avoid walking on a sidewalk, I did. Because when I looked down at the cracks in the concrete, I never saw anything but

Nic's blood.

I nodded immediately. "Okay."

Tilting his head from side to side, he cracked his neck, and, then in a voice filled with emotional gravel, he started with, "I can't… It's too—"

I rose to my knees. "Penn, honey. I said okay. Trust me, I get it. Rip it up. Whatever you need to do for you. You do it, okay?"

The color returned to his face as the most brilliant gratitude flittered through his eyes.

And then it was my turn to be surprised.

He walked inside, turning to the door as he shut it. "And I'm gonna fix your bed."

In the grand scheme of things, it was small. He'd done a lot for me in the short time he'd been there. But that? For a girl like me? Well, that one meant a lot.

Chills detonated across my skin. "What did you say?" My damn nose started stinging again, and then it was all about the blink.

He scowled at the floor as he walked toward me. "A bed. You need one. I'll get a frame set up. New mattress and box spring. This damn carpet has to go first. I'll put some wood down. See if I can match the rest of the—" He abruptly stopped at the foot of my bed. "Shit… Are you crying?"

I shook my head. But I totally was.

"Cora, baby," he whispered, dropping his knees to the mattress before pulling me into his arms.

Barely holding myself together, I went willingly. He settled on his side, then juggled me until I was facing him and resting on his arm.

Kissing my forehead, he rumbled, "What's going on in that head of yours?"

I hadn't cried in front of anyone in over a decade. And, damn it, I'd done it twice just that night. I let out a groan and tried to swipe under my eyes. "Just another allergic reaction."

"About the carpet or the bed?"

"About you caring where I sleep."

His brows pinched together. "Of course I care. Why wouldn't I?"

I peered up at him, my vision swimming with unshed tears. "Because no one ever has. I take care of people, Penn. They don't take care of me."

Another one of his shadows flashed through his features. I couldn't figure out if those happened when he was trying to cover his true emotions or when they finally escaped his walls. With his next words, I stopped caring.

"You've given enough. Now, you need to learn how to take," he stated as fact. "If I can do something to make your life even a fraction easier, I'm gonna do it. Whether it be something small like a bed or changing the bald tires you got on your car. Or something big like dealing with those piece-of-shit Guerreros—I'm gonna handle it."

"Why?" I croaked.

His forehead crinkled. "Why do you always ask me why? Is it so unfathomable to you that someone would actually want to help you?"

"Yes!" I exclaimed, sitting up. I crisscrossed my legs and faced him. "That doesn't happen for me. If I want something done, I find a way to make it happen. If there isn't a way, I find a way to make one. Don't get me wrong. I'm grateful.

188

So damn grateful for everything you've done, right down to you sitting here, having this conversation with me." I sucked in a shaky breath. "But I'm going to be honest: I don't know what to do with all of this. Two weeks ago, I didn't know you existed. Two days ago, you were avoiding me like the plague. Now, you're vowing to buy me a new bed? They aren't cheap, Penn. Do you even have money for that?"

"I got a little put away. Worked my ass off for it too. That means I get to spend it however I see fit. Like on a bed for a good woman who deserves a decent night of sleep more than anyone I've ever met."

Stunned into silence, I could do nothing but stare at him.

He thought I was a good woman.

I mean, I *was*. I knew that to the core of my soul. But hearing it again after all those years? That hit me deep. It was a gift all of its own.

"You…" I shook my head, unable to trust my voice.

"And, now, she's in shock," he mumbled, rolling to his back, taking me down with him. "Two weeks ago, I wasn't sure I existed, either. Two days ago, I was struggling with how I felt about you. Though it seems we got that figured out." He kissed the top of my head. "Two minutes ago, you told me I could rip out the carpet in your bedroom because you recognized that it was important to me. You gave me that, Cora. No questions asked. No explanation needed. This is me giving something back to you. And dry up the tears, because it's not exactly a grand act of heroism like saving the population of humpback whales. I'm simply helping you get a bed that isn't on the floor." He groaned and shifted to the left. "And one that doesn't have a broken spring in the middle of it."

Note to self: Hide my accounting textbook somewhere else.

With my heart soaring, the strangest feeling took up root inside me. I couldn't pinpoint it. But I thought it might have been akin to the feeling of a massive boulder being lifted off my shoulders. Whatever it was, with one hundred percent certainty, Penn had been the one to take it from me.

Sniffling, I cuddled into his side, allowing my tense body to relax as I curled around him. "Have you given a lot of thought to saving humpback whales?"

"Not for a second. Though, if you find it on your list of needs, I'll give it a little more."

The tears came back, but for once in my life, they weren't because I was sad, or overwhelmed, or trapped in a life I so desperately wanted to escape.

For the first time in, well, forever, I didn't want to be anywhere else.

Smiling, I squeezed him tight and tangled our legs together. "If you keep this up, I'm going to go broke cooking you thank-you dinners."

He chuckled but said no more.

Eventually, I fell asleep—not staring up at Nic's stars, but rather tracing the black ink on Penn's forearm and listening to the strong and steady rhythm of his heart.

Some hours later, he woke me with peppered kisses over my face and asked me to lock the door behind him.

Then the girls started calling to check in—chaos finding me all over again.

But for those hours wrapped safe in his arms, the calm had been intoxicating.

One I could easily get addicted to, whether he wanted

me to or not.

And, lucky for me, Penn didn't seem to heed his own advice about not getting used to being with me, either. Because, after the night of Maury Poppins and Toolbox Thai food, there weren't many nights where Penn wasn't in my bed.

CHAPTER NINETEEN

Cora

"Mmm," I purred as he kissed down my chest. "Take it off."

We were on week two of Penn ignoring my sexual pleas—and I was going insane.

Every night, we made out like teenagers. But like the good teenagers with good parents who filled their heads with fears about getting pregnant from oral sex.

Penn never went below the belt, which was nice a week ago. Now, it was obnoxious.

"Slow, Cora," he murmured.

"One of these days, I'm going to spontaneously combust."

"Far as I know, that has never actually happened to a person."

I arched off the bed. "Then I guess you'll have the privilege of witnessing a scientific phenomenon. Congratulations."

He chuckled, palming my breast, kneading as he continued kissing down to my stomach. It felt so incredible that I couldn't bring myself to complain anymore.

Well, that is until he got to the elastic waistband of my sleep shorts. His tongue trailed a wet path, making me desperate all over again.

Lifting my hips off the mattress, I pleaded, "Okay, then, take those off."

I felt his smile, and then his teeth grazed over the sensitive flesh above my hip.

"Oh God," I cried as a burst of pain morphed into pleasure and then radiated between my legs. "Please."

"I gotta get back to work, baby," he murmured, kissing his way back up my stomach. "And you gotta get back to talking."

I threw my head back against the pillow. "You are such a tease."

"Don't act like you're the only one suffering here." He rolled his hips, his hard length finding purchase against my thigh.

"Penn," I breathed, hooking my arms under his and turning into him. "Neither of us has to suffer. You know that, right?"

He pecked my nose, grinned, and then he was gone. "Tonight, we do. Because I want to hear what you got to say."

He tossed me my tank top, which I'd thrown nearly halfway across the room the second his lips had met mine. It'd made him laugh. Putting it back on made me want to cry. "Ah, the curse of a good storyteller."

"Precisely." He winked, something so beautiful that I released a breathy schoolgirl sigh.

This again made him laugh, but he did it shaking his head. And then he got back to work, prying up the tack boards that had once secured my carpet.

He'd ripped that up a few nights before. He'd cussed the

whole time. But when he'd thrown it over the railing and into the parking lot, his whole body had sagged like it had taken every ounce of his strength with it.

Truth be told, I'd hated that carpet too. It was an ugly brown that had made the whole room feel dark and dreary. Seeing Penn's reaction had made me hate it that much more.

I was still using my old mattress, but according to him, it was only until he got the new wood floors down. I wasn't sure how big this savings account Penn had squirreled away was—or how I felt about him spending it on me—but I wasn't about to tap into my Freedom Account. I'd been siphoning that off the Guerreros for the last five years. So, if he was adamant about getting me a new bed, then who was I to argue?

I flipped to my stomach, put my elbows to the bed and my chin in my hands, and watched the muscles in his back ripple beneath his plain white tee.

"Stop creeping and start talking," he ordered without looking at me. He tossed another strip of wood into the small pile in the center of the room.

I rolled my eyes. "Fine. None of the girls would ever rat us out."

"You positive about that? Because I gotta be honest: I don't give a damn what anyone has to say about us, but I can't imagine Marcos or Dante would be real happy to find out we have something going on. I don't want one of the girls running their mouth about how much time I spend over here, giving the Guerreros an excuse to pop up unannounced when I could be out at the hardware store or chauffeuring Drew's ass home from a bar."

I crossed my legs at the ankle, bent at the knee, and

rocked them back and forth above me like a true coed. "Yeah. Trust me. They hate Marcos and Dante."

"Then why do they work for them?"

Now wasn't that the million-dollar question. "Different reasons, I guess." I shifted uncomfortably. "The first floor is here because they love the job."

He quirked an incredulous eyebrow like anyone who wasn't in the business would.

"Yeah. I know. It's a hard concept to understand. But some like the attention. Some like the money. Some just don't believe they can do any better. But trust me, Penn. If they weren't here, they'd be working somewhere else."

He scoffed. "You're telling me they're here by choice?"

"I guess, in one way or another, we're all here by choice."

His eyes flashed dark. "Including you?"

I shot him a tight smile. "Lie. And yes."

"Jesus," he muttered. "So, what about the girls on the second floor?"

"They're the new ones or those who haven't made up their mind yet. Most have been assaulted by Dante in some form and are still confused about how they ended up here and haven't really decided if they want to stay. I keep a special eye on them."

He threw another tack board into the pile. "And what if they want to leave? Can they?"

I lifted a shoulder in a half shrug. "Physically? Yes. With the right support system, they could get out. Dante would probably go after them, but it's been done before. It could be done again. But it's mental sometimes. The abuse before they get here. Women don't find themselves in this life because they seek it out. They find themselves here because the world has beaten them down to the point that even the darkest knight looks like a hero."

Kneeling in the corner, he stopped what he was doing and gave me his undivided attention. "Is that what happened to you after Nic? Dante start looking like a hero?"

My stomach rolled. "No," I answered firmly.

He arched a dark brow. "Lie?"

"God's honest truth. Dante has always been the villain in my story."

"You want to elaborate on that?"

I held his gaze. "Truth. No."

His face flashed hard, dozens of follow-up questions dancing in his eyes. But I wouldn't answer any of them—at least not with the truth.

"Dante's good at what he does." I shifted back to the original topic. "He gets into their heads and pulls all the right strings that will make them believe that this is the best life they can ever have."

"Tell me you don't believe that, Cora."

I allowed the truth to blaze from my eyes. "No. I don't."

He looked visibly relieved. It would have been sweet had it not been insulting.

"I'm not stupid, Penn. I'm not brainwashed. I'm not... whatever you think about me."

He lifted his hands in surrender. "Whoa, slow down. I don't *think* anything about *you*." He paused, breathed a curse, and then continued. "That was a lie. I actually think a lot of things about you. But none of them are bad. Okay?"

I cut my eyes to the door to avoid his scrutinizing gaze.

"I don't want anyone's pity."

Out of the corner of my eye, I saw him rise to his full height. Then his boots thumped on the concrete as he walked over, the mattress dipping when he sat on the edge. I tried to roll away, but he didn't let me go far. Using one hand, he guided my head into his lap and then used the other to hook my legs so I was curled like a kitten around him with my thighs flush with his back.

His face was soft, his posture relaxed, and his voice raw as he leaned in close and pointedly stated, "Then you'll get none from me."

I focused on his stomach. "It didn't seem that way—"

"I'm here too, Cora. You were right. We do all have our reasons. I'm just trying to understand yours." He brushed the hair out of my face, the tips of his callused fingers trailing across my cheek and down my neck. As if he knew what it meant, he stopped before he reached my star necklace. "And that means getting to know *you*. So if you have secrets you're not ready to share yet? Fine. Play your game of lies. But don't ever mistake my asking questions or wanting to know everything about you as some kind of judgment or pity."

Damn. That was sweet.

And it made me feel like crap.

My cheeks heated. "Sorry. I haven't done the talking thing with anyone in a long time. I mean…I talk *a lot*. But not usually about myself."

"It's okay. I'll fuck this up, too. I'm not exactly the most open man in the world."

"No, you definitely aren't." I hazarded a peek up at him.

He was smirking. "You got something you want to ask me?"

"Oh, about a million things."

"What do you say we play a little Truth or Lie tit-for-tat? I think I'm done working for the night."

I smiled wide. Partially because I was beyond eager to learn more about the mysterious Penn Walker, but also because being done working meant he'd probably lie in bed with me, talking and holding me close until I fell asleep.

"I see you like this idea."

I nodded several times.

He slanted his head toward the top of the mattress. "Come on. Get under the covers."

I watched with rapt attention as Penn unlaced his boots, set them at the foot of the bed, hit all the locks on my bedroom door, and then slid into bed beside me. I giggled as he wrestled me into a comfortable position on his chest.

Once his arm was crooked behind his head, he kissed the top of my head and mumbled, "Shoot."

I decided to start out small. "Favorite color."

"Truth. Blue."

"Light or dark?" I tilted my head to peer up at him and he put his chin to his chest to look down at me.

"Nope. Tit-for-tat. My turn. Favorite food."

"Lie. Veggies." I winked.

He chuckled. "You forgot I saw you maim that cupcake a while back."

Grinning, I bulged my eyes at him. "I said lie."

He glared at me, but he did it with twitching lips.

"How old were you when you lost your virginity?" I

asked, teasing my fingers under the hem of his T-shirt.

His eyebrows shot up, and he caught my hand, stilling my ascent up his chest. "Who says I've lost it?"

It was my turn to glare.

And his turn to laugh.

When he sobered, he answered and then continued with the rapid-fire questions. "I was sixteen. Danielle Rogers in my bed while my parents were at work. Favorite flavor ice cream?"

"Chocolate."

"Shocking," he deadpanned.

"Did you graduate high school?" I asked.

"I did. Top of my class."

My mouth fell open. "No shit?"

"Your surprise isn't doing good things for my ego. What about you?"

"I got my GED a few years ago," I replied, suddenly feeling super inadequate.

He gave me a reassuring squeeze on my hip. "Don't say it like that. Hard work is hard work. Be proud of that, Cora."

My cheeks heated under his praise. "Did you go to college?"

"Um..." He swayed his head from side to side. "Lie. Florida State."

I laughed.

He shrugged. "What about you?"

I chewed on my bottom lip. I'd been in college for years, taking one class at a time. At first, that had been all I could afford. Cash hadn't always been easy to come by. But, more recently, time had been the hardest commodity to come by.

Most of the classes I took were online, but without a computer at home, I had to hit the local library. My coming and goings weren't monitored by any means, but that was only because I'd never raised suspicions. If I started disappearing for hours a day, who knew what would have happened. Flying under the radar was always the safest. And that included keeping my mouth shut about my accomplishments even when I wanted to shout it from the rooftops.

I shot him a flirty wink and parroted, "Lie. Florida State."

"Right," he chuckled. "Your turn."

I snuggled deeper into his side. "Do you have a relationship with your parents?"

"They're dead," he answered curtly. "Drew's all I got left."

Wincing, I whispered, "Sorry."

"Don't be. They lived a good life. Loved each other. Loved me. I loved them. Nothing to feel bad about." He was silent for several seconds after that, lost in reflection. So I allowed him his time, but I did it while lazily drawing circles over his abs.

He abruptly cleared his throat. "Shit. Ah, okay. I'm up." His hand anchored in the curve of my hip, trailed up my side. "You got any friends?"

"I have a lot of friends."

"No, Cora. I don't mean the women in this building. I mean girlfriends that you stay on the phone bullshitting with for hours on end. Or get dressed up, go out to a bar, and cut loose with, laughing too damn loud while annoying every patron in the building, yet still attracting the eyes of every man."

"Oh. Then no."

"What about that Catalina?"

My head jerked back and my entire body turned to granite at the mere mention of her name. "What?"

He gave me a squeeze. "Relax. I'm only asking because you mentioned you two used to be tight, and short of River and Savannah, I haven't seen you be anything even resembling tight with anyone else."

I narrowed my eyes. "I mentioned we used to be tight?"

He put his chin to his chest and looked down at me. "Yeah, babe. While you were trying to kick me out of your apartment and accusing me of reporting back to Manuel."

I blinked, racking my mind. I rarely said anything about Catalina. Though that particular night, I hadn't been thinking straight. My aching heart and furious mouth had been running that show, so it wasn't exactly impossible that I'd mentioned something. I just didn't remember it. Which, depending on what I'd said, could be a dangerous thing. Even if I'd only said it to Penn.

"What else did I say?"

"Nothing. Just that and that you didn't know where she was followed by a whole lot of, 'Get the fuck out.'"

I blew out a relieved breath. "Okay, good."

His brows shot up, crinkling his forehead. "Something you want to tell me?"

I pursed my lips and shook my head. "Nope. And truth. No, I don't have any girlfriends that I get dressed up and go out with. That's not a luxury I've ever had. Not when Cat was still around and not since she's been gone, either. Though that does sound fun. Maybe when the weather gets cold again and things slow down, I'll suggest a night out to some of the girls."

He shifted, inching down at the same time he pulled me up until we were sharing the same pillow. "You can talk to me. You know that, right?"

"Course," I whispered, pecking his lips. It was only a half-lie. I did feel comfortable talking with Penn. I loved this little game of tit-for-tat. But not at the risk of Catalina's life. "My turn. How'd you get the name Penn?"

He frowned, ignoring me. "You miss her?"

My stomach knotted—at the question and the answer. "Every day."

"You think she's still alive?"

I didn't want to hear the alarm bells.

I didn't want to feel the hairs on the back of my neck rise in warning.

And I definitely didn't want to see the rapt interest as he held my gaze waiting for my reply.

But it was there. All of it.

And it made a panic build within me until I was ready to bolt.

"I'm going to grab something to drink. You want—" I turned away and started to sit up, but his hard front became flush with my back. His strong arms folded around me from behind, tight enough to restrain me, loose enough that I could easily escape.

Pure Penn.

"I hate that you're alone," he rasped. "I hate that you spend ninety percent of your time trapped between these four walls. I hate that the only friends you have are women who need you rather than want you. I hate that you have no family to lean on. And, while I fucking love that every night you're waiting for me to get here, I fucking hate that I'm not shoving people out the door in order to spend time with you. You need good people in your life, Cora, and Catalina is the first and only person I've heard you mention as being that to you. So I'm sorry if talking about her upsets you, but if there's something I could do to get that back for you, I'd like to at least try."

His explanation mildly relaxed me, dulling even the loudest alarm bells, but as it was so often said: the road to hell was paved with good intentions.

"The best thing you could do for me is to *stop* talking about her," I hissed over my shoulder, my pulse thundering in my ears. "*If* she's still alive, it's because she doesn't want to be found." I placed my hand over his and threaded our fingers together. "Yes, Penn. I miss her. Yes. I'd give anything to have her back. But knowing she's not stuck living with her abusive husband and that she's out of reach from her psychotic father and brothers? Well, that does more for me than any girls' night out."

"Shit," he breathed, his arms convulsing around me.

"You might mean well, but I'm begging you to let it go—let *her* go."

He nodded, his chin resting on my shoulder, as we both faced the dingy wall on the other side of my bedroom.

He was staring at nothing.

I was staring at the trim above the doorjamb and envisioning the two hundred thousand dollars hidden behind it.

It wasn't enough.

Not yet.

But I was getting closer.

And, therefore, so was Catalina.

"It's a family name," he whispered before placing a kiss on my shoulder. "Dad, Grandfather, Great-Grandfather. We were all Penn."

I nodded and glanced at him over my shoulder. "Maybe we should quit for tonight."

Half of his mouth tipped up. "Probably a good idea."

Without further conversation, we both settled in for the night.

Penn on his back.

Me on my side, my leg thrown over his hips and my arm draped over his stomach.

I could have stayed like that for the rest of my life. I hadn't fallen asleep yet, but I was already dreading him waking me up so he could leave in a few hours.

"Spend the night tonight?" I asked, kissing his chest.

"I always do."

I slanted my head back to look up at him. "No. You either wake me up to leave or leave when the girls wake me up to check in."

His face was soft, his eyes filled with genuine affection—such a vast difference from the man who had first walked through my door a month earlier. "Babe, your girls call or text all night long. The last usually wake you up at five. Even when I'm in my own apartment, I wake up by five. I'm not racing out of here to crawl back into bed at my place. I leave so I can get a cup of coffee, go for a run, take a shower, throw back some breakfast, and then get to work by seven."

My brows furrowed. "You go for a run every morning?"

"Yep."

"Really?"

He flexed his abs under my hand. "I'll say it again: Your surprise is not doing good things to my ego."

"No," I defended, pushing up onto an elbow. "You definitely look like a man who works out. It's just I didn't realize you ran every day."

He smiled. "There's a lot you don't know about me, Cora. Which is exactly why we're laying in bed, playing Truth or Lie. You'll learn." His arm tensed around me, and his lids fell shut even as he aimed them up at the ceiling. After sucking in a deep and content breath, he finished with, "We'll both learn."

Like so often with Penn, I fell asleep that night with a smile on my face.

After a slow and toe-curling kiss, he left bright and early the following morning to go for his run.

And because I figured Penn running meant he'd be hot, sweaty, and possibly shirtless, I got up bright and early too and drank my coffee at the railing overlooking the parking lot.

I was right on all accounts.

When he came jogging back up, he was hot.

So sweaty.

Very, very shirtless.

And as he stared up at me, his chest heaving, his hands on his hips, his abs giving the most incredible cameo with his every breath, and a humor-filled grin stretched across his handsome face, I decided that it was my newest routine.

CHAPTER TWENTY

Cora

"Pivot!" River yelled as Drew and Penn carried my brand-spanking-new mattress up the last flight of stairs.

"Oh my God, stop."

She giggled. "You have to understand that, when you force a person to watch all ten seasons of *Friends*, at some point, there *will* be consequences." She shot me a huge grin. Then she cupped her hands around her mouth and repeated, "Pivot!"

Laughing, I gently slapped her arm. "Stop. He bought me a bed. Don't make him regret it."

Savannah gave me a nudge from my other side. "The man bought you a bed that he gets you naked in before he sleeps in it with you every night. I don't think he's going to be regretting anything for quite a while." She winked.

My mouth slacked open. "I will have you know that the *only* thing Penn does in my bed is sleep, thank you very much."

"Ah, he can't get it up. Don't take it too hard. He's old—"

"He can get it up!" I exclaimed entirely too loudly, just

as Penn appeared with one end of the queen-sized pillowtop mattress.

"I can get what up?" he grunted as he backed past us.

Drew appeared a few steps later, holding the other end and flashing me a knowing smile.

I rolled my eyes and then shot Savannah a death glare that only made her giggle. In a sugary-sweet—and hopefully distracting—tone, I replied, "The bed. That's all. Nothing more." I shuffled to the side, bumping Savannah out of the way so the guys could get through the doorway to my apartment.

River let out one last, "Pivot!" as they made their way inside.

When they disappeared toward my bedroom, I hissed at Savannah, "Would you hush? First of all, it's none of your business what Penn and I do or do not do in my bedroom. Secondly, he's *not* old."

"So you're telling me you've been together for over a month and you haven't put out yet?"

Uncomfortably, I looked at River, who was suddenly— and thankfully—enthralled with her shoes.

"Again. None of your business." I lowered my voice and hissed, "But no. I have not *put out* yet." I kept the *not for a lack of trying* to myself.

Her eyes flashed wide, and then all at once, her face paled. "Holy shit. You're seriously not fucking him?"

My back shot straight. The crap Savannah said never surprised me anymore. She had no filter whatsoever. But it was the pure terror contorting her face that made my heart stop.

Eying her curiously, I replied, "No. I'm not."

Diving forward, she grabbed both of my shoulders and gave me a hard shake. "Why not!"

"Hey!" River yelled, attempting to wade into the middle of whatever the hell was going on.

"What is wrong with you?" I snapped.

Savannah's crazed, green eyes bored into me, suffocating panic rolling off her. "You have to have sex with him! He'll either leave, find it somewhere else, or he'll take it. Men don't wait!" She gave me a hard shove, sending me stumbling back. "If you want to keep him, you need to stop with the games and give him what he wants."

My stomach sank as bile crawled up my throat. "That's not the way relationships work, honey. Penn would never—"

"Yes, he would!" Her voice cracked, and her hands trembled as she tried to shove me again.

I caught her wrists before she had the chance. "Stop it," I seethed.

She only got more worked up. Tears spilled from her eyes as her face turned bright red. "He's a man! He *will*, Cora. And then he will leave. So, please, I'm begging you. Just give him what he wants. We can't afford to lose him."

I stopped dead in my tracks. "What do you mean *we* can't lose him?"

It was River who answered. "She means Marcos and Dante haven't been back since Penn and Drew got here. Not even after Angela. They've never been gone this long, especially not after something like that."

This was something I knew and had been doing my

best not to harp on. Having Penn as a distraction had made it easier.

What was not easier was knowing that the girls had taken over my position as Head Worrier.

I cringed when realization dawned on me. They liked Penn. He was nice to them; Drew was too. The Walker brothers paid the girls a few dollars here and there to help clean up after jobs or fold their laundry. Penn had even sat Savannah down once after dinner at my place and helped her with homework. I was a fool for not seeing it coming. River and Savannah had finally met a decent man, and now, they were terrified of losing him.

I attempted a deep inhale, but I found no air. Not with the staggering weight of the lessons those girls had already learned in their short lives blanketing the room.

The men in River's life were sociopaths, criminals of the worst kind.

And Savannah, underneath her clothes, still wore burns and scars from her father.

They both hid the aftermath of their abuse well for the most part. But shit like that didn't fade into the background in a matter of weeks or years. For most women—myself included—it became the focus of every single decision they made for the rest of their lives.

The past wasn't always the past. Sometimes, it was nothing more than a distorted spotlight illuminating your every step, no matter how beautiful that path in the present might be.

It was a light that couldn't be broken.

Or outrun.

Not even when it burned out.

Sometimes, the only thing that could shade the pain was learning that bigger and brighter lights existed.

Ones that shined the truth, warmed your freezing skin, and healed your tattered heart.

It didn't have to be a man. It could have been *anyone*.

A friend. A family member. A stranger.

Or even a woman just as trapped as you.

Releasing her wrists, I gave her a sharp tug and pulled her into a hug. She struggled against me, but there was no fight in it, and seconds later, silent sobs racked her body as I wrapped her up tight.

"You don't have to sleep with someone to make them stay in your life, Savannah."

"You won't know until it's too late," she croaked, burying her face in my neck, her thick, red ponytail tickling my nose.

Motion at the mouth of the hall caught my attention. I glanced up and found Drew standing there, leaning against the wall as if he'd been there for a while, his fists clenched so tight that his knuckles were white. He was staring at Savannah's back, but I didn't have time to focus on him before I felt Penn's heat behind me.

Annnnnd they'd been listening. Fantastic.

Penn was careful not to touch me or break my hold on Savannah.

But he was very much there, sandwiching me between the broken girl in my arms and the man she desperately wanted to save us.

His voice was like a rock, steady and firm, as he leaned over my opposite shoulder and aimed his words at her. "Seven hundred years, Savannah."

Her body locked up tight, but Penn kept talking.

"That is how long a man who cares about a woman would wait to sleep with her. They don't leave. They don't lose interest. And they sure as fuck don't take something that doesn't belong to them. A man doesn't take. A man doesn't manipulate you for your body. A man doesn't give the first fuck if your hair and makeup are done. He doesn't even care if you force him to watch stupid-ass musicals with your girls. A real man would wait those seven hundred years, his belt cinched tight, because every single second he gets to spend with his woman is a reward of its own."

My breath caught and my insides melted as I peeked over my shoulder at him.

"Don't talk to me like I don't know how men work," she sniped. "You want one thing. And if she's not giving it to you, you'll find someone who will."

"Honey, stop," I pleaded. "This is stuff between me and Penn. It's doesn't affect you."

"That's a lie," River chimed in, stabbing a finger in my direction. "Admit it. *Everything* you do affects us. Right down to who you are or aren't sleeping with. How the hell do you think this is going to end? The Guerreros buying you and Penn a wedding present? Offering to hold the ceremony here at the building? Dante is *never* going to let you go. And you are lying to yourself if you think he is."

The pain amplified as the fragments of my heart shattered into a million pieces. "So I should roll over and let him win?"

"Hell no!" she yelled. "You get some freaking help. What

we want to know is: Is Penn that help?" Her eyes filled with tears. "Truth. I also felt better about your relationship when I thought you were sleeping with him. Because he always came back. But, now, I'm wondering if he's only coming back because he enjoys the chase. What happens when he stops? And, worse, what happens when he leaves? Word *will* get around. Even if it's just a snitch at the grocery store. Where is Penn going to be when they do show up? Because we all know where *you'll* be."

Out of the corner of my eye, I saw Penn jerk, and then his back straightened, making him seem taller. She wasn't wrong. I'd been living in a dreamland if I thought I wouldn't pay in one way or another for being happy. But I got to experience that so rarely that it felt worth the gamble.

Now though? After seeing the girls like this? I wasn't so sure anymore.

"River," I breathed, holding my arm out so she could join Savannah in my embrace.

She backed away. "No. I don't need a hug, Cora. I—*we*—need answers. And we need you to be honest." She paused and sucked in a deep breath. "Truth or lie."

I reached up and caught my star necklace, nervously sliding it back and forth over the chain. I had no idea what she was about to ask, but I couldn't promise that I'd tell her the truth. "Okay. Go ahead."

She shook her head. "Not you. *Him.*"

I looked back and found Penn staring at her.

His tongue snaked out to dampen his lips as he cocked his head to the side. "Shoot, kid."

"Are you going to take care of her? And I mean, *really*

take care of her. More than cupcakes and stupid dinners."
She took a step toward him. "I'm talking putting your entire
family's life on the line against the Guerreros if and when it
comes down to it?"

Every head in the room turned to Penn as he silently
stood there. Uncomfortably, but still confident, he looked at
the floor, shifting his weight from side to side for an agonizing amount of time that probably calculated closer to seconds than the hours it felt like.

Penn and I were just starting something. And that was
a big commitment they were asking for. And, unfortunately
for my heart, hearing the answer was an even bigger commitment, because there was no going back from it. I wasn't ready
to lose him, thus losing a piece of myself, but if his answer
was anything other than a conclusive, unquestionable yes,
that was exactly what I'd have to do.

"You don't have to answer that," I whispered.

"Yes. He does," Savannah said, stepping out of my arms.

I held my breath until my lungs burned. Penn had told
me that he'd be there for me in the little deal we'd made, but
this seemed like something bigger—something real.

When he finally looked up, his face was granite, but his
eyes were blazing like a fire was brewing in his soul. "I don't
have any family left. I have nothing left to lose. Nothing they
can take away from me."

Yeah. That sucked.

Momentarily.

He folded his hand around mine, adding, "Except for
Cora."

An explosion of emotion happened behind my lids. I

couldn't blink them fast enough to keep the moisture at bay.

After bringing my hand to his mouth for a quick kiss, he gave River back his focus. "And, by extension, that means you and Savannah too. So yeah, River. I'm gonna do whatever the hell it takes to keep Cora safe. And that is one hundred percent the truth."

Savannah's chin quivered, but she squared her shoulders and looked him straight in the eye. "Even if that means getting her out of here and taking her away from us?"

My eyes flared as guilt iced my veins. "No," I swore, taking a giant step forward.

Cool and calm, Penn used our entwined hands to pull me back to his side. "You think she'd leave you behind?" This was asked in that *hey, that sounds like a good idea* way rather than the rhetorical *you cannot be serious* way.

"Penn," I scolded.

They were suffering and he was toying with them? I attempted to snatch my hand from his, but he only held it tighter.

"Answer," he pressed.

They looked at each other, silently communicating, tears falling from their eyes.

River finally offered me a sad smile. "No. She wouldn't leave us."

Love detonated inside me—until it was Savannah's turn.

Her thin body trembled as she avoided my gaze and admitted, "I don't know."

"Savannah," I breathed, her confession slashing through me, cutting me to the bone.

"Then you need to open your eyes, kid," Penn said

roughly. "Yeah, Cora and I have something going. It's good. Every day that passes, it grows stronger and deeper. But I would never try to take her away from you. Because, God's honest truth, she wouldn't come."

Savannah's head popped up, disbelief etched in her features.

"Yeah. You heard me. This woman would willingly throw me and everything we have together in front of a bus for so much as asking her to leave you two. We've been spending a lot of time together, but quite honestly, it's embarrassing how much she's filled my ears with you girls."

My heart stopped as I witnessed the most beautiful relief wash over both of my girls. Head to toe, they sagged. But Penn wasn't done yet.

"Savannah, your favorite color is purple and not because you like it, but because it makes your eyes pop. Also, could you please teach Cora to do her eyebrows like yours? Swear to God, every night, she gives me a ten-minute dissertation about how she can never get hers to look like yours. You'd be saving my eardrums a lot of trouble if you could take care of that."

My mouth fell open as I craned my head back to look up at him.

"And, River," he continued. "Not even kidding, if you could cool it with all the A's, I'd be much obliged. And stop growing while you're at it. I think you've gotten two inches taller since I've been here. Cora's not ready to look up to you, yeah?"

Savannah's whole face lit up like he'd presented her with the highest acclaim.

River shyly looked down at her shoes, a giant smile stretching from ear to ear.

And with my heart pounding, yet simultaneously struggling to beat, I stared at him in absolute awe.

I'd never once talked about Savannah's eyebrows. Honestly, I'd wished she'd tone them down. And she did wear purple a lot––Penn must have noticed. And River, yes, she made A's; she was smart as a whip. And it wasn't going to be long until she was towering over me, but I couldn't remember ever voicing this to Penn.

I loved my girls. I'd claw my way out of a grave before I ever left them behind.

But every word out of Penn's mouth had been a bald-faced lie.

And the gratitude I felt inside made my knees weak. Penn had used things he knew or had observed to make them feel loved in ways simple words never could have properly conveyed.

I'd always hated lies. I'd spent most of my life having them fed to me. As far as I was concerned, they only lulled a person into a state of false security.

But right then, I'd never been so grateful for anything in my life.

My damn eyes started to water again as Penn revealed just how bright his light truly was. He'd been protecting us from day one.

Pulling the shower curtain.

Cleaning Angela's apartment.

Sitting outside my door.

And he'd been waiting. Maybe not seven hundred years.

But he'd been there every night, talking and spending time getting to know me with little to no expectations.

And he understood that I'd *never* turn my back on River and Savannah. So much so that he'd lied to them to make sure they knew it, too.

No matter how much I tried to forget about it, I still had that distorted spotlight of my own. And for the first time since Nic died, I felt a cool shadow on my face as Penn blocked it out.

I blinked. Like, a lot. Penn had already declared that he was taking care of me. But this was different.

This was a promise.

A vow.

An undeniable truth.

And, worst of all, it gave me hope.

Nothing in the world had ever disappointed me, broken me, or destroyed me quite like hope.

And feeling that with Penn? Well, it scared the hell out of me.

I turned into his chest to hide my face from the girls.

His strong arms folded around me as I burst into tears.

"So, as you can see, I'm here. You're all safe. No matter what. Now, if you could head out and say a prayer for me, Cora's about to chew my ass for telling you all the things we talk about in private," Penn said, curling me close.

River coughed, like maybe she had a few emotions of her own that she didn't want to reveal. "Yeah. Okay. I, uh…I think we should go to bed now."

"Sure," Savannah whispered, all the fight gone from her voice. "Bed. Sounds good."

I heard their feet on the wood as they hurried down the hall, pausing only for a few mumbled goodnights.

Drew was next. "I'm gonna head out, too. You good to set up that frame on your own?"

"Yeah, man. Thanks for helping."

"Not a problem." Drew patted my back. "Night, Cor."

"Night, Drew," I replied into Penn's chest.

When the door finally shut, Penn dipped his head and put his lips to my ear. "You okay?"

I shook my head.

"Good not-okay or bad not-okay?" he asked.

"I'm not sure yet." A wave of tears clogged my throat until I was barely able to get a word out. "You...you lied to them."

He kissed the side of my face. "Not all lies are bad, babe. Sometimes, they're necessary. We've been spending a lot of time together. They're kids. They just needed to hear that they're still the most important thing in your life."

My breathing shuddered and I brought a hand up between us to cover my mouth, talking around it as I replied, "They are. They so are."

"I know. And, now, they know it, too."

I couldn't get close enough as I wiggled into his arms. "God, Penn. How are you so incredible?"

"*Finally*, she asks a how instead of a why."

I peeked up at him. "Huh?"

He grinned. "Few weeks ago, you'd have been asking me *why* I helped you. Tonight, you asked *how* I was so incredible. That's a big step, Cora."

He wasn't wrong. It was a huge step for me.

And it had happened so effortlessly.

Kinda like falling in love.

Blink.

Blink.

Blink.

"Shit, you're gonna cry again," he mumbled.

I face-planted in his chest again. "But I think it's a good not-okay this time."

"You want to figure it out while I put your new bed together?"

"You're handy with a screwdriver, so I'm not sure that's going to be enough time."

He chuckled. "Right, but at least, this way, when you're done thinking and I try to kiss you into being better than good not-okay, we'll have a comfortable surface."

I choked a laugh. "You're a really sweet guy, Penn. Saying all that to the girls. Doing nice things like getting me a bed. Promising to take care of me."

"Making you cry all the time," he added to my list.

"No. Not that. I told you that was medical."

He laughed, sliding his arms around my waist and pulling me flush with his front. "Then what is it, baby? Because, from where I'm standing, none of those things seem bad."

"They're not bad. They're really amazing."

And they were. But nothing in my life stayed amazing for long.

He grinned. "Good. Because I like doing those things for you. And I'll especially love eating the thank-you dinner you'll hopefully cook for me tomorrow night." His head came back down so he could nip at my earlobe and he murmured,

"I vote we throw it in reverse and go back to where it all began with turkey bacon burgers and beer."

I offered him a genuine—but very forced—smile.

I could do that. I could cook him that dinner. I could sit in my room while he put together my bed. I could even lie in the aforementioned bed and let him kiss me breathless all over again.

But what I could *not* do was hope that I was going to be able to keep him.

Because, the minute I did, he'd be as good as gone.

"Okay. I can do that."

He pecked my lips. "Despite the cupcakes and cash I've been slipping them, I'm not sure your girls like me."

"Well, they're gonna have to get over it, because I think after tonight we have an official relationship status."

He kissed me again, this time with a smiling mouth. "Woman, you're insane. We've had an official status for weeks. I spend every damn night in your bed."

I slid my hand around his waist and down to his firm ass, giving it a long and lingering squeeze, throwing in a moan for good measure. "You know, for the record, none of this would have happened tonight if we were having sex."

His eyes flashed wide, and his smile grew. "Is that so?"

"Yep."

"Well." He returned the ass grope, kissing me as he groaned down my throat. "The good news is we got seven hundred years to remedy that."

I slapped his chest.

"The bad news is I gotta run next door and get my tools. Go get changed and two beers ready. I'll be right back."

I glowered as he stepped away, but it only made him laugh.

However, with heat licking at my core, I found not the first thing funny.

The wolf whistle I threw his way as he walked out the door with my gaze glued to his ass remedied that though.

CHAPTER TWENTY-ONE

Penn

"What's the chance you're here to bring me some amazing food Cora cooked to thank us for helping with the bed?" Drew asked, standing at the microwave, counting down the seconds until whatever the hell frozen dinner he'd popped in three minutes earlier would be done.

"None," I clipped, walking past the kitchen to the bedroom. I navigated around the foot of the new bed I'd bought at the same time I'd gotten Cora's. Hers was nicer. But considering I'd not slept in my own apartment since our first date, it was really a purchase for Drew.

The microwave beeped as I dug through my toolbox in search of my Allen wrench.

"That was some heavy shit tonight," Drew said around the tail end of a three-bite burrito that was exactly one step above eating cardboard.

"Those kids are smarter than they look."

"Well, your bullshit was top-notch. All that 'and, by extension, you and Savannah are safe too.' You sold the hell out of that crap."

"It wasn't crap," I said, going to my closet to grab a pair of sweats to sleep in.

"I'm sorry. What?"

"I said it wasn't crap."

He arched an incredulous eyebrow. "Yeah, asshole. That's the part I heard, but surely, you misspoke."

I tossed my sweats over my shoulder and gave him my full attention. "Change of plans. The three of them. Package deal."

He ground his teeth. "Fine. When this is all over, we'll turn the kids over to Social Services. It's gonna kill your woman though."

I sat on the edge of the bed and began unlacing my boots. "She's not my woman. But she's not gonna be here when we leave, either."

He barked a laugh. "First of all, I'm not touching the 'she's not my woman' bullshit you just laid down. I do not have time to talk you off that ledge after I tell you that she's in love with you. And, worse, you've got it fucking bad for her."

My gut wrenched. This was not news to me. No man could spend as much time as I had with a woman like Cora Guerrero without catching it bad. And I'd seen the way she looked at me—all dreamy and lovestruck.

The way she held me every night when she fell asleep, her soft curves pressed so tight against my side that it was like she was trying to crawl inside me. She never tossed. She never turned. And when she was woken up by one of the women in the building, she only moved far enough away to grab her phone and then she was right back at my side.

Then there was the way she cried when I did sweet things

for her. And those sweet things were utter bullshit. Sweet would have been replacing her piece-of-shit car, buying her designer handbags, or taking her to five-star restaurants just to hear her moan with every bite. No. The only sweet I could give Cora were simple necessities.

Earlier that week, I'd noticed she was running low on body wash while I was taking a shower at her place, so I'd picked it up while I was at the grocery store. She'd gotten all dewy-eyed and acted like I'd given her the world in that fucking three-dollar bottle of suds. I'd had to leave after she'd said thank you for the hundredth time for fear of exploding.

She deserved more.

She deserved better.

She deserved the fucking best.

Gaining Cora's trust had been far easier than I'd ever thought because she expected so little from a man that just showing up every night had her falling in love with me.

And fuck me. Sitting there, experiencing the world through her reactions, bringing her that stupid soap, and watching her eyes dance with pure joy as I carried the top-of-the-line mattress that I'd told her had only cost three hundred dollars up to her apartment had me falling in love with her too.

Cora was far from naïve, but her bar was set so low in life that everything was new and magical. I couldn't imagine the wonder that would have filled her eyes if I'd taken her to the beach, or overseas, or, fuck...to Ohio. She'd have been thrilled, laughing the whole time, bouncing up and down, racing from chain restaurant to chain restaurant like Cleveland was the new Paris.

And that shit was infectious—like the goddamn plague. Because it was killing me.

Weeks earlier, I'd had an emotional meltdown from even contemplating spending time with that woman.

And now, every day, I was losing my mind figuring out how I was ever going to let her go.

It was safe to say Cora was no longer under my skin. She was a part of me. And regardless of how it ended—which was more than likely with me in a grave—she was going to flourish.

That meant not only did we have to make sure *she* got out of this okay, but that *she, River, and Savannah* got out of this okay.

I'd given those girls my word. I was keeping it.

I stopped with my boots and looked up at Drew. "I told you no matter the cost."

"And I told you we'd make sure nothing blew back on her."

"Not good enough anymore. I'll follow through. I'll find Catalina and her kid. I'll do whatever I have to do. But, at the end of the day, I want her out of here. I want her in a fucking cushy pad where she can breathe free and easy, those two girls at her side."

He raked a hand through the top of his short, brown hair. "No. No. No. We do not have the resources for that."

Shooting to my feet, I pinned him with a glare. "I have the resources. And I'm getting them out of this mess as soon as possible."

"Penn, she's got a record. You know this. Cora's staring down that third strike like a T-ball player facing a major league pitcher. And you're gonna help her walk away with two runaways, one of whom is a junkie? That shit's gonna catch up with her. And it's gonna put her away *for life.* You're not thinking straight. We can find Catalina's daughter, then take Cora out of here. *By herself.*" He took a long step toward me. "Do *not* forget why we are here. You are not the savior in this story. It is not your responsibility to save those girls. I accepted your 'nothing happens to Cora' declaration, but this is one promise we can't follow through on."

When I was a kid, I used to stare at those optical illusion pictures until I went cross-eyed. I'd never been able to see the dolphin jumping out of the water or the palm tree on an island popping out in three dimensions. But every time I'd passed one of them at the mall, I always tried.

Right then, staring at Drew was a lot like that.

Only he was the palm tree in this scenario because the man in front of me, talking about leaving thirteen and sixteen-year-old girls behind, was not in any way, shape, or form the man I knew.

"Who are you right now?" I asked, tilting my head from side to side as if the picture would change.

"Who am I?" he repeated incredulously. His eyes flashed dark, and his face contorted with stone-cold fury. Hooking his thumb at his chest, he snarled, "I'm the man who spent two years rotting in prison, kissing Manuel Guerrero's ass, all but dropping to my knees to suck his cock for one goddamn clue to find out who the hell killed my *sister.*"

"And she was my wife!" I moved fast, bumping my chest with his. "Vengeance does not mean turning your back on the rest of the world."

He laughed, but it held no humor. "You need to get the fuck out of my face right now. I'm not going to let you screw this up over some fucked-up need to save these girls because you couldn't save Lisa."

A blast of adrenaline hit me so hard that it blurred my vision. Luckily, he was only inches away, so it wasn't like I needed a roadmap.

Rearing back, I slammed my fist into the side of his face. Drew followed it up with a punch of his own, both of us falling to the floor. We rolled around, exchanging blows, knocking shit over as we went. He put a gash in my left eyebrow, and I split both of his lips open.

It was not rare for Drew and me to have a brawl. When we were in college and I told my best friend I was in love with his twin sister, they actually became quite common. But this was one of the worst.

For the first time in all four years since we'd sat down and planned this whole kamikaze mission of revenge, we were standing on different sides of the fence.

Countless punches were thrown.

Head.

Body.

And since the rules of professional boxing didn't apply to bedroom brawls…

Back of the head and below the belt too.

We were both sweaty, bleeding, and out of breath by the time the last punch was thrown.

"Fuck, man. I think you broke my rib," he groaned, settling beside me on his back.

"Good," I mumbled, not mentioning my own aching side.

We lay on that floor side by side, staring up at the ceiling, panting and moaning as we discovered new injuries.

"Well, that was therapeutic. Look at us handling things all responsibly and shit. My probation officer would be thrilled."

I shook my head, wincing when I found a goose egg on the back of it. "How did this happen?" I asked around the lump of reality in my throat. "*How* are we here right now?"

"You don't have to be." He turned his head to face me, but I didn't look at him. "What if you go home, Penn?"

"No," I replied immediately.

"Come on. Hear me out. You take Cora *and* the girls back to the beach. I know you still have the house. And I'll stay here and finish this once and for all."

My blood pressure rose. "No way. That wasn't the plan. You did your part. You stole the car and got to Manuel."

"Hey hey hey. I stole *two* cars, thank you very much."

I laughed sadly, remembering the first time I'd picked him up from jail. He'd climbed into my Audi, cussing and screaming. He was quite possibly the first man in history to be mad about being released with a slap on the wrist. He remedied that by stealing car number two and earning himself two years in prison.

"Yeah, you did. And, now, it's my turn." I finally gave him my eyes. "That was the plan, Drew. You sacrificed whatever time you were in jail. And I'd sacrifice the rest of my life. Whether it be in a cell or in a coffin. That was the plan."

"But that was before Cora."

"No." I shook my head adamantly. "I'm not the man for Cora. This isn't my last stop. I can't drag her into this. She's incredible, and I want her out of here. But I can't offer her any more than that and you know it."

He huffed a laugh. "You're full of shit. You know that, right? You've been more alive since we got here than you've ever been. And that includes with Lisa."

My face got tight, my chest aching with bone-crushing agony. "Don't do that."

"You loved her. No one here is doubting that. But Cora's more your speed. You love taking care of that woman. Every time she giggles, you light up like a pussy-whipped Christmas tree."

I laughed as he kept talking.

"Lisa was something else though. She was independent to a fault. Trust me, I spent nine months in the womb with her. I don't care what the doctors tell me—I distinctly remember her trying to off me at least once with her umbilical cord."

We both smiled. It wouldn't have shocked me if he was right.

Drew wasn't ready to step off his soapbox. "She loved you. But she loved the adventure of life more. You weren't cracked up for that. You created an empire tearing down beach houses and building overpriced hurricane-proof mansions in their place. Last I checked, that did not leave a lot of time for travel or gumshoe-detective work. Which was all Lisa had ever wanted. I could have told you that before your first date." He reached over and slugged my arm, hitting a spot that was already bruising. "That is if you had actually asked me before jumping into bed with her behind my back. I'd like it noted on the record—you did *not*."

I dabbed at my brow to see if I'd stopped bleeding. I hadn't, so I sat up and peeled the shirt over my head and then pressed it to my eye before reclining back down. "It's been fifteen years, Drew. It's time to let that shit go."

"All I'm saying is Cora's different for you. I've seen it with my own eyes. She makes you happy, Penn. And I will not judge you for wanting to hold on to that."

"I can't. I made a promise."

"And I'm letting you out of that promise. I'll take care of this."

In theory, it sounded like a great offer. But my heart, my soul—my *conscience*—wouldn't allow it. Emotion rained down over me, slicing me from all angles.

"You're right about Lisa," I said. "She was a free spirit in so many ways. But she needed me once. And I wasn't there. I can do both things. That would make Lisa happy. I'll get the girls and Cora safe and then I'll finish what we started."

He stared at me before giving his attention back to the ceiling. "You sure about that, Shane?"

My whole body jolted. My heart stopped. And in my very next breath, I remembered why I was there.

One in. One out.

"Please, Shane."

"Positive."

CHAPTER TWENTY-TWO

Cora

I was waiting on Penn to come back from getting his tools when my phone started ringing.

"Oh my God, you actually saw the bat symbol!" I exclaimed, lifting it to my ear.

"Uhhhh," Catalina drawled. "What?"

I glanced around my empty apartment. River and Savannah were locked in their room, hopefully sound asleep after the night's emotional turmoil, but more than likely, they were watching TV or playing on their cell phones.

"I've been hoping you'd call. I need advice."

"Yes. You should leave tonight."

I rolled my eyes. "I have five classes left. I promise I have one foot out the door. But that's not what this is about."

"Five classes will take you a year at the speed you've been going."

I stopped pacing. "Can we put a pin in the college discussion and talk about the fact that I met a guy?"

As I suspected it would, the line went silent.

"Yes, I'll hold while you process that tidbit of information. And while you are wrapping your head around it, I feel the need to go ahead and tell you that he is unspeakably gorgeous. Like the Voldemort of gorgeousness."

"He was pretty hideous in the movies, so I'm not sure that's a fair comparison."

With a giggle, I switched the phone to my other ear. "His name is Penn. He and his brother are the maintenance guys who took over for Hugo."

More silence.

And then a lot of *not* silence. "Are you insane!"

I pulled the phone away from my ear to avoid losing my hearing, but she kept right on yelling.

"Cora, what the hell?"

"They aren't Guerreros. They're...Walkers. Drew served time with Manuel."

"Oh my God!" she cried. "That's worse!"

I sank back down on the couch. "Relax. They aren't like that. They're good people."

"No one who associates with my father is good people."

"Well, Penn's never met him. But trust me, they are nothing alike."

"Oh my God. Please tell me you didn't mention me."

I huffed. "Psh. Now, you're the insane one. I'm insulted you'd even ask that."

"Oh thank you, Lord."

Without a bed set up for me to flop down on, I walked to the den and settled deep into the corner of the couch, pulling my knees up to my chest. "The Lord had nothing to do with this. I'd never risk you or Isabel for a man. Even if he is insanely gorgeous, and kind, and thoughtful, and—"

She made a gagging sound. "You done yet?"

"Don't be jealous. One day, Prince Charming will come for you too. He'll throw rocks at your window. Then, in a very regal British accent, he will ask you to let down your leg hair so he can climb up."

"Ew!" She burst into laughter.

It was a stupid joke, but there wasn't much I wouldn't say to make Cat laugh. She did it so rarely that I sat there grinning like a maniac as she lost herself in humor.

When she finally sobered, she whispered, "God, I miss you."

"I miss you too. But, assuming you didn't see the bat symbol and weren't calling to hear all the juicy details about he who shall remain nameless, to what do I owe the pleasure of this call?"

"Hmmm…poverty," she replied.

I suddenly sat up, putting my bare feet to the floor. "What now?"

"My power's been shut off. Which we both know is nothing new, but the lady whose house I usually clean decided last minute to spend the summer in Maine, visiting her grandson."

"*Why?*" I whined.

"I have no idea. Apparently, she likes him or something. The problem is: This leaves me high and dry until I can find something else."

Catalina had spent her life as the crowned princess of the Guerrero family. Sure, they'd treated her like shit, talking down to her and using her as a pawn for whatever they needed. But the shoes she'd walked in may as well have been encrusted in diamonds. She'd never worked, and when Manuel had convinced her to take one for the team and marry the district attorney, Thomas Lyons, she hadn't moved down the food chain. Right up until the day she left it all behind, she drove a Jag, lived in a seven-thousand-square-foot mansion, and had all of her clothes delivered by her personal stylist. On the outside, it was my dream life. On the inside, it was the same hell I lived in only with slightly better decorating.

Thomas beat her on the regular, forced himself on her when she tried to tell him no, and verbally abused her to the point that it may as well have been physical. She asked her father for help, but Manuel needed to keep Thomas under his thumb in order to stay out of jail.

They were an unstoppable team. Manuel the crime lord with his hands dipped in both prostitution and drugs and Thomas the crooked and narcissistic district attorney who thought he was above the law.

But in the miracle of all miracles, Cat got out. And, now, she was living paycheck to paycheck cleaning houses. To hear her tell it, she'd never been happier. She always sounded lonely to me though.

"How much is it?" I asked.

"No. I'm not worried about the power. We'll make do. However, Isabel is still sick. I can't get her better. Doc said it was tonsillitis last time, and the antibiotics seemed to clear it up, but it's back. She's freaking miserable and running a fever. Which, when it's a fourteen-year-old, means she's making me miserable too. I need to get her back to the doctor."

"Damn, that sucks for both of you. How much is it?"

She sighed. "Well, a doctor's visit for the uninsured goes for the low, low price of about two hundred bucks a pop these days, but I still have sixty from the last time you gave me money. You shouldn't be giving me extra, though it's come in handy recently."

I smiled. "Just not handy enough."

"Exactly."

I stood up and walked to the front door. Putting my eye to the peephole, I peered out, finding no sign of Penn heading back this way. "All right. Let's break this down. Power bill?"

"Eighty-seven dollars."

"And the doctor is two hundred. How much were her antibiotics last time?"

"Thirty-eight and some change."

I squinted one eye, mentally rounded up, and then carried the one. "Okay, so three twenty-six."

"Minus the sixty," she corrected.

"No. Not minus anything. You need some padding. These constant trips to drop off are dangerous for both of us. I'm gonna bring you two grand. Tonight. Pay all your bills and then pay ahead a month. Give yourself some wiggle room until you can find a new job."

"All that doesn't cost two grand, Cora," she replied, but I heard a cry of relief muffled by her hand.

"Well, you didn't let me finish. *Then*, with whatever's left, I want you to find a bakery, buy a dozen chocolate cupcakes, and binge all weekend pretending I'm there with you."

This time, she didn't even try to hide her sob. "I can't take that much from you. That's your ticket out."

"*You're* my ticket out. We're in this together, remember? Besides. I'll get it back. I haven't submitted the bills to your brothers this month yet. I'll figure a way to work that money back in."

Her voice cleared, fear overtaking the emotion. "Cora, don't. That's a lot of money to explain away."

I made my way down the hall to my bedroom, locked the door, and slid the chair in front of it, holding the phone between my shoulder and my cheek. "Don't worry about me. I got five off them last month. And, this month, I've got Penn's receipts from the hardware store. Couple of extra zeros here and there and we're in business."

I snagged a dirty T-shirt from my hamper and climbed onto the chair. After using my thumbnail to pry off the wood trim at the top of the door, I wrapped the shirt around my hand and removed the pink insulation, revealing clear plastic bags stuffed with more insulation. I grabbed one, dropped it to the floor, then shifted the rest around until they once again looked like a solid wall of fluffy fiberglass.

"Cora, please. You have to be more careful. Especially now that you're sleeping with the maintenance guy."

I curled my lip and replaced the trim. "Why does everyone think we're sleeping together?" I climbed down, grabbed the bottle of Wite-Out I'd long since replaced with touch-up paint, climbed back up, and set about sealing the joints until it looked perfect again. I'd hit it with some dryer lint once it dried a bit. It had taken me a while to perfect the art of making things faux dirty. But, in that building, nothing drew attention like cleanliness.

"Uhh…because that's what adults do when they're dating someone. Wait—are you not sleeping with him?" she asked.

I rolled my eyes. "Technically, yes. He actually just bought me a new bed. But if you mean sex, then no."

She was silent for a second. "I thought you said he was hot?"

"He is! He's all the things. He bought me cupcakes, and pulled up my carpet and put wood floors down, and lied to the girls tonight, telling them how much I talked about them when I didn't."

"Wow. He sounds like a real dreamboat," she deadpanned.

I laughed. "I promise he really is. And good to me. So freaking good."

"All right. All right. I'll give Voldemort the benefit of the doubt. But keep your secrets close, Cora. Do not trust this man. Do not give him ammunition to take back to my family."

I huffed. "I know. I know."

"I just worry."

I grabbed the baggy of insulation off the floor and carried it to the closet, where I shook it out on top of the safe. A rolled-up wad of five thousand dollars fell out.

"You don't need to worry about me. I've got this covered." I peeled off half, and then locked the rest of it in the safe. I liked to keep a little cash in there in case of an emergency. Say...Marcos or Dante showed up and accused me of stealing money. Twenty-five hundred dollars and a beating would be enough to feed their salacious appetite for justice, leaving my secret stash above their heads and five years' worth of work intact.

"Are you going to drop it off tonight?" she asked uncomfortably. "No rush or anything. I thought you mentioned that or something."

"Relax. I've got the cash and I'm headed to my car now. It's over an hour drive, but I'll be there soon."

"I love you, Cora."

"Love you too. Take care of yourself and tell Isabel to get better."

Her voice smiled. "Will do."

We hung up at the same time.

Penn still wasn't back, and much to my dismay, my bed and him kissing me into better than good not-okay was going to have to wait.

After opening my texts, I shot off a message to River and Savannah that I was leaving to run an errand. When the text bubble didn't pop back up from either of them, I thanked the god of tears for making people sleepy afterward.

After one last message to Penn, I purposely left my phone on the counter and headed out.

Me: Hey, I had to run out for a few. Keep an eye out for Savannah and River. They're already asleep. I'll hit you up when I get back. Xoxo

CHAPTER TWENTY-THREE

Penn

Ten minutes before I lost her...

"Calm down, Mr. Pennington," the 911 operator urged into the receiver of my landline.

There was no calm left in the world. Not as they stood over her, their filthy hands in her hair, holding her to the bed, blood profusely seeping from stab wounds on her chest and stomach.

Her pink shirt was red.

I couldn't focus.

I couldn't breathe.

Everything was in fast forward and *slow motion.*

The knife in the air came too fast.

Her attempts to fight back were too slow.

I knew I was yelling. I was vaguely aware of the gravel shredding my throat, but what I was saying never passed through my brain.

Visceral rage rushed out of me like a dam had been broken in my soul. But, with nowhere for that violence to manifest, it was worthless.

I was worthless.

My wife was dying.

And I was absolutely worthless.

"Mr. Pennington, take a look around. I have police officers on standby. We just need to figure out where she is."

"She's in a hotel!"

"Where? Do you know the name of the hotel?"

I paused as an onslaught of every emotion I'd ever experienced peeled the skin from my body. "I...I don't know. Somewhere in Chicago."

Another stab.

Another cry.

Another plea.

"Get the fuck off her!" I roared so loudly that my body vibrated.

It was all I could do.

Her screams echoed in my ears even as they held a hand over her mouth. Her legs kicked wildly, her hands clawing at the men attacking her.

Acid forged valleys in my veins.

"Look around the room," the operator urged.

The adrenaline fueling me like gas to a fire made searching the room while they tortured her impossible. But if it could help her...

"Oh fuck," I groaned, forcing my mind to cooperate. Frantic, I scanned the room. "There's a blue bedspread. And... and...fuck!"

His fist landed across her face, blood spraying on the wall. I felt it in my gut.

Pain exploded inside me.

The only things stronger were the guilt and desperation

clouding my vision.

I'd never felt more helpless in my entire life. It was killing me.

And, worse, it was killing her.

"Take a deep breath, and try to focus, Mr. Pennington," the woman ordered, drawing my attention to the task at hand.

"Okay. Okay. Shit. There's, uh, a desk, a fucking TV."

"What else? See if you can see a phone or notepad. Anything that might have the name of the hotel on it."

I thrust a hand into the top of my hair and brought my cell closer to my face for inspection. "No. Nothing. It's a fucking cheap-ass hotel room. It looks like every other budget hotel in the world."

Another punch.

Another stab.

Another cry.

I broke.

Falling to my knees, I threw myself at the mercy of any god who was willing to listen. "Please. Please, I'm begging you. Please, God. Help me find her." My voice shattered along with my heart. "Help me find her. Please. Please help me."

Please: I'd never hated a word more.

"Where is she!" I roared at Drew, the pressure in my head threatening to split me in half.

"Relax. She'll be back," he replied with his back to our apartment door, preventing me from leaving.

"Move!" I snarled.

"You're not going over there and waking those kids up.

Her text said they were already asleep when she left and that she would be back in a few. You need to calm down before she does get back and sees you acting like a madman."

"Don't you dare tell me to calm down. You know what the fuck I've been through." I sucked an exasperated breath in through my teeth. My eyes were wild, and my chest didn't feel much better.

She'd been gone for three hours.

Three fucking hours was not *a few.*

The first hour, as I'd paced a path in the parking lot, my mind screaming, my heart thundering in my ears and my anxiety skyrocketing, had not been *a few.*

The second hour, as I'd driven around the city, searching every possible location, constantly texting Drew to see if she'd shown back up but always coming up empty, was not *a few.*

And the third hour, as I'd destroyed our apartment, time-traveling from the past to the present through memories in my mind until I wasn't even sure where I was anymore, was not *a few.*

One thing I knew.

Something had happened.

Whether it was Marcos or Dante or…fuck. I don't know who. Something had happened to her.

And once again.

I had no idea where she was or how to help.

And I was suffocating, buried six feet deep in the what-ifs.

I'd called.

And called.

And fucking called.

She never answered.

And when I'd gone into the hall and heard her phone ringing in her apartment, my entire life had ended all over again.

She was gone.

I had no way to reach her.

And…and…

"Please, Penn. Please!" Her voice screamed in my head.

Fuck.

I choked on the bitter acid of reality. "We have to find her."

He bulged his eyes. "She's not Lisa, Penn. She'll come back."

"And if she doesn't!" I yelled, the sound echoing around our apartment. "I swear to God, Drew, if they so much as touched her, I—"

His hands landed on either side of my head, his palms covering my ears, his fingers biting into the back of my skull, and his face filling my view. He spoke slowly and definitively, but he couldn't hide the concern in his brown eyes. That same concern was currently burning a hole straight through me.

"She. Will. Be. Back."

"No." I shook my head repeatedly before stepping away. "We need to get back out there and look for her. Let's go together. Get the gun. We'll head over to Dante's."

"You already drove by Dante's, Penn. Her car wasn't there."

"Well." I planted a shaking hand on my hip and searched through my mind for any possible theory that would enable me to not only find her, but also bring her home—alive. "Maybe they weren't there yet."

He once again got in my face, his hand landing hard on my shoulder. Steady and confident, he said, "Penn. Brother. Listen to me. She left her phone, and knowing her attachment to the women in this building, not to mention River and Savannah, that was not an accident. Let's be logical here. Maybe she doesn't want to be found. Maybe she doesn't want to be *tracked*."

I swallowed hard. Hope spiraled like a vortex inside me, and I was so desperate that I was willing to cling to anything—even a tornado. "Catalina," I whispered.

"Bingo," he replied with a smile.

That hope lasted exactly one second.

"You think they caught her?" I intertwined my fingers, resting them locked on the top of my head, and started pacing again. No air found my lungs, but with every step, my panic grew. "They must have followed her." Every muscle in my body flexed painfully as that god-awful scene played out in my subconscious.

Same hotel room.

Same blood.

Cora's body.

"Fuck!" I boomed. "Fuck, fuck, fuck!"

It was my every nightmare come true.

I'd watched Lisa die. Castrated to help her.

And there we were again. Full circle. Only, now, it was the one woman I wasn't sure I could survive losing.

Not like that.

One day, she'd be gone, living her life, smiling and

laughing. Free of the clouds of hell that had been following her for the majority of her life. *That* I could survive.

But this?

My stomach rolled. "Oh God."

Finally, he answered.

With the sound of a car pulling into the parking lot.

My head snapped up at the same time my body shot forward. Drew wisely stepped out of my way as I reached him. Then I snatched the door open and flew down the steps as fast as my legs could carry me.

"Hey!" she chirped, looping her broken purse over her arm, a glowing, white smile on her face.

I marched toward her, my heavy strides devouring the distance between us as my gaze raked over her from head to toe and back again.

Her eyes were free of tears.

Breath filled her lungs.

Not a droplet of blood tainted her blue tank.

She was alive.

She was okay.

She was...

"Where the fuck have you been!"

CHAPTER TWENTY-FOUR

Cora

I froze, the smile on my face falling as his crazed eyes continued to race over me.

"Excuse me?" I snapped.

He stopped in front of me, anchored his hands to his hips, and bit out, "You'll be back in a few? A few?" He laughed with negative amounts of humor. "Three fucking hours is not a few!"

"Okay?" I drawled, glancing up and finding Drew standing on the third-floor balcony. Even at that distance, the relief painting his features was staggering.

When I shifted my gaze back to Penn, I got my first real look at him. His eyebrow was split and swollen, and smears of blood disappeared into the hair above his temple.

My.

Heart.

Stopped.

"What happened to your face?" I rushed out. "Oh God, where are the girls?" I started to race past him, but he caught my arm, pulling me up short.

"Asleep," he clipped, but his face was so filled with anger

that it offered me no comfort.

"Then what's wrong?"

His hand got tight on my arm, and then every hair on the back of my neck stood on end as he dragged me closer. His upper body loomed over me as he leaned forward, bringing his face to mine, where he seethed, "Where the fuck did you go for three goddamn hours without even taking your phone?"

I blinked. I didn't recognize the man holding me so harshly. He was an utter stranger.

His jaw was tight, ticking at the hinges.

The veins in his neck bulged as if they were trying to escape his body.

And his eyes—they were not those of the man who held me every night as I fell asleep. They were wide, furious, and downright malevolent.

My mouth dried, a seed of fear settling in the pit of my stomach. But before I allowed it to grow, I made one last-ditch effort to see if my Penn was still in there.

I stared up at him, refusing to show him any weakness, and demanded, "Let me go."

His eyes darkened, but his hand fell away in the next beat.

I blew out a ragged breath and slapped a hand over my heart, which was attempting to break free of my ribs. "What the hell is going on with you right now? Who'd you get into a fight with?"

"Drew," he replied.

I slanted my head in confusion. "Any particular reason?"

"How about we worry less about my fucking cut and

more about the fact that you left."

"Yeah. And I sent you a text."

"No. You sent me a text saying you'd be back in a few. And then you were gone for three fucking hours. I've been losing my goddamn mind thinking something had happened to you."

While I hated that he'd been so obviously fretting, it made me all warm inside to know he was worried about me.

Placing my hand on his bicep, I gave him a reassuring squeeze. "Penn, baby, everything's fine. I had to run an errand."

His brow furrowed and his chest heaved. "For three hours?"

"Yeah. *Three hours*. And, now, I'm tired. So can we go upstairs and talk about this in bed? We'll just flip the mattress onto the floor and you can put it together tomorrow night." I released him and started toward the stairs.

The crunch of his boots on the gravel followed behind me.

"Where'd you go?" he asked roughly.

I rolled my eyes and kept going. "To run an errand. I already said that."

"What errand?" he demanded when we hit the second floor.

With twisted lips, I slowly turned to look at him over my shoulder. "It's none of your business. I had something to do. I did it. I'm home. It doesn't matter anymore."

"It matters to me!" he yelled—without actually raising his voice at all.

There was no way I could tell him about Catalina

needing money. But I wasn't real excited to lie to him, either. And if I said the word *lie* before giving him whatever reason I hadn't come up with yet, I didn't think it would placate him much.

I started toward the third floor. "Are you going to yell at me all night? Because, if so, I'm gonna take a pass on hanging out."

"I swear to God, Cora. I will only ask you this one more time. Where the fuck did you go?"

Like nails on a chalkboard, it made my skin crawl. He sounded like every man I'd ever had in my life. And not in a good way.

"None of your business," I shot back.

To his credit, he didn't touch me again.

To my credit, my head didn't explode as he followed me up so closely that his boot shared the same step with my flip-flop half the time.

Drew was gone when we hit the third floor.

And so was my patience.

I refused to respond anymore as I shoved the key into the doorknob, unlocking it before repeating the process on the deadbolt and swinging it open. I might have been angry, but I liked his face, so rather than slamming the door shut behind me and risking any further injury, I left it open.

"Where did you go!"

I walked to my bedroom, rubbing my temples. I did not have the energy to deal with anything else. "Penn, *please*. Be quiet. The girls are asleep. And I'm tired. And it's freaking late."

"You're seriously not going to answer me after that

bullshit tonight? For fuck's sake, Cora, I deserve a goddamn answer."

"No," I snapped, dropping my purse on the floor and turning to face him. "I'm not—" I stopped midsentence, unable to continue.

He wasn't mad.

He wasn't being a dick.

He wasn't like *any* man I'd ever had in my life.

Because, with one look at him, I realized he was flat-out terrified.

"Penn," I breathed, my heart jumping into my throat.

His chest rose and fell with great effort. He leaned into the forearm he had propped against the doorjamb as if it were the only thing holding him up and his eyes morphed into dark puddles of grief.

"Shit. Okay. Okay. It's not a big deal. I went to drop off some money for one of the girls." I hurried over to him and placed my hand on his stomach.

He shook his head, his face the perfect picture of desolation.

"Hey," I whispered. Lifting his free hand, I kissed the back of it. "I'm fine. We're both fine. Come on. Let's sit down."

He took me literally, sinking to the floor only inches inside the doorway, his legs bent with both feet planted on the wood and his head hung low.

I slid down to join him, settling at his side but facing him. I hooked my arm around his leg and leaned against it. "What's going on?"

He closed his eyes and scrubbed his jaw as though he could rub away whatever cloud had invaded his head. "I was so fucking scared."

I inched closer. "Baby, I'm right here."

"No, Cora. I thought you were *gone*. I didn't know where you were and I had no way to get in touch with you. No way to know if you were safe. No way to know if you were alive or…" He shook his head, unwilling to finish. "All I could see each time I blinked was losing you the same way I did…*her*. Only, this time, I wouldn't even know I was losing you until it was too late. I couldn't go through that again. Not with you. Never with you. You're supposed to win. You're supposed to be happy. You're supposed to get out. You're supposed to *live*."

Hindsight: That should have been the exact moment suspicion slithered over me. But he was rambling in the middle of an emotional breakdown. A lot of what he was saying didn't make sense. But it was all sweet, and it was coming from somewhere deep inside his closet of fears.

"I know, baby."

"You can't end up like her, Cora. And, tonight, knowing you were out there, with no way for me to reach you… No way to protect you." He stared off into the distance, sucking in through his teeth like he was breathing through the pain of a knife gliding across his skin.

It was pain I felt for him as guilt exploded inside me. He hadn't known where Lisa was the night she'd died. He blamed himself specifically for that.

And there I was, giving him attitude for asking about where I'd been—for *caring* about where I'd been.

"I'm sorry," I whispered.

He grabbed the back of my head, pulling me toward him before tucking my face against the curve of his neck. "I can't lose you, Cora. Not like that. I can't. I just can't."

"I'm not going anywhere," I swore while peppering apology-filled kisses up his neck. I leaned my torso in front of him until he lowered his legs to allow me the space to climb into his lap. "I promise I'm not going anywhere."

"You don't know that. You have to be more careful," he rumbled, turning away so I couldn't see him, but the devastation couldn't be hidden.

I kissed across his cheek—the stubble tickling my lips—over his nose, and up and down every inch of his face I could reach, murmuring, "I do know it, Penn. Because I'll be with you. You'll make me safe. I believe you."

His head cranked to the side like I'd slapped him, and he groaned, "I gotta get you out of here. Fuck. I gotta get you out of here."

I didn't have the chance to ask what he meant before he rose to his knees with me securely held to his chest and laid me down on the wood floor, his body coming down on top of me.

My legs fell open—an offer he did not refuse. His hips wedged between my thighs as his mouth sealed over mine in the most desperate of kisses I'd ever received.

It was slow and searing.

Sad, but loving.

Brutal, but honest.

It was all the points of light that made up Penn Walker.

"I'm done with the games," he murmured, supporting his weight on one hand beside my head, his other frantically shoving my shirt up. "I can't lose you, Cora. I *can't.*"

I sat up only far enough to finish the job of removing my

shirt while promising, "You won't."

"I will. But I swear on my life I'll make sure you win." His tone was so jagged that I could barely understand him, and less than a second later, I gave up trying. "I need to feel you, baby. Say you trust me."

I gave it exactly zero consideration before I replied with, "I trust you."

He stilled, hovering above me. His gaze traced over my face, searching for what I could only assume was hesitation. "Truth, Cora?"

"Truth. Please, Penn."

And that was all it took.

With one foot, he kicked the door shut.

With one hand, he tore the cup of my bra down, exposing my breast before dipping low and sealing his hot mouth over my nipple.

Sparks detonated inside me, radiating all the way down to my clit and everywhere in between. His hand found its way to my other breast, where he plucked and kneaded in time with his tongue.

I arched off the floor, eager and wanton.

And Penn gave.

He licked and sucked, groans rumbling from his throat, teasing my skin and taking me even higher.

Panting, I threaded my fingers into the top of his hair and got lost in the sensation.

Every swipe of his tongue was followed by a nip.

Every nip was followed by a long, soothing lave of his tongue.

Every lave was followed by a roll of his hips, revealing

his thickening cock.

And every roll stole gasps from both of our throats.

It had been too long, and I was climbing that peak of ecstasy fast, but this wasn't going to be enough to carry me any further.

Sitting up, I tugged his shirt over his head and then followed it up by unhooking my bra and allowing it to slide down my arms.

"Fuck, you're beautiful," he rumbled, his gaze anchored to my breasts like a teenage boy.

I almost laughed, but my cheeks heated under his praise. I'd never been particularly shy, but…

Penn was gorgeous. In so many ways. And not because he was all sleek power and defined muscles, though that didn't hurt. Penn was gorgeous because he was all the things that hadn't existed in my world for over a decade.

Frantic and fevered, I sat up, going straight for his jeans. He caught my hands as I fumbled with his button.

"I'm done with the games too," I told him. Fire hit his eyes, causing a surge of heat to pool between my legs, but I held his feral gaze. "I trust you. I want you. I need you. Now, Penn."

He moved fast, his mouth sealing over mine as he yanked my shorts down my thighs without even touching the zipper. Then he paused only to repeat the process with my panties.

I tugged on his jeans until he rose to his feet, his arm hooked around my back, taking me up with him. Then I dangled in his arms as he used one hand to send the mattress leaning against the wall crashing to the floor with a loud thump.

I giggled at his urgency. But Penn was all business.

I landed on the bed first, watching with rapt, mouthwatering attention as he stepped out of his jeans. He was long and thick.

But more, he was ready.

I squeaked as he dropped his knees to the mattress and folded over me with his hands on either side of my head, his body hovering over mine. He kissed me again, chastely at first, breathing me in with a reverence so genuine that it made my eyes sting.

I wanted to talk to him. To once again reassure him that I was okay.

But we'd done enough talking.

And as his mouth opened hastily, his tongue snaking out to tangle with mine, and his fingers slipping between my legs, it was clear he agreed.

My head flew back against the mattress, costing me the loss of his mouth, but I could focus on nothing but the glorious pressure building with only a single touch.

He latched on to my neck, rough and desperate, licking and sucking, driving me to the edge as his fingers played between my legs with the skill of a piano player, hitting every single note my body had to offer.

I moaned incoherently.

He swallowed them like they were his favorite meal.

I cried out, fighting the orgasm off, not ready to let go.

He found my clit, circling and rolling until it was impossible to hold out any longer.

"Oh God," I breathed, the coils inside me tightening almost painfully before springing to life with pure euphoria.

My breathing shuddered as he thrust two fingers inside me, stretching me and coaxing, adding another layer to my release until I wasn't sure how long I'd been falling.

My head was spinning as my body pulsed and I rode out the final currents when I felt his mouth come down to my ear.

"This is the truth, Cora. This. Right here. You and me. This moment. This feeling. *This* is the truth."

My eyes popped open, his turbulent gaze staring back at me. "Penn?" But that was all I got out before he guided his length inside me, filling me completely.

Penn made love to me that night.

Like, real, actual love.

But there was something sad about it.

He never stopped kissing me, but it wasn't heated or frenzied.

His hands never stopped roaming and caressing my body, but it was like he was engraining my every curve into his memory.

He drove into me slow and sweet like he was savoring every stroke.

It was absolutely incredible—and a little heartbreaking.

I came twice more, his name tumbling from my lips each time.

By the time Penn came, we were both covered in sweat, our lips raw, my legs aching. But I was completely sated—inside and out.

He held me as we slept, just like he always did.

But it wasn't the same.

Even if I couldn't figure out why.

CHAPTER TWENTY-FIVE

Cora

Me: Hypothetically speaking, if I were to make you a birthday dinner, what day of the year would I make that?

Penn: On my birthday.

Me: So, like, Tuesday?

Penn: My birthday isn't Tuesday.

Me: So Wednesday?

Penn: Not then, either. Where ya going with this?

Me: Hopefully somewhere with streamers and party hats.

My phone started ringing in my hand. Penn's number and a sneaky picture I'd snapped of him smiling while talking to his brother popped up on my cracked screen.

"Hello, gorgeous," I whispered seductively.

"Baby, my hands are covered in drywall mud. I type one more text to you and my phone is going to become a sculpture."

Things had changed in the two weeks since Penn and I had finally taken our relationship to R-rated. I wanted to say it was for the better. It felt like the better each night as he climbed into my bed and kissed me breathless before sliding inside me. Or when River and Savannah would leave for school and he'd come over and shower with me. Neither of us got very clean during those showers, but they were effective in other ways.

But it was different.

We still smiled.

We still laughed.

We still played Truth or Lie tit-for-tat.

But the weight that had once only been in his eyes now loomed all around him.

He stared off into space a lot more, and his questions about my past got deeper. He asked about Nic. How it had felt when I lost him? What was the hardest part? Where I would have liked to be if I'd never gotten trapped by the Guerreros?

And, surprisingly enough, I told him a lot of truths.

For all intents and purposes, Penn and I were growing closer by the day.

But there was something between us that I couldn't figure out.

It'd come out eventually––everything did. I just had to hold on until he was ready.

"Drew kinda sorta mentioned that you were a Gemini."

"Oh, he *kinda sorta* mentioned this, did he? It fell into casual conversation? 'Oh hey, Cora. Penn's a Gemini,'" he teased.

"Well, no. Not exactly. I may have asked him when your birthday was and he may have refused to answer, citing that he 'ain't no snitch.' But, when I offered him the leftover Swedish meatballs from dinner last night, he cited that 'Even snitches gotta eat,' and told me you were a Gemini, which according to my research started last week. I pressed further, but not even homemade cookies could make him give me the actual date. So…I'm hoping I haven't missed it and it's like… Thursday?"

He laughed. "Next Thursday, babe."

I blew out exaggerated relief. "Thank goodness. I still have time to plan."

"Plan away. But, just so we're clear, I'm not wearing a fucking party hat."

"Okay. Fine. But how do you feel about a piñata?"

"Fucking hell," he breathed. "And on that note, I gotta get back to work. You cooking tonight or you want me to grab some takeout?"

I groaned. Takeout sounded amazing, but… "Savannah requested tacos."

"They got takeout tacos at a restaurant too."

I huffed, "No, I already bought the stuff. If I don't cook it tonight, the meat will go bad."

"All right. Your call. Hit me up if you change your mind."

"Will do."

"Bye, babe."

"Bye, Penn."

When the connection was severed, I sat there for several minutes, my eyes glued to my phone, pure happiness radiating through me as I basked in the normalcy between us.

My *life* was insane. My *world* was insane. But Penn made it all so manageable.

It was all kinds of wrong.

I'd spent too long trying to escape that place to become content now.

But, with Penn, the days weren't as long.

They weren't as hard.

And I had more than enough reasons to smile.

But staying had never been an option. I had plans. Plans that used to be my only reason for survival.

Plans I now had to force myself to follow through with on a daily basis.

Life with Penn was comfortable: the one thing I couldn't afford to be.

"What about the girls on the third floor?" he asked as we lay in bed later that night.

Unfortunately, we were fully clothed. River and Savannah were still awake, but my fingers, toes, and everything in between were crossed that the taco coma would consume them soon enough.

I lazily traced the defined ridge of his pec beneath his T-shirt. "What about them?"

"While back, you told me about the first- and second-floor girls. But not the third."

"Oh. They're the ones who want out," I admitted.

"And you help them?"

"I do what I can, but ultimately, I'm only one person."

"Bullshit. One person," he breathed, catching my hand to stop the movement. "You do the work of an army around this place. You need to own that."

"I don't know. I feel like a racehorse with four broken legs most of the time."

His hand spasmed around mine. "How many girls have

you gotten out?"

I chewed on my bottom lip. "Forty-nine."

He let out a low whistle. "That's a lot of lives for a legless racehorse to save. But I can see how that would be hard on you."

My head perked up. "Hard on me?"

"Yeah. Watching people achieve something you want. That can't be easy."

"It's hands down the *easiest* thing I've done. Those girls. They were mine. Sure, they were the ones who ultimately made the decision to get out. Some went back to school. Some made amends with friends and family in exchange for a place to stay. Some got clean. Whatever it was, they did that. But I helped. So that, in its own way, freed me too."

His face got soft, his eyes warming. "What would it take to make *you* free, Cora?"

I didn't have to think. I knew the answer to this question better than anything else. "One million, one hundred thousand, six hundred, eighty-four dollars."

His eyebrows shot up.

I offered him a tight smile. "And ninety-nine cents."

His face was priceless. "Come again?"

I laughed. "Between high school equivalency programs, housing, new wardrobes, counseling, and a few rehab programs, that's how much it would cost to free all the girls in the building."

"I didn't ask about the girls in the building. I asked about you."

"Oh. Okay. Then only… One million, one hundred thousand, six hundred, eighty-four dollars. If I'm out of here too,

I can forgo the ninety-nine cent celebratory candy bar from the Stop and Shop."

He glowered. "I'm serious."

"I'm serious too. If I just up and disappear one day, where does that leave them?"

"I'm not talking about Savannah and River. Obviously, they'd go with you. But the rest... They're grown women."

"Yeah. Most of them are. But age doesn't dictate your situation. A person can be a hundred and five and still need help."

His face twisted in disbelief. "So you're telling me, if someone comes in here and offers you a life raft, you're going to refuse it because it won't fit thirty-plus women?"

I narrowed my eyes. "No. I didn't say that at all. But you gotta understand: I spent too many years hoping and praying for a life raft. I found a few. But they all fell apart before I made it over the first wave. To get me out of this life, I'm going to need an ark. The kind you have to build on your own. Because, *when* I get out of here and get my feet under me, I'm coming back until every last girl is out." I paused and offered him a half shrug. "And who knows? Maybe I'll pick up a drowning man along the way."

He scowled at me, lips pursed, forehead crinkled, and something between awe and absurdity dancing in his eyes.

I huffed. "Stop looking at me like I'm crazy. I—ooph," Before I could get another word out, I was on my back.

Penn was on top of me, his upper body pinning me to the bed. "You *are* crazy, Cora. There's no other way to look at you," he rumbled as his mouth came down on my neck.

I gasped, slanting my head to the side while he slid a

hand up my thigh to hook my leg around his hip.

"You're also beautiful," he murmured between kisses, the scruff on his jaw teasing a path for his hot breath coasting across my skin. "And so incredible that I can't decide if I need to have you certified as insane or nominated for sainthood."

I wrapped my arms around him, turning my head to give him more access to my neck. "A vacation in a padded room does sound peaceful, but I don't know if they allow conjugal visits." I felt his lips on my neck curve into a smile. "I also don't know if there's some sort of celibacy vow involved with being a saint. So perhaps I should do some research and get back to you on that one."

"*Perhaps* you should." He went for my shirt, but he froze when we heard Savannah and River arguing in the hall. "Okay," he drawled, moving off me and rolling onto his back.

I laughed as he threw his arm over his face, a very noticeable bulge showing behind his sweats.

"Soooo…truth or lie," he said.

"Nuh-uh. My turn. What do your tattoos mean?"

"I don't actually know." His lips thinned as he lifted his arm above us, turning it as though he were inspecting it for the very first time.

"What do you mean you don't know? You picked them out, didn't you?"

"I guess I did," he answered absently, his focus landing on the inked gears on the back of his left hand.

It was a complex design—by far the most intricate of his tattoos—that made his hand appear mechanical, filled with nuts and bolts rather than bones and blood. A circle of Roman numerals surrounded it, giving it the effect of a porthole into his flesh. For several beats, he stared at it, opening and closing his fist, the tendons making the ink dance.

"So why'd you get that one?" I pressed.

He chuckled, but it sounded a little sad and a lot broken. "I blindly chose it out of the artist's portfolio. I opened to a random page and stabbed a finger down." The skin between his eyes crinkled, and then, as though he couldn't stand to look at it for a second more, he dropped his arm to the mattress. "It didn't matter what it was. I just needed it to be there." He went silent.

Physically, he was still there. Holding me the same way he had been only seconds earlier.

Mentally, he was at least a million miles away. But the longer he remained quiet, the more I thought a million miles and four years was probably more accurate.

His chest rose as he sucked in a deep breath, and he held it far longer than I'd thought possible.

I waited patiently. Of course I was curious. I would have loved the truth about that tattoo. Mainly why he was having such a visceral reaction to a simple question. But I didn't want the answer at the price it was costing him.

I slid my hand over his stomach and hugged him as tight as I could. "Lie. It's okay."

"I hate lying to you."

"It's not a lie if you tell—"

"It's still a lie, Cora."

"A wise man once told me that not all lies are bad."

He sighed but said nothing else.

We lay there together for a long time.

My head on his chest. His hand on the curve of my hip.

Perfectly normal.

Awkward as hell.

When his breathing finally evened out, I glanced up to see if he'd fallen asleep. His eyes were still open, aimed up at the four words Nic had once written in glow-in-the-dark stars across my ceiling. I hadn't known it when he'd put them there, but those four words became more precious to me than any "I love you" he'd ever uttered.

After he was gone, they were a reminder to live when I didn't want to.

To breathe when it felt impossible.

To keep going when all I really wanted to do was quit.

As far as I knew, Nic hadn't been able to see the future, but the day he'd chosen to write *those words* on the ceiling above our bed, he'd proved that he knew me better than anyone else ever would.

One in. One out.

Now, lying there with Penn, I could only hope they were offering him even a morsel of the comfort they'd given me over the years.

I placed a kiss to the underside of his jaw. "You don't have to tell me anything."

"Yeah, I do," he mumbled. "It's just that there's not always a lie to give. Not everything is black and white. Sometimes, the most important details are found in the gray. So, with that in mind, this is all I have for you tonight." His eyes found mine, that weight inside them heavier than ever. "Truth. My tattoos mean *nothing*."

I eyed him warily. "That didn't seem like a nothing reaction, Penn."

"It wasn't. But it's still the truth."

I narrowed my eyes, searching his face. But, in true Penn fashion, he sucked in a breath, held it for several seconds, then blew it out and went right back to normal.

So. Freaking. Weird.

"I believe it's my turn again," he announced.

"Oh, no. This game is officially over for the evening." I started to roll away but only made it to my back before he caught me.

"What happened to no pity?" The corners of his mouth lifted playfully, but his eyes were still sad and I hated it more than I could ever explain.

"Oh, I don't feel bad for you. All that emotional upheaval. I'm concerned for your heart. You aren't exactly a young man anymore."

His eyes lit. His mouth split. And then he came back to me.

Burying his face in my neck, he burst into laughter.

It was a stupid joke, something I suspected he recognized too. But, in a life like ours, where the dark and dismal were far more prevalent than the light and humorous, you took the few moments of levity you could get.

Penn spent the night wound around me.

I talked.

He listened.

I laughed.

He kissed me.

And, eventually, when we were sure the girls were asleep, he made love to me.

I knew every inch of his body.

His favorite color was blue.

His favorite meal was turkey bacon burgers.

And his tattoos held both a lot of meaning and none at all.

However, the true Penn Walker was still a mystery to me.

But from that day forward, within every word he spoke—every truth, every lie, every sentence, and every syllable—I looked for the gray.

Little did I know, that was all I'd ever find in him.

CHAPTER TWENTY-SIX

Cora

"**S**urprise!" I yelled as Penn returned from his run at twenty past the crack of dawn. He was hot, sweaty, and shirtless—just the way I liked him.

He eyed the pan in my hand, complete with the numbers three and eight burning on top, as he walked over, pressed a chaste kiss to my lips, and then asked, "What did you do, woman?"

"So, I know you don't like cupcakes. Which is a travesty in and of itself. But it's your birthday, so I made you a little traditional dessert from your native area of the southern United States that you may recognize as blueberry cobbler."

He blinked at me. "I'm from Florida."

I pushed the pan toward him. "I know. Blow 'em out."

"Florida's not the South, Cor."

I rolled my eyes. "I know how to read a map. I'm pretty sure Florida is as south as you can get in the U.S."

His lips thinned, suppressing his smile. "No, babe. Florida is not *the South* in terms of the culture. It's a literal melting pot for people from around the world. You drive up into Georgia, you'll find your cobbler. In Florida, though, that piñata you were talking about the other day or a tube of Bengay depending on which coast you're on would be more appropriate if you wanted to do something reminiscent of my"—grinning, he tossed me a pair of air quotes—"*native area.*"

"What! Seriously?"

He laughed. "You mentioned you haven't traveled much. But how far south have you been, babe?"

I twisted my lips. "Indiana?"

It was his turn to be shocked. "Seriously?"

I shrugged. "I don't get out much."

He cocked his head to the side. "How far you been north?"

"I'm not sure. What's the northernmost room in the building?"

"Jesus," he breathed.

"Now that you mention it, I'm a little offended I haven't been invited on any of the Guerrero family vacations." I winked and he rewarded me with a laugh.

He dipped his head, blew the candles out, and then brought his smiling mouth to mine for a lip touch. "Good news though. I fucking love cobbler." He punctuated it with another lip touch.

My proud grin stretched across my face. "Of course you do. It has fruit in it. That's, like, the anti-chocolate."

He laughed again. "Nature's sugar is better for your body."

"Then I probably shouldn't tell you there's, like, a whole bag of good old-fashioned processed white sugar in it too."

"I'm gonna pretend I didn't hear that."

"Good. Now I feel better about part one of my Florida-themed birthday party."

He quirked an eyebrow. "What's part two?"

I sauntered up the stairs, calling over my shoulder, "You'll see."

"Oh. My. *God*." Drew gasped as we guided Penn to the railing overlooking the building's postage-stamp backyard.

I'd sent them both home from work early with strict instructions to stay away from the windows.

Penn had grumbled. Because Penn.

Drew had grinned huge and offered me a high five. Because Drew.

"What is it?" Penn asked. His eyes were covered with a scarf blindfold I'd all but had to hog-wrestle him into putting on.

"Your woman just professed her undying love for me." Drew stopped and bit his knuckle. "Dear Lord, she's topless."

"What!" Penn snapped, going for the scarf.

I barked a laugh, slapping his hands away. Then I leaned over the rail and yelled, "Hey! Tops up. The guys are coming."

This was received by a symphony of cheers, groans, and curses, but within a few seconds, everyone was covered again.

Only then did I take Penn's blindfold off.

"Happy Birthday!"

All the girls parroted me from below

Penn blinked a million times, adjusting his eyes to the bright sun—or possibly the sight of over twenty bikini-clad women relaxing on towels and lounge chairs.

I'd bought four small kiddie pools, three bags of play sand, and a bag of decorative shells, thus transforming the backyard into a Floridian paradise. Or as close as I could get for the low, low price of fifty-three dollars.

Penn's head swung in my direction. "What in the…"

"I told you she loved me," Drew whispered.

I snapped my fingers in his direction. "No touching."

He leaned over the railing to get a better view. "I can look though, right?"

"Go for it."

Rubbing his hands together, he shot down the stairs, leaving Penn and me alone on the third floor.

"Part two?" he asked, circling his arms around my waist.

I squeaked when, rather than bending down to kiss me, he lifted me off my feet, bringing me up to his mouth.

"Welcome to Florida, baby. Since you're stuck in Illinois this year, I figured I'd bring the beach to you. Everybody pitched in this morning, helping me set up. Brittany even opened up her apartment as the bar. She's making cocktails complete with little umbrellas and neon straws. Keep an eye on Savannah though. I already had to snatch two out of her grip."

Penn chuckled, putting me back on my feet. "You didn't have to do all this, Cora. Really, it's just another day."

"No, Penn. It's your birthday. We *celebrate* birthdays. Nothing is a given. Nothing is promised. Nothing is guaranteed. So, when you have the chance to put on a bathing suit, lie in the sun, dig your toes into the sand, and drink fruity cocktails with umbrellas and neon straws while surrounded by people you care about, you *do it*."

He stared down at me, his gaze clear, his mouth smiling. But that all-too-familiar shadow flittered across his face. "You're the most amazing woman I've ever met."

"You're not so bad yourself."

His hand slid down to my ass. "You gonna be wearing a bikini?"

I swayed into him, looping my arms around his neck. "For a little while." I pecked at his lips. "But my goal is to end the day very, *very* naked."

"So there we were, four women, three of which were in heels, pushing this car to the edge of the parking lot. 'Just pop the clutch,' they said. 'It's easy,' they said." I lifted my drink in the air. "They lied! I was rolling down that hill like a soapbox derby star. I couldn't get the damn thing to crank. Nor could I get it to stop. I had no less than twelve heart attacks before I thought to pull the parking brake."

Everyone laughed as we sat in a semicircle around one of the baby pools. Penn and I were sharing a lounge chair. His feet were on the ground on either side, a beer in his hand, and I was sitting between his legs, leaning back against his chest, and halfway through my third piña colada.

It had been a really freaking good day. It was Penn's birthday, but the smiles on the women's faces as we all swapped stories and picked on each other like the family we truly were had me vowing to do something like this at least once a month. They deserved some downtime, not time locked away in their apartments, isolated from people who loved them.

And days like that were reminders of how much I did

love them. Each and every one of them. No matter how big of a pain in the ass they could be sometimes.

"You need another drink?" Penn whispered into the top of my hair as the girls carried on around us.

I craned my head back to see him and replied quietly, "You want birthday sex tonight?"

His eyes lit. "I wouldn't turn it down."

"Then no. Three is enough."

He dipped, kissing my lips. But I wasn't done with one. Snaking my hand up, I cupped the back of his head and pulled him down for a few more.

"Oh shit," someone breathed like they'd never seen two people in love before.

In love?

Shit, were we in love?

Just being able to ask myself that question was more than I'd ever thought I'd have again.

I hummed, kissing him again.

"Cora," someone hissed, but I waved them off, causing Penn to laugh against my mouth.

And then it was over.

The joy.

The happiness.

The comfort.

That hope that had been enveloping me, warming me, and feeding my soul since Penn had arrived? It exploded. And, as I'd expected, it slayed me in its wake.

"Well, this is cozy," Dante snarled behind me.

I froze, my pulse coming to a screeching halt before skyrocketing.

Penn shot to his feet, and I scrambled up after him, desperate to get between them.

"Hey, Dante?" I croaked, trying and failing to keep the shake out of my voice.

With a hand on my stomach, Penn stepped around me. "The fuck are you doing here?"

Dante laughed, unsteady on his feet but no less malevolent. His pupils were the telltale size of pinpricks, and the exposed skin beneath his white button-down was sweaty and red. God only knew what he'd taken that day. He was crazy as it was, without drugs adding to his unpredictability.

I swung my gaze around the yard, searching for Drew. He'd handled Dante once and nobody had died. Maybe he could do it again. I blew out a loud breath of relief when I found him prowling our way, a dark scowl hidden beneath a plastic smile.

"What's up, brother!" Drew called out on his way over.

As Dante turned his unfocused eyes away, Penn whispered in my ear, "Go. Lock yourself in your apartment."

I swallowed hard. If they tried to keep me from Dante, something he viewed as his property, it would only exacerbate the situation. The easiest and safest way was for me to face him and take whatever he wanted to dole out until his drugged-out mind got bored or passed out.

"No," I replied. "I'll handle this."

Penn grabbed my arm, hauling me against his side, and seethed, "The fuck you will."

I glared at him and then snatched my arm away. I could argue with Penn later, when Dante was gone and we were both still breathing.

Slapping on a smile, I stepped forward just as Drew arrived at Penn's side. "I didn't know you were coming over. Can I get you a drink?"

He chuffed. "A drink. A fucking drink." He glanced around, searching for an audience, but the women had wisely scattered. "I find one of my fucking whores riding the janitor and the bitch asks if I want a drink?"

"I wasn't—"

"You making him pay, Cora? Swear to God, you better not be giving my pussy out for free."

Penn hit my back, but I gave his hand a quick squeeze, silently begging him not to do anything stupid. Insults from Dante were a way of life. They didn't bother me. Though, if the suffocating rage firing off Penn was any indication, he could not say the same.

And Drew, well… "You got something to say, or are you just here to listen to yourself talk?"

"Shit, are you fucking her too?" He waggled his finger between Penn and Drew. "One in each hole, or are you two taking turns?"

Drew laughed like he actually found Dante humorous.

Meanwhile, Penn jerked, his straining chest getting even tighter at my back like it was costing him a great deal of effort to keep his hands at his sides and not planted in Dante's mouth.

I gave him another squeeze, whispering, "Please don't. He'll leave in a minute. Just wait."

Penn didn't reply, but he didn't move, either.

For me, it was a huge victory.

Getting Dante the hell out of there would have been an

even bigger victory.

"So, what can I do for you? Did you need something?" I asked.

He turned to me and smirked. "Oh, right. So here's the thing. I had a chat with Chrissy yesterday. I don't know if you remember her, but apparently, Marcos turned her out a while back." He scratched the back of his head. "That bitch is crazy. Made my damn ears bleed, she was talking so much. She wanted to come back, went so far as to lie to me and tell me you were keeping one of my personal girls as a pet."

The blood in my veins caught fire as the air in my lungs turned to sludge. But I fought it all back, showing him no fear as I scoffed, "What? That's nuts."

He smirked. "Yeah. Some bullshit about a redhead. I didn't know what the fuck she was talking about, so I decided to stop by and check in. See if you knew."

I could barely think with the thundering of my heart in my ears. "Nope. I'm just as clueless as you."

He shoved a hand into his pocket. "That's what I thought. Cause you wouldn't lie to me, would you?"

I shook my head, a sinking feeling settling in my stomach.

He grinned sardonically. "'Cause you remember exactly how much you have to lose, right?"

"Right," I breathed, nodding repeatedly.

He tipped his head at Penn. "Like, say, you start fucking this asshole and get the idea in your head that maybe you don't belong to me."

"Oh for fuck's—" Drew started, but I threw a hand out to silence him.

Stepping away from Penn, I forced a smile around the

fire in my throat.

They were words I'd said before.

Words I'd once believed.

Words that had nearly destroyed me.

Words that I now knew were the biggest lies I'd ever told.

"I belong to you, Dante. I'm not sleeping with anybody. I would never disrespect all you've given me like that. I'm a Guerrero. Always and forever."

He smiled, sick and twisted. "Lies have consequences, Cora."

"I know. But I'm not lying."

He held my stare, searching with glassy eyes.

I stared back, showing him nothing but the truth he wanted to see.

"Okay. As long as we're clear." He turned on a toe and drunkenly staggered toward the parking lot.

That was the exact moment I realized something was wrong.

Seriously, terribly, *gravely* wrong.

Dante never gave up that easily. Not until I had paid hand over fist for whatever he'd so much as thought I'd done.

"Where are the girls?" I whispered to Penn, my hands trembling as I watched Dante make it to his car.

Time stopped and the ground opened, releasing the demons from hell in the five seconds it took for him to reply.

"I don't know."

He might not have known, but suddenly, it was all too clear that Dante did.

"River!" I screamed.

CHAPTER TWENTY-SEVEN

Penn

D rew and I took off at a dead sprint toward the stairs, Cora's terror-filled cry fueling my every step. I led the way, my feet pounding on the concrete as I took the stairs three at a time. Drew was right behind me.

Out of the corner of my eye, I caught sight of Dante pulling out of the parking lot as I rounded the last curve to the second floor.

That son of a bitch.

That fucking fucking son of a bitch.

If he'd touched those girls…

I'd wanted to kill him for breathing the same air as Cora. Then hearing her say she belonged to him? Dante was lucky he'd walked away after that.

But if he'd done anything to River or Savannah, he'd never find himself that lucky again.

When I reached the top, I went straight for the door to Cora's apartment. My shoulder slammed into the wood, though the door refused to open. I shook the handle, but it wouldn't budge.

"River! Savannah!" I yelled, pounding my fist against

the wood.

"Move," Cora choked out as she finally made it up to us, her keys already in her hand. She twisted both locks open and carefully shoved the door open.

The chain didn't catch.

It had been locked from the outside.

Dante was one step closer to his coffin.

"River!" she screamed.

A deep thudding sound came from down the hall. After passing by the girls' empty room, I threw Cora's bedroom door open—only to screech to a halt when I saw River and Savannah on the other side.

It should have been a relief, but neither of them was okay.

River was wearing a makeshift gag, tears streaming down her frightened face. Her hands were bound by an electrical cord, which was anchored to the very same bed-frame I'd bought Cora. The bed had been pulled clear across the room, and River was on her knees, next to a blue, lifeless version of Savannah. White foam trickled from her mouth while a syringe lay haphazardly discarded on the floor at her feet.

"No!" Cora screamed.

I flew straight to Savannah first, dropping to my knees beside her. My heart was in my throat as I prayed with everything I had for the first time since I'd sat on that phone with Lisa. No one had helped me then. I didn't know if there was a God anymore, but if there was, I needed him to actually show up this time.

"She has a pulse," I declared, rolling her to her side.

Drew jumped into action, shoving a finger between her lips, sweeping vomit from her mouth.

"Oh, thank you," Cora breathed. "Is she breathing?" she asked, her hands frenzied as she fought with the gag in River's mouth.

"Yeah," I said with hope. But, while Savannah's breaths were visible at her chest, they were shallow, each one taunting me as if it could be her last.

And then a rusty knife hit my gut when I lifted her lids. Her hollow, green stare was already cloudy.

Cora finally got the gag off River.

And then the world stopped.

Everything I'd spent four years searching for suddenly fell into my lap, but in that moment, it didn't seem important anymore. Not with innocent kids dying. Women being taken advantage of, manipulated, abused. Not with people like Dante and Marcos Guerrero walking the street.

It was that exact moment that my purpose shifted, but surprisingly enough, my goal remained the same.

"Mom!" River screamed, diving into Cora's arms with her upper body, her hands still tethered to the bed.

I saw Drew's body jerk, so I shot my head up. Shock and confusion registered on his face as he stared with narrowed eyes at Cora embracing…

Her daughter?

"It's okay. It's okay. It's okay. I've got you. It's gonna be okay. Everything's going to be okay," she chanted.

"He made her take it," River cried as Drew used a pocketknife to cut her free. "She told him no. But he made her. He said he would take her away. Back to his place, where she belonged."

Cora palmed River's tear-stained face. "Did he give you anything?"

"No."

"Pills, food, drink, anything? River, think!"

"No! He didn't touch me. He just tied me up so I couldn't get you. Oh God, Mom. Is she going to be okay?"

"Yes," Cora answered definitively. "She's gonna be fine. Everything is going to be fine. She just needs to sleep it off." With tears in her blue eyes, she turned to me. "Right, Penn?"

I wanted to say yes. But I couldn't lie to her. Not about this.

"No, baby. She needs to go to a hospital."

Her face paled, but her words were resolute—a pep talk for herself. "No. We don't do hospitals. She's going to be fine. She just needs to sleep it off."

I reached out and squeezed her shoulder. "Cora, baby. She needs—"

"No!" she yelled, her desperation morphing into anger. "Pick her up and put her in her bed. I'll keep an eye on her. She's gonna be *fine*."

But you couldn't sleep off an overdose. Not if you ever wanted to wake up.

"Get her in the truck," I called out to Drew. I tried to gather Cora in my arms, but she fought against me, becoming feral as she tried to keep Drew away.

"Don't you dare touch her. She's not going anywhere."

Wedging my way in between her and the kid, I said bluntly, "Then she's going to *die*."

Her body turned to stone, so I gentled my tone.

"Look at her. We gotta get her to a hospital so they can help her. God only knows what Dante gave her. Or how much. He was trying to punish you. Punish *her*. I would not be surprised if he gave her enough to put down a horse. She needs a doctor, baby. Or she's gone."

She burst into tears. "But she's gone if you take her too, Penn. She's an underage runaway. Social Services will get her and they'll send her back to her family in Indiana. Her father will beat her within an inch of her life and her mother will give her more drugs to numb the pain. The kid has been an addict since she was twelve. She gets back in that life, she won't get out. She'll end up back on the streets with nowhere to go, using and selling her body to pay. I will never see her again."

Pressure built in my chest until I wasn't sure I could take it anymore.

Plain as day, Cora's heart was breaking.

My heart was breaking for her.

But she wasn't thinking clearly.

She was thinking like a mother.

I was thinking like a man who would have done anything to take the pain away from his woman.

No matter the cost.

One in. One out.

I wrapped her tight in my arms, as if I could keep her from falling apart, and pointedly tipped my chin at Drew.

"No!" Cora wailed as he took the cue and lifted Savannah off the floor, carrying her with hurried steps out of the bedroom.

Her whole body shook with waves of despair.

I kissed the top of her head. "I'll get her back. I'll take her to the hospital and drop her off at the emergency room. That's all we can do for her right now. The minute she is healthy again, I swear on my life, I will get her back for you. I promised you I would make them safe. And I will. But I gotta do it *now*. Time is a big factor, and us standing here arguing isn't helping her."

"Oh God, you're right. Go take her," she croaked, stepping out of my arms. "Check her pockets before you drop her off."

"What?" I asked, backing toward the door.

"He did this to me too. When River was a baby, I almost died and then spent a year in prison because he planted heroin in my pocket before dumping me on the side of the road."

My bones turned to concrete, and my vision flashed red. "Are you fucking kidding me?"

She shook her head, hooking her arms around River's shoulder and pulling her into her chest.

Yeah. Dante was a dead man.

"Right, okay. I need to go. Lock the door behind me. I'll be back soon as I can."

"Take care of her," she whispered.

"I will. I swear."

Despite the distance only being a few miles, it was the longest drive of my life. As the only member of the family without a record—yet—I carried that girl in my arms straight through the front doors of the emergency room, yelling for help like a madman. As soon as they got her on the gurney, I sent up a prayer for her and then ducked out the same way I'd come in.

Drew was idling at the curb when I climbed back into the truck. "She gonna make it?" he asked.

"I have no clue," I replied, scrubbing my hands over my face. "I want them dead. Both of them. If there is one Guerrero left walking this Earth, it's too many."

He kept his eyes on the road as he turned into traffic. "River's gotta be a Guerrero."

My head snapped to his. "You thinking she's the one?"

"I don't know. This doesn't make sense."

And he was right.

None of it made sense. Not since day one.

After Lisa died, I'd been a cyclone of pain. I'd thrown hundreds of thousands of dollars at private investigators, searching for answers. I hadn't been able to save her, but bringing the men responsible to justice became my obsession. The police had written her murder off as a robbery gone wrong, both suspects killed by officers. But I'd spent twenty-nine minutes watching those two men beat and torture her for sport.

That wasn't an accident.

That was personal.

All initial signs pointed to the Guerreros. But we couldn't get any solid proof. And, while killing those pieces of shit in Lisa's name wouldn't have cost me a single night of sleep, it also wouldn't have soothed the searing failure engulfing my soul.

That was when Drew, who'd been burning at the stake beside me, decided we needed to handle it ourselves. He stole two cars in order to get himself locked away in the same prison Manuel Guerrero had been sentenced to. And then Drew did what he did best—he became a chameleon.

That was how he learned about the meeting.

That was how we found out someone had asked Manuel to put a hit on a nosy reporter who was getting too close.

And that was when Manuel had bragged about how strong his family was, stating that he'd allowed his young granddaughter to make the final decision.

According to Manuel, the child had declined to issue the woman's death, proudly stating that Guerreros didn't take orders from anyone.

But my wife still died the very next day.

Whoever had been in that room with Manuel and his granddaughter that night had Lisa's blood covering their hands, and it didn't matter the sacrifice I had to make, whether it be rotting in a cell or in a body bag. I would make them drown in it.

Like I'd told Cora all those weeks earlier: The world was an ugly place. It was filled with more sinners than saints. More hate than love. More chaos than kindness. And that was not because the world was filled with bad people. It's because the good ones stayed silent.

I was the sinner in this story. With a heart filled to the brim with hate and a mind overflowing with vengeance and chaos.

But I would *not* stay silent.

"Manuel specifically told me he had only *one* grandchild, Penn. I listened to him rave about her for hours on end."

I turned in my seat. "And you heard him say it was Catalina's daughter, Isabel, who was there that night?"

285

He slammed the heel of his palm down on the steering wheel. "No. He told me it was *his* granddaughter. His *only* granddaughter. It had to have been Isabel."

"Unless it was River and we've had the answer at our fingertips all along. Shit. We were so focused on finding Catalina we couldn't even see what was sitting right in front of us." I rubbed the center of my chest as if I could ease the pain. "Goddamn it, I've been asking the wrong questions all along."

We both fell silent, lost in our separate but parallel thoughts.

"Okay, we gotta figure this shit out. What are the chances River isn't Nic's?" Drew asked.

"If Cora's her mom, she's Nic's. She's never been with anyone else." *Except me.*

And, if I had my way about it, she'd never be with anyone else, either.

But what next?

Did I just forget about the people responsible for Lisa's murder because I'd met Cora?

Ride off into the sunset together? Love heals all wounds? Bullshit. Bullshit. Bullshit.

I'd warned Cora about the fire inside me.

I'd told her if she got too close it'd burn her too.

And now, we were all up in flames.

"This has to end," I told Drew. "Marcos, Dante, Cora, fuck...*Penn Walker*. There's gotta be a better way, Drew. There's *got* to be a better way."

He took his eyes off the road long enough to look over at me. "Admit you love her. I want to hear it out of your mouth before I agree to help you break her."

I stared out the passenger-side window, biting the inside of my cheek until I tasted the metallic tang of blood. The world rushed by. The sun followed us, trees and cars blurring as we passed, and clouds moving in slow motion above our heads as the opaque moon hung in the sky, waiting for its turn to shine. Not even an hour earlier, Cora had been sitting in my lap, drinking piña coladas, carefree and giggling.

That was the life I wanted for her.

That was the *world* I wanted for her.

One in. One out.

"I just want her to be free. Even if that means she has to be free of me."

CHAPTER TWENTY-EIGHT

Cora

"So, she's your daughter?" Penn asked from the double bed beside us.

River's soft snores hummed in my lap, but even though she'd cried herself to sleep nearly an hour earlier, I continued stroking, soothing, and playing with her hair.

The minute Penn had gotten back from dropping Savannah off at the hospital, he'd ordered us to pack a bag. He and Drew had stood guard at the door while River and I had gathered a few things, and then we were off.

Cussing and cringing every step of the way, Penn took us to a hotel. And not a cheap one. I didn't know how he was paying for it. But I was too shaken to care.

I'd have emptied my entire Freedom Account to escape that apartment for the night. I hadn't been able to blink without seeing River tied to a bed and Savannah's limp body on that floor. I was so completely and utterly numb that I couldn't even feel the fear anymore.

Dante had manipulated my feelings to keep me in check for years. But, this time, he'd stepped it up a notch. It wouldn't be long before torturing people I loved became his preferred method of control.

Penn would be next. No question about it. Maybe Drew too.

Then…

He'd never touched River. But, one day, that would change.

I couldn't risk that she'd be there when it did. I couldn't wait any longer. It was time to go, even if that just meant getting River and the money to Catalina. Whatever happened to me after that, I could deal with it.

"She's the reason Nic and I got married," I replied, twirling a lock of her hair around my finger. "Funny thing, back then, I'd thought getting pregnant at sixteen was the scariest thing that could happen to me. God, I was so naïve. Nic was scared too, but he had this way about him that always made the bad seem manageable. Manuel lost his mind though. Forbid Nic from having anything to do with me." I smiled at the memory. "The next day, Nic bought me an engagement ring. The day after that, he paid a homeless guy a hundred bucks to pretend to be my dad, and we got married at the justice of the peace."

My breathing shuddered, the happiness of those days colliding with the pain of all the years that followed. "The Guerreros have never accepted her. They don't even acknowledge that she's Nic's. They blame me, and thus her, for his death. Because, rather than trying to save himself, he died protecting us."

Tears rolled down my cheeks. But I couldn't swipe them away fast enough to hide them. I didn't know why I bothered anymore. Penn had seen me cry more than anyone else in my entire life.

I wasn't sure if that was a good sign or bad one.

He moved to our bed, sitting at my feet and resting his hand on my shin, nestled beneath the covers. "Why didn't you tell me?"

I glanced up at him, using my shoulder to wipe the dampness off my chin. "Because it's not safe for people to know. So many girls have come through that building over the years with one thing in common: They've all been abused by Guerrero men. You think I wanted to advertise that a member of the family was just upstairs, sleeping under the same roof? No fucking way. I was a Guerrero by marriage. She's one by blood."

"How many people know?" he asked.

"I don't know. I don't think any. When we first arrived at that building, I'd just gotten out of jail and River was about a year and a half old. Manuel had custody of her while I was locked away, so like a knife to my heart, he'd taught her to call me Cora. It ended up working in our favor. I told everybody she was the daughter of a working girl who had died and that it was our responsibility to make sure she had a better life. In all the years that I lived in that building, I only had to tell that lie once. It's gotten passed down like folklore. But I'll tell you what. The women in that building take care of her. They don't treat her like one of the new girls coming in. They treat her like somebody who's going to get out." I went back to staring at her. "When she was little, we used to get into our pajamas, pile into bed, lock the door, and pull the blankets over our head. She'd lie there for hours, looking at pictures and listening to stories about Nic. That's when she started calling me mom." My heart ached watching River's long black lashes fluttering with REM. I could only hope she was dreaming of a better life. "She slips up sometimes."

"Damn it, Cora. You have a daughter. Why didn't you ever leave? Just take her and run?"

My head shot up. "You don't think I tried? Jesus, Penn. I tried so damn hard from the very first day. At Nic's funeral, Dante kneed me in the stomach so hard I started bleeding. I was four months pregnant, my husband was dead, and I had twenty dollars to my name. So I packed the little I had and went home. My father took one look at my swollen belly, called me a whore, and slammed the door in my face."

"Jesus," he breathed.

I got quiet when River stirred in my lap, her arm hugging my legs, trying to get closer even in sleep.

"Marcos found me that time," I whispered when she settled again. It was like I'd opened the floodgates. The truth wouldn't stop pouring out of me. "They hated me, but they couldn't let me go because they *needed* to hate me. It was an enemy of Dante's who killed Nic. He'd pissed some people off, so they came for his family. Dante blames himself and takes every bit of that self-loathing out on me. After she was born, I tried to leave, but he made sure I ended up in jail instead.

"After I got out of lockup, I was just so thankful to have my daughter back that it didn't seem worth trying to escape again. I started running the building and settled in for what I hoped would be a decent life for the two of us. But Dante never let me breathe easy. It was way worse back then too. It was rare for a week to go by without him stopping in to take his anger out on me. I tried running two more times. The first landed me in the hospital for a week. The second in jail on another drug charge." I twisted my lips and mumbled, "Strike two. But that wasn't the worst of it. While I was there, Manuel used his good old son-in-law, Thomas Lyons, to have me labeled as an unfit parent in the eyes of the law. I lost custody of River to Manuel."

Penn shot to his feet, his face contorted by a snarl. "How is that even possible?"

"Shhh. Keep it down," I scolded, but River didn't budge.

He lowered his voice, but not his anger. "You're telling me a judge awarded a criminal custody of a child?"

I leaned forward and hissed, "I was the criminal, Penn. I was the one who tried to get away. I was the one who failed her."

"That's a load of shit. I didn't even know she was yours and I still knew you were a good mom."

"Not good enough, though. After that, I was *literally* stuck. I couldn't turn to the cops. My only saving grace was that Manuel didn't actually want River. He gave her back to me on the condition that I shut up and do my job. If I stepped out of line, he took her from me. Maybe for a day. Once, I didn't see her for a month. During that time, I didn't know what they were doing to her. I didn't know if she was safe. I had no options, Penn. It was a cruel game that she and I both paid for until finally I stopped trying." Straightening my back, I looked him right in the eye. "That *doesn't* mean I gave up. That *doesn't* mean I accepted this life for her *or* for me. I just needed some time to figure it out. And Catalina gave that to me."

He gave my leg an urging squeeze. "What do you mean?"

"Thomas asked her to testify against her father. And she did. Manuel went to jail. Marcos took over. He has no interest in River whatsoever. So I managed to get custody back."

He arched an eyebrow. "I thought Thomas and Manuel were partners."

"They were. Back in the day, they were unstoppable. Manuel would feed Thomas intel on the drugs and prostitutes in the community. In turn, Thomas would take down the Guerreros' competition while earning himself a solid conviction for his record."

"So what changed that?"

I scoffed. "Power trip. Both of them were riding it high. Manuel thought he was running the show. Thomas disagreed. River told me that Thomas started catching some heat and Manuel didn't feel like helping him out. They quit being partners and Thomas won."

Penn suddenly shot to his feet like the bed had been electrified. "What did you say?" he gasped with wild eyes.

"Um…Thomas won."

Intertwining his fingers, he locked them on the top of his head. "Because the Guerreros don't take orders from anyone. But Isabel is a Lyons, not a Guerrero."

I eyed him warily and drawled, "Riiight."

He started to pace, his eyes flashing around the room without actually landing on anything. "When did this happen? When did Manuel and Thomas stop working together?"

"I don't know. Why?"

He spun to face me. "Cora, think!"

My head snapped back at his rough tone, but his face was nothing but a plea.

"I…um… Cat's been gone for three years now, and that was after the trial. So maybe four, five years ago. Why? What the hell is going on?"

His eyes fluttered shut, his head fell back between his shoulders, and his whole muscle-covered body sagged in a way I'd never seen before. It was like a weight had not only been lifted from his shoulders, but from every cell, right down to his DNA.

I gently guided River off my lap and made my way over to him. Resting my hands on his stomach, I asked, "What is going on? Talk to me."

His arms looped around me, pulling me into his chest. His heart was pounding, but his body remained slack. "I should have asked you. The very first day. But, as much as I hated to admit it, I was in awe of you from the moment I saw you. You were this gorgeous woman staring up at me, so filled with fear that it made you fearless. I was jealous, baby. Because fear and anger and resentment had been dictating my life since the day I watched her die."

A chill prickled my skin. He was making no sense, but it sounded like a confession flowing from his soul.

I rested my chin on his chest and peered up at him. "*What* are you talking about right now?"

He didn't answer my question as much as he just continued. "But then I would have missed having you. It was worth it." He smiled, his forehead crinkling with pain. "You're a good woman, Cora. A good mom. A good *person*." For the first time since I'd been with Penn, he reached up and tapped the star hanging around my neck. "One in. One out. No matter how hard it gets. You keep breathing."

My eyes filled with tears as Nic's words from the past came back at me from Penn's mouth. As far as I could remember, I'd never told him that story.

But Penn fell asleep under those stars every night too. Maybe it was a given.

He dipped low and touched my lips. "It's been a crazy day, baby. Lie down with me?"

I nodded, ready for nothing more.

Penn and I climbed into bed that night. He assumed his position on his back. I assumed mine with my head on his chest. I didn't think I'd ever fall asleep that night. I spent at least an hour staring at River in the bed beside us, watching her chest rise and fall while stressing about if Savannah's was doing the same thing.

Was she okay? How was she feeling? Was she scared?

Could Penn really get her back for me?

Sleep eventually devoured me.

So much so that I didn't feel him climb out of bed.

I didn't hear him whisper, "I love you," when he kissed me on the forehead.

And I completely missed the door clicking behind Penn Walker as he walked out of my life for the very last time.

CHAPTER TWENTY-NINE

Penn

One week before I lost her...

"Hey! There's my hunk of a husband," she cooed through the speaker of my phone, but the screen remained black.

I fought with my suit coat, trying to shake it off with one arm while keeping the phone steady with the other. "I can't see you."

"Hang on. The internet is shit here."

I set the phone on the granite island in the middle of our closet and turned my fight on my cufflinks.

"What about now?" she asked.

I leaned over to see the screen. "Nope. Still black."

"What about"—her beautiful, smiling face suddenly appeared on the screen—"now."

"Nope," I lied, biting my bottom lip to suppress a laugh.

"Ughhh!" she groaned, bringing it to her face. Her nose scrunched adorably as she squinted, clearly not wearing her contacts.

"You out of contacts?" I asked, starting on my button-down, the promise of a T-shirt calling my name.

"Huh?"

I could see straight up her nose as she flipped the phone in every which direction. I wasn't able to hide that laugh. "Lisa, stop. I was kidding. I can see you."

Her toffee-brown eyes perked as she stretched her arm out, allowing the rest of her face to fill the screen. "Is it working?"

After tugging on the soft, washed-out cotton of whatever vintage band T-shirt my hand had hit first, I picked the phone up and shot her a smile. "Yeah, crazy. It's working. How's it—what the hell are you wearing?"

She glanced down at the skintight scrap of black leather that was wrapped around her midsection and replied, "A dress."

"Absolutely," I replied, walking back to our bedroom and settling on the bed, "if you were Catwoman. But, seeing as how you are a mere human with no feline reflexes or expert combative skills, I'm going to ask again: What the hell are you wearing?"

She huffed. "You forgot the whip."

"You have a whip!"

She laughed wildly. "No, Shane. Catwoman has a whip. I was just correcting your seriously lackluster comic book knowledge."

I glared at her.

She smiled back.

"The dress, Lisa. Explain."

She walked across the room, propping the phone against her computer, tilting and angling until I could see most of the room. She backed toward her suitcase which was opened across the foot of the bed, clothes hanging out on every side. "I'm supposed to be seducing a man. You caught me before I had the chance to change."

"Oh wow," I deadpanned. "Exactly what every man wants to hear from his wife." I leaned in close as she peeled the dress over her head to reveal a sexy-as-sin pair of black lace panties and no bra. I sucked in a sharp breath through my teeth. She'd been gone for over a month this time, and I'd missed more than just her dinner company. "Whoa, slow down," I objected as she pulled a pale-pink nightgown on.

"Not tonight, Pervy McGee. I need to tell you all the things I've learned this week."

I rolled my eyes and collapsed back on my bed, holding the phone above my head. "That doesn't sound nearly as exciting."

"I can't hear you for shit. My phone's been on the fritz. Let me grab my earbuds."

While she searched the room, I grabbed the remote and flipped the TV on. The ticker from the stock market's end of day scrolled across the bottom as a news anchor rambled about the country's unemployment rate. I hit mute.

"Okay. That's better," she said.

"Good news: Amazon's stock prices climbed again today. I might actually be able to afford to keep you golden in our golden years."

"Oh, please. I'm gone the minute you start balding."

I clutched my heart. "Hey!"

"I'm kidding. You know I have a thing for Mr. Clean." She winked. "Now seriously, listen to this shit. I think I found a way to get that woman out."

"What woman?"

"Cora," she stressed. "The Guerrero woman. The one that was married to the guy who was gunned down."

"The madam?"

Her lips thinned as she scowled. "She's not a madam. But yeah. Her."

"She wants out?"

"Seriously, Shane. Do you ever listen to me when I talk?"

"Oh, I listen. Let's see if I've got this right. My wife is currently infiltrating a whore house like she's Geraldo Rivera. As of last week, she had been *promoted* to the third floor—whatever the hell that means. And three nights a week, you get dressed up like a hooker, go to a hotel room where you pretend to meet with rich men who give it to you all night long, when you're really just bullshitting with your husband via FaceTime. Then, when it's all over, I go to sleep with blue balls while you withdraw cash out of *our* bank account to pay your pimp. Trust me, Lisa. I hear what you say, but if you don't want me showing up there and dragging you home caveman style, you're going to have to accept what kind of details I choose to commit to memory."

We both glowered. Hers broke first.

"Anywho... So Cora. She's this woman who runs the building for the Guerreros. She used to be married to the youngest one. But I swear she looks like she's like eighteen now, so I don't know how that's possible, but I digress. So she and I were talking last week and she told me about her ex. Oh God. It's such a sad story, Shane. She still wears this star necklace that he gave her, and get this: Before he died, he wrote on her ceiling in glow-in-the-dark stars. She told me she used to get really overwhelmed, so he wrote the words 'One in. One out.' As a reminder that, no matter how hard things get, everything will be fine as long as you just keep breathing."

"Damn," I whispered. "That's rough. He died, right?"

"Yeah. Long time ago. But, when she was forced to move here from their old place, she brought them with her. Stuck them right back up the way he had them." She paused and glanced around the empty room before lowering her voice and rushing out with, "A few nights ago, I broke into her apartment while she was gone and planted a hidden camera under a cluster of some of them." She slapped a hand over her mouth like a kid who had said a curse word.

I shot upright, my mouth falling open as I stared at my wife. "What the fuck, Lisa! Where the hell did you get a hidden camera?"

"The internet. They delivered it right to my doorstep."

I flared my eyes at her. "At the whore house? Addressed to Lisa Pennington?"

She waved me off. "No. I'm not stupid. I made sure it came to Lexy Palmer."

I gritted my teeth. "Not helping."

"Relax. It's fine."

"It's not fine. You told me when you left for Chicago that you were just following up on a tip about those missing women and the modeling ads in the paper. Now, you're living there and planting hidden cameras? You gotta stop this bullshit before you get yourself killed. You are not a detective, Lisa. I let you do this because—"

"You don't *let* me do anything. I'm here because I *want* to be here and I feel passionate about it. And, because, if I don't help Cora Guerrero, nobody will. She's incredible, Shane. She has no idea that she's the only thing keeping this entire operation running. The Guerreros *need* her. She's the one who takes the women for STD testing and makes sure everyone stays on birth control. She talks to them and actually *listens* when there's a problem. She makes every single one of them feel special. For example: She makes us call when we get home every night. She does, like, a head count, and if you don't check in, she'll be beating down your door first thing the next morning. These women have never had anyone care about them. But Cora cares, and because of that, the women stay. If somebody just got her out of here, the whole damn thing would fall apart."

Frustration built in my chest. She had that excited tone to her voice that did not bode well for me. When Lisa got her mind set on something, there was no stopping her. I never doubted that she loved me, but our marriage was never what she set her mind to. I took the back seat to every one of these little adventures she went on. I was fucking sick of it. I could have asked her to come home. She wouldn't have done it. Not until she'd accomplished whatever harebrained mission she had her heart set on. This time, it was Cora Guerrero. Next time, who the hell knew. The only thing that was certain was that there would be a next time. And a time after that. And a time after that.

Money didn't mean much to me. I'd made a fortune buying foreclosed beach property up and down the coasts of Florida when the housing market had crashed. But time with my wife? That was getting rarer and rarer by the year.

Pinching the bridge of my nose, I suggested, "See if you can throw some cash at her. Get her out of there. Get *you* out of there. Whatever it takes to get you home. I don't care."

"That's the thing though. She *has* money. Last night, I was watching some of the video. Above the frame of her door, she has this, like, secret compartment where she keeps a shit-ton of money. It's all wrapped up in insulation. I have no idea how much is up there. But it was more than a little rainy day fund."

I sighed, my head starting to pound. "And let me guess: You've got a plan."

She smiled wide and toothy. "Yep."

"Do I want to know?"

She swayed her head from side to side. "Probably not."

Dread filled my gut. "Is it at least legal? Do I need to get a criminal attorney on retainer?"

She mocked horror. "Of course it's legal. Who do you think I am?"

"You know, honestly, I have no idea anymore."

She rolled her eyes. "Okay, maybe we should stop talking about me. What have you been up to?"

"Work."

She twisted her lips. "That's it?"

I looked down at my watch. "That and I'm supposed to meet Drew for beers in an hour."

"Oh! So he's speaking to you? That must be nice. He hasn't answered my calls in weeks."

"Yeah, well. He hates your Nancy Drew bit just as much as I do. However, he chooses to ignore it, while I've learned to embrace banging my head against the wall."

"Hardy har har har. Tell him I said I love him. And that he sucks. And, if he doesn't answer his phone next time I try to call, I'm never speaking to him again."

CHAPTER THIRTY

Cora

I slapped around on the nightstand as my phone started screaming beside me. I blinked at the time, finding it well past three.

My head was groggy with sleep as I pressed the little green button and lifted it to my ear. "Hello?"

"Where are you!" Brittany screamed.

Instinctively, I pulled the phone away from my ear. "Jesus, stop yelling."

"The building is on fire, Cora. Where are you?"

I shot upright, my whole body coming awake with a blast of adrenaline. Slinging the covers off me, I jumped from the bed. "What!"

"Cora," River called, sleepily sitting up.

"Get dressed," I hissed at her, before asking Brittany, "How bad is it?"

"It's… Cora, it's gone. All of it. The fire department is here. Police are crawling everywhere." Her voice broke as she started crying. "Where are you?"

My breath lodged in my throat, and I slapped a hand over my mouth. "I'm…I'm at a hotel."

"Do you have River with you?"

I glanced over at her and saw her dragging her hair into a ponytail with frantic eyes leveled on me. "Yeah. She's right here. Listen, who's with you? Everybody was supposed to be working tonight except Jennifer. I need a head count, Brit. Get in contact with everybody you can. I'll try too. Say nothing to the police until I get there. We're on the way." I looked back at the bed, finding it surprisingly empty.

My pulse spiked as I searched the room, but there was no sign of him. My mind spun, trying to figure out if sleep was still clouding my memories. But he had definitely been there with me when I'd fallen asleep, his heartbeat playing in my ear like my favorite lullaby.

Maybe he'd gotten up early and gone out for a run. Yeah. That had to be it.

"Did you hear me, Brit? I need accountability on *everyone*. I'm gonna call Marcos—"

"He's here already," she rushed out. "Or at least his car is. Dante's too. I haven't seen them though."

Surprise hit me like a brick wall. Why the hell would they be there this time of night?

And then she slayed me.

"Penn's truck is here too. Have you seen the guys?"

My heart seized, chills exploding across my skin. I didn't realize I'd dropped the phone. I hadn't actually formed a full thought before I found myself standing in the hall, pounding on the door on the other side of us.

Drew opened the door with a hand raised to block out the bright light of the hallway. "Jesus, woman."

"Where's your brother?" I shrieked.

His hand fell, alarm hitting his face. "With you?"

Fear slammed into me like a runaway train. I threw a hand out to catch myself when my knees threatened to buckle.

"Mom?" River squeaked, diving toward me.

Drew swooped in, hooking me around the waist before I hit the floor.

"Oh God." My stomach rolled, threatening to revolt as the panic overtook me.

Dante's words from the day before echoed in my mind, slicing me deeper each time. *"Lies have consequences, Cora."*

This wasn't happening. It wasn't possible.

First, Savannah. Now, Penn.

No.

Penn was going to walk up any second, pull me into his arms, and tell me there was nothing to worry about.

He had to.

"Cora, say something," Drew urged.

"There was a fire at the building," I whispered. "Penn's truck is there." I didn't want to say it.

I didn't want it to be true.

I *needed* it to be a lie.

"So are Dante and Marcos's cars."

River gasped.

Drew let out a string of curse words, but his only reply was, "Let me get my boots."

I stood on my own, shaking, propped against the wall, as they both dashed into action.

I vaguely remember River dropping my flip-flops in front of me. I must have put them on, because I was wearing shoes when Drew guided us into the back of a cab.

"'Cause you remember exactly how much you have to lose, right?"

Numb and unable to focus, I clung to the star around my neck, pleading to God, Nic, and the entire universe that I was wrong.

River held my hand, whispering reassurances as we drove, while Drew sat beside me, his thigh flush with mine as he silently stared out the window.

The moon was still high in the sky when we pulled into that dirt parking lot. Hope that it wasn't as bad as Brittany had made it out to be sprang inside me as I saw the tall silhouette of the building, but the flashing red-and-blue lights of fire trucks and police cars painted the true story.

It was gone, only the stairwells and a mountain of burned debris remaining.

I climbed out of that cab faster than I'd ever moved before, running toward the building like I could stop it from being real.

"Ma'am. Ma'am. Ma'am!" a cop called, rushing toward me as I ducked under the caution tape roping the area off.

"Penn!" I yelled, the lingering smoke in the air choking me. I coughed, gasping for air through my panic.

The officer stepped in front of me with his arms stretched wide, blocking my path, but I fought to get around him.

"Miss, calm down. Do you live here?"

"Did you find any people in there? My...my boyfriend. I think he's inside. You have to help him." I gripped the front of his uniform. "Please. Please. I'm begging you. You have to save him."

His eyes flicked to a firefighter who almost imperceptibly

shook his head.

Agony erupted like a volcano inside me. "No!"

Drew appeared at my side, a ghastly look on his face matching my own. "Cora, come here." He grabbed the back of my neck the same way Penn had done so many times before and curled me into his front.

And I cried, tears soaking the front of his shirt. "He's out for a run. I know it, Drew. He's just out for a run. He'll be right back. He'll be *right back*."

Lies—I needed them more than oxygen.

I was never going to be able to survive the truth.

Not again.

Not. Again.

"Okay, Ms. Guerrero. You're free to go whenever you'd like. This will remain an active investigation, but given what we were able to pull off Mr. Walker's security camera, this seems pretty clear-cut."

I stared at the officer. Looking right at him, but not seeing him.

Penn had security cameras. Good to know.

"Thank you," I whispered.

I was sitting in the back of a police car, wrapped in a blanket.

Numb.

Broken.

Ruined.

And free.

The bodies of Marcos and Dante Guerrero had been

recovered from the ashes, along with the body of another male, his arms and legs still bound to a chair when they'd found him.

I couldn't look. I couldn't see him like that. I couldn't remember him the way I remembered Nic every night when I closed my eyes: dead.

Drew identified his body.

And I sat there, in the back of a police car, wrapped in a blanket.

Numb.

Broken.

Ruined.

And free.

Miraculously, all the girls had made it out. Only Jennifer had been off work that night, and thankfully, she'd been out at the club, dancing and having fun.

The money in my wall was gone. According to the fire inspector, the flames had originated on the third floor, more than likely my apartment. Five years of secrets, scrimping, and risking my life to swindle money from the Guerreros' monthly accounts was just poof—up in flames.

And I was sitting there, alone, homeless, and broke in the back of a police car, wrapped in a blanket.

Numb.

Broken.

Ruined.

And free.

I couldn't wrap my mind around why Penn, Marcos, or Dante had been at the apartment that night. I'd played out at least a hundred different scenarios in my head, but I couldn't come up with an answer.

At least not one that brought him back to me.

He shouldn't have been there. He'd been in bed. Safe. Breathing. Holding me. And now...

I was sitting in the back of a police car, wrapped in a blanket and fileted open, my heart having been torn from my chest one last time by the Guerreros.

Numb.

Broken.

Ruined.

Finally free, but more trapped than ever.

"Cora," Drew said, squatting in the open doorway, a cigarette dangling between his fingers. "River's ready to go."

I glanced up to find her leaning against the hood of the police car. She'd walked away from me the minute the cops had started asking me questions. They'd cornered her next, but she'd kept her distance ever since.

"They found a few things," Drew said. "Everything's wet and covered in soot, but I think some of it's salvageable. You want to come take a look?"

"No," I whispered.

He stood up and glanced around the parking lot.

The girls had trickled by all morning, fielding questions from the cops with practiced answers that didn't include prostitution. Then they'd offered me tight smiles before trickling out. There was only one fire truck left. One cop car. Marcos's Mercedes. Dante's BMW.

And Penn's truck.

I was sitting in the back of a police car, wrapped in a blanket.

Numb.

Broken.

Ruined.

And—

"Cora, come on," Drew whispered. "I gotta get out of here before I lose my shit. I'm begging you. Take a look at your stuff and then let's call a cab and go back to the hotel."

He'd just lost his brother. If I'd had the ability to feel anything, I'd have felt bad for him.

I attempted to swallow, but my mouth was dry. "Yeah. Sure. Let's go." Robotically, I climbed out, releasing the blanket before taking his proffered hand.

He led me to a pile of random odds and ends the firemen had recovered from inside the building. The majority of it wasn't mine. I picked up a charred photo album, flipping through two pages before dropping it back down. It was Ava's. I'd let her know it was there.

A spark of emotion ignited behind my eyes when I saw my small fireproof safe beside the remnants of all of our lives. At least I wasn't destitute. There should have been a couple thousand dollars in there. Enough for River and me to use on a hotel and to eat for a few weeks while I tried to get back on my feet—if that was even possible anymore.

After dropping into a squat, I twisted and turned the combination of River's birthday and my wedding anniversary until the door popped open.

And then everything stopped.

The Earth.

My heart.

Time.

There was no money in that safe. No pictures of River when she was a baby. Nor the few I had of Nic and me. The extra keys to the building were missing. So was River's and my birth certificates and social security cards. The safe was empty except for Penn's truck keys and a hand-written note that read, *One in. One out.*

I swung my head to Drew, but his expression told me he was just as puzzled as I was.

"What the…" he breathed, reaching around me to pick the keys up.

My hands trembled as I lifted the scrap of paper in his direction. "What does this mean? Did he put this here?"

He shook his head, staring at the keys in his hand. "I have no fucking clue." He took off, jogging to Penn's truck, and I followed him every step of the way, blood roaring in my ears.

He snatched the driver's door open, and I shoved around him. Fantasizing about finding Penn just casually sitting behind the wheel instead of in the body bag he'd been carried off in.

He wasn't there and it hit me like a thousand rusty arrows falling from the sky.

The cab of his truck was clean. Just the way Penn liked it. Not so much as an empty coffee cup in the holder. Just his magical toolbox abandoned on the floorboard.

And then I saw it.

A single green glow-in-the-dark star on top.

I dove in after it, tears springing to my eyes. I couldn't tell if it was one of Nic's from my ceiling. There were no defining marks. But it had definitely been placed there for me. I turned it in my fingers, examining every angle, searching for a clue or a key that would make this entire nightmare stop. When I came up with nothing, I tucked it in my palm and fumbled with the latch on the toolbox, my fingers so intoxicated with hope that it took several attempts.

I finally sprang it open and everything stopped all over again.

The Earth.

My heart.

Time.

My mouth fell open as twin rivers streamed down my face.

Stars. Nic's stars. All of them. The tiny balls of adhesive I'd rolled between my fingers still clinging to the backs.

All of my pictures and paperwork were beneath them, and as I lifted the edge to search through the contents, I discovered that Penn's toolbox really was magical.

Stacks of cash.

My cash, complete with little pink strands of insulation still clinging to the corners.

I cupped my hands over my mouth, the tears coming harder, the source even deeper within me. "How...how did he know?" I croaked.

I think Drew answered, but I had no idea what he said because a small, white paper on top of one of my papers caught my eye. It was a white rectangle banking slip dated a week ago, the words *cash withdrawal* typed in black letters across the top.

The amount at the bottom was one million, one hundred thousand, six hundred, eighty-four dollars...

And ninety-nine cents.

"Oh fuck. Fucking fuck fuck fuck," Drew muttered, drawing my attention his way.

I leaned over the front seat and followed his gaze down to two massive black duffel bags wedged into the floorboard. They'd been covered by a sleeping bag, but when he unzipped the one closest to him, it revealed a mountain of neatly packed stacks of crisp hundred-dollar bills.

But it was three quarters, two dimes, and four pennies that shredded me.

"What would it take to make you free, Cora?"

Oh God.

"So you're telling me, if someone comes in here and offers you a life raft, you're going to refuse it because it won't fit thirty-plus women?"

Oh. *God.*

He'd done it. It had cost him his life, but he'd done it.

For me.

"What is happening right now!" I cried.

Drew lifted his hands in surrender and told me a truth. "Honest to God, I have no idea."

CHAPTER THIRTY-ONE

Savannah

One week later...

"Girl, you have no idea how good it is to be out of there." I fought the wind to get a light.

Kerri continued inspecting her chipping fingernails. "Your dad still a douchebag?"

"Worse." I gave the cigarette a deep inhale. The act of my lungs expanding made the bruises on my ribs scream.

After spending a few days in the hospital recovering, I'd been home five days. Though "home" might have been a bit of a stretch. I was back where Social Services had deemed I needed to be. The very same place I'd traveled to hell to escape.

Part of me wished they'd have let me die that night. In a lot of ways, it would have been easier.

For everybody.

I couldn't think about it.

It didn't matter.

I blew out a cloud of smoke. "Anyway, my mom said, if I can get her two hundred bucks tonight, she can score us some H."

Her mouth gaped as she swung bulging eyes at me. "Two hundred bucks? Where the hell are we gonna get that kinda cash?"

I leaned forward, adjusting my boobs to reveal more cleavage, and then shimmied my skirt up another inch. "You think I'm standing on this corner for my health?"

"Shit, Vannah," she whispered, shifting her eyes up and down the street. "This place is crawling with cops."

"Yeah, but in about fifteen minutes, all the bars are gonna be closing, sending hundreds of drunk, horny men staggering out. Ripe for the pickin'."

"Oh hell no. I ain't sucking no dick. I told you Ronnie and I were getting serious."

I twisted my lips and arched an eyebrow at her. "Ronnie got two bills?"

She crossed her arms over her chest. "Nope. But he ain't got no STD either."

I rolled my eyes. "Fine. Then go." I made a shooing motion. "But don't expect me to share."

Her eyes narrowed on me as if she were looking at a stranger. "Girl, you have lost your damn mind. You spent too long living with Mama Prostitute. She done—"

"Shut your fucking mouth!" I shoved a finger in her face. "You don't get to say a goddamn word about her. Do you hear me? Nothing. *Ever.*" I couldn't even think about Cora or River without becoming physically ill.

I'd woken up at the hospital alone and abandoned. I'd waited for her to show up. Waited for her to sneak me out of there. I didn't even care about going back to Dante if it meant going back to her.

My parents had arrived instead.

"You know what? I don't have to take your bullshit. I'm out."

"See if I give a fuck," I muttered, watching her blond hair sway as she navigated the cracked sidewalk in a pair of black stilettos. It was no skin off my back if she wanted to go home and ride Ronnie's pencil dick all night.

Even if I was jealous that she had somewhere to go.

No sooner than she disappeared around the corner, a jet-black Audi R8 pulled up in front of me. The dark tinted window rolled down, and a deep baritone rumbled, "You working tonight?"

I leaned down, squinting to make him out in the light of the dashboard. "Depends on who's asking."

His hand appeared at the open window, five one-hundred-dollar bills fanned out between his fingers.

That was the right answer.

"I am now," I chirped, dropping my cigarette, not even bothering to toe it out before taking the cash and climbing into his car. "So where you taking me tonight?" I asked seductively, tucking the cash in my bra.

"First?" he growled, locking the doors. "Rehab. *Then* I'm taking you back to where you belong."

My head swung in his direction.

Furious blue eyes I'd recognize anywhere glared back at me, but just as quickly, they softened. He snaked a hand out and gave the back of my neck a squeeze as he whispered, "God, it's good to see you breathing again."

I gasped, tears filling my vision. "Penn?"

The story continues in

THE TRUTH ABOUT US

Coming September 13, 2018

OTHER BOOKS

Retrieval

Transfer

Guardian Protection Agency

Singe

Thrive

The Fall Up Series

The Fall Up

The Spiral Down

The Darkest Sunrise

The Brightest Sunset

The Truth Duet

The Truth About Lies

The Truth About Us

The Wrecked and Ruined Series

Changing Course

Stolen Course

Broken Course

Among the Echoes

On the Ropes

Fighting Silence

Fighting Shadows

Fighting Solutude

Savor Me

ABOUT THE AUTHOR

Born and raised in Savannah, Georgia, Aly Martinez is a stay-at-home mom to four crazy kids under the age of five, including a set of twins. Currently living in South Carolina, she passes what little free time she has reading anything and everything she can get her hands on, preferably with a glass of wine at her side.

After some encouragement from her friends, Aly decided to add "Author" to her ever-growing list of job titles. So grab a glass of Chardonnay, or a bottle if you're hanging out with Aly, and join her aboard the crazy train she calls life.

Facebook: www.facebook.com/AuthorAlyMartinez

Twitter: twitter.com/AlyMartinezAuth

Goodreads: www.goodreads.com/AlyMartinez

Made in the USA
San Bernardino, CA
24 August 2018